Open Hearts

Stealing Hearts, Book 3

K. Evan Coles

For information contact:
http://www.kevancoles.com

Edited by Beth Greenberg

Book and Cover design by K. Evan Coles

Published by Wicked Fingers Press

Some hearts are made to be opened.

Jae-seong Bak has never been in love. He prefers to let his personal life take a backseat to his career as a nurse, especially since no-strings hookups with men he's glad to call friends have always felt like more than enough.

After years of moving around the United States, Jae takes a job in his home city of Boston, arriving just in time to celebrate his brother Ty's engagement. In reconnecting with friends and family, Jae befriends Emmett McNeil, a young chef and Ty's future brother-in-law, whose own bad luck with love hasn't dampened his enthusiasm for life.

As the summer passes and Jae and Emmett help their families plan the wedding, the spark between the two men ignites, though each agrees to keep their hookups under wraps in order to prevent potential drama. Taken off guard by the depth of his feelings, Jae backs away, only to find that going back to being just friends with Emmett is much harder than he ever could have predicted.

Now, standing with Emmett as their siblings make their vows, Jae must decide if he's really content to hold the man he loves at arm's-length or if taking a chance on more is in the cards.

Dedication

For my son, who makes me laugh every day.

And for Jayme Yesenofski who read my manuscripts so many times in the past and gave me such wonderful feedback and flails. I miss you so much, friend.

Many thanks to Barb Payne Ingram for eagle-eyed proofreading. And all my gratitude to Helena Stone, Randall Jussaume, Beth Greenberg, and Shelli Pates, who generously donated their time to help fix my words. You all have no idea how much I appreciate your feedback on this story.

A big thank you as well to the readers in my Facebook Group— Emily, Kaila, Stacy, Marrybell, Heather, Crystal, Helen, Randall, Victoria, Li, and others— who shared their experiences with me and helped me better understand living with food allergies.

Contents

Copyright Acknowledgements

K. Evan Coles

.

Chapter One

January 2018

"These blini are weird."

Jae-seong Bak glanced up at the young man standing opposite him. "Weird how?" He set his gaze on the trio of mini pancakes arranged across the young man's cocktail plate, each topped with a daub of white cream and black caviar pearls. "Weird as in oddly shaped or weird like this party is about to come down with a case of epic food poisoning?"

The young man chuckled and set the plate on the cocktail table between them. "Weird as in I'm not sure they've been made with the right kind of flour." Plucking a canapé from the plate, he bit into it, eyes narrowing as he slowly chewed. "Traditionally, blini are made with wheat or buckwheat flour," he said, "and these are suspiciously lacking in nuttiness."

"Ah." Jae smiled. "I haven't had any, so I'll have to take your word for it."

"Not a fan of caviar?"

"I'm not a fan of crème fraîche. Or anything dairy, for that matter."

"Blini are made with milk, so you've dodged a bullet twice. You must be Jae-seong." The young man wiped his fingers with a cocktail napkin, then held his hand out to Jae. "Emmett McNeil," he said. "Amelia is my sister."

"Nice to meet you, Emmett—I've heard a lot about you from

1

Ty."

Setting down his vodka tonic, Jae shook hands and tried not to stare.

Running late after a long shift at the hospital, Jae had missed the introductions between the two families who'd gathered in this Boston Waterfront restaurant to celebrate Amelia McNeil's engagement to Jae's brother, Ty Bak. Jae had worked his way around the room since his arrival, introducing himself to Ty's friends and future in-laws, aware Emmett would be in attendance. Jae had been blissfully ignorant the man was his type to a T until now, however, all golden-brown curls and wide-shouldered athletic frame, with a flashing smile that made Emmett's dark blue eyes sparkle.

Not that Jae had noticed.

Fiddling with the leather bracelet he wore on his right wrist, Jae ran a finger over the medical alert medallion attached to the band. He made sure his voice held a teasing note when he spoke again. "Did you peg me for a Bak because I look Korean or because Ty told you his brother can't drink milk?"

"A little of both." The tips of Emmett's ears turned pink as he grinned. "I can see a resemblance to your dad when you smile, and Ty's told me more than once that you're tall. You brought up the dairy thing, though."

"That's fair."

Emmett smiled wider. "You just moved back here from L.A., right?"

"Two weeks ago today," Jae said. "I think I'm finally over my jet lag, thank God. I'm a Nurse Anesthetist and working late shifts on a sleep deficit has been painful."

"Ty told me you were a nurse. And you work with surgical teams?"

"Usually, yes, though sometimes a shift will take me into the Emergency Department or ICU." Jae shrugged. "It probably sounds weird to say I move around too much to be bored but there's some truth in that, too."

"I get it. Maybe Ty told you I'm a chef?"

"He did. And my friend Zac told me that you and your friend Aiden run one of the hottest food chains in the city so yeah, I'll bet you're always on the move too." Jae enjoyed the obvious pleasure on Emmett's handsome face. "Endless Pastabilities, right?"

"That's us!" Emmett seemed almost to glow from the inside out. "We park an EP truck outside of your hospital at least twice a week. But hey, I didn't know you were a friend of Zac's. I'm guessing you met through the job?"

"Through school, if you can believe it. Zac and I shared an apartment for a while and got each other through our grad programs—it all feels like a million years ago." Jae shook his head. "We stayed in touch after I moved out of state and he was the one who told me about the job at Mass Eye and Ear. He also swears you guys serve stuff on the food truck that a guy like me can eat."

"We totally do. EP cooks vegan options every day and you can order dairy-free for delivery." Emmett frowned. "We'd also have done a better job of putting out those options for this party."

"What do you mean?"

"I know for a fact that Ty and Amelia spoke to the restaurant staff about food you can eat but I don't see it anywhere."

Jae raised his eyebrows. "They did?"

"I told you he wouldn't believe it," said a familiar voice from behind them.

"*Gah.*" Emmett nearly bobbled his drink, then aimed a glare at his sister and Ty, neither of whom appeared even remotely sorry for startling him. "You guys have got to stop sneaking around like that."

Amelia hid a giggle behind her hand, but Jae saw irritation mixing with the amusement in his brother's expression, an emotion Jae saw on Ty's face far too often when they met.

"I didn't say I didn't believe it," Jae said gently. "I was just surprised. Pleasantly, by the way, and thank you very much for thinking to do that."

"It was Emmett's idea, actually." Like her brother, Amelia was fair and lightly freckled, with blue eyes framed by long, curling lashes and an infectious grin. "Ty and I knew we needed to do more than just pick dairy free foods, and Em was the first to suggest putting some things aside."

"It's a simple way to limit cross-contamination." Emmett glanced from his sister to Jae. "*If* everyone pays attention and follows all the rules, that is. Hang on a sec and I'll grab a tray from the kitchen."

Jae's mouth fell open as Emmett turned on his heel. "Wait, what?"

3

Emmett was already gone though, slipping his big frame through the crowd with ease and a word for nearly everyone he passed.

"Um." Jae bit his lip. "Crap. I didn't mean for that to happen."

Amelia waved him off. "It's fine, seriously. You've no doubt made Emmett very happy by giving him something to do. My brother loves feeding people, even if he's not the one cooking."

"We also think he's been going a bit stir-crazy," Ty added. He shared a look with Amelia and his eyes, rounder than Jae's but the same dark brown, glowed. "Emmett and his partner have been up in Portland since Christmas starting another branch of the business. They've been living in a vintage Shasta trailer which, while cool as hell, has got to be cramping their style. They're used to a faster pace here in Boston and we're pretty sure Emmett's counting down the days to when he and Sean can move back."

Partner, huh?

Jae swallowed down a sigh. That figured. Every attractive guy he'd met since moving back to Boston was already in a relationship. Then again, Emmett's unavailability was probably for the best. Even thinking about a hookup with Ty's future brother-in-law smacked of a disaster waiting to happen. Emmett was also clearly far too young for Jae, who, at forty-three, was better off sticking with men closer to his own age.

"So, the move to Portland isn't permanent?" he asked, more to distract himself than anything else.

"Definitely not," Amelia said. "Em's whole life is here in Boston. He wants the stores and trucks in Portland to do well, of course, but he'll be more than ready to move back home by the time spring rolls around."

"Amelia, dear, where has your brother gotten himself off to?"

Jae nodded to the middle-aged woman who had bustled over to them. He'd heard a good deal about Emmett and Amelia from Ty over the last two years, but less about their mother, Margaret, who lived in Virginia and rarely returned to the Boston area. Jae had found her engaging and liked that she seemed to have bonded with Jae's own parents, seemingly unbothered by the Bak family's Korean-Caucasian mix, not to mention Jae's out and proud status. However, he also knew that Margaret's relationships with her children were strained, and particularly with Emmett who'd been labeled a rebel by his parents in his late teens.

4

Margaret certainly looked exasperated now even talking about her son, her forehead creased in a frown that Amelia met with one of her own. "Em will be right back, Mother," she said. "He went to check on some of the food we had set aside for Jae."

Margaret heaved a big sigh. "Of course, he did. I swear, I thought that boy would outgrow his love of playing waiter by now. No offense to you, Jae."

"It's fine." Jae fought off a wince at her obvious scorn. What the hell? Did Margaret McNeil not understand what her son did for a living?

"Mother—" Amelia started, only for Margaret to speak over her.

"I asked him for one thing tonight, Amelia," she said. "To stand with his family in your father's place."

"Which he's done, repeatedly." A fond smile brightened Amelia's expression. "Em helped Ty pick out my ring, you know, and he used his contacts to help us find a venue for the wedding. He helped the Baks plan this party and he's taken a ton of time off from work to drive down here and help us organize."

"As any man should do for his sister." Margaret made a tsking noise with her tongue. "We're here to celebrate you and Ty, not your brother's ability to read a catering menu."

Ty cleared his throat. "Emmett's done a lot more than manage a menu."

"That hardly matters, Ty." Now Margaret was smiling. "Tonight is about your engagement, and the happiness you and Amelia have brought to your parents and me by deciding to start one of your own. A grandchild or two will be wonderful additions to the family, even if I have to travel to meet them."

"Um." Ty's eyes went slightly wide. "Margaret, Amelia and I are—"

"Not even married yet," Amelia said with a snort. "You need to slow your roll, Mother. Sure, Ty and I have talked about having kids, but the decision is a ways down the road."

Jae bit back a laugh at Ty's vigorous head bobbing.

"A *long* ways." Ty slipped his arm around Amelia's waist. "Heck, we still have housemates at our place! We're nowhere near ready to even plan for a baby right now."

Margaret waved his words off with a chuckle. "I'm not in any

5

great rush, dear—you and Amelia will get there soon enough. My point is that the two of you are clearly planning for the future, unlike Amelia's brother who can't make up his mind about *anything*, not even where he wants to live." She sniffed, her mouth turning down at the corners. "The boy doesn't even have a real home at the moment, nor does he seem to care."

"That's not actually true, Mother. It's just that the home I live in right now happens to be on wheels."

Oh, thank God.

An odd mix of guilt and relief went through Jae as Emmett swooped back in and set a tray down before him. Under normal circumstances, Jae's mouth would have been watering at the sight of the beautifully arranged canapé. The palpable tension among the McNeils was hard to ignore, however, and Jae hated knowing that—whatever problems Emmett had with his mother—his own inability to eat like everyone else in the room had set off this disruption. Ty's frown just made Jae feel worse and it took real effort to put on a happy expression.

"Thank you," he said to Emmett. "You really didn't have to do this, Emmett."

"Oh, I know," Emmett said, his tone far easier than Jae had expected. "But I wanted to make sure the right tray came out and avoid any kind of great food trauma."

"Well *I* may be about to suffer from food trauma because these look delicious." Amelia had set her hands on her hips, humor dawning on her face. "Why weren't these put out for everyone?"

"Because your fiancé refused to even taste the vegan options." Emmett aimed an accusing look in Ty's direction.

Jae couldn't resist jumping in. "Ty's always been a big meat eater," he said to Margaret, whose frown had started to thaw. "My ma had to sneak vegetables into his food when we were kids, like adding grated zucchini to spaghetti and meatballs."

"You shush." Ty set a hand over Jae's mouth. "Don't you go giving my wife-to-be any crafty ideas, bro."

"Too late! You need to give me more recipes." Amelia held a palm up for Jae to slap. "And I definitely want to make whatever is on these cucumber slices, Em."

"I've got you, girl." An air of great satisfaction settled over Emmett's whole person. "I can talk you through the ingredients right now, so Jae-seong knows exactly what he's eating." He

6

cocked an eyebrow in Jae's direction. "You ready for that, tall guy?"

"Ready as I can be, I guess," Jae replied with a laugh, then took a step closer to the table so Emmett could begin.

Chapter Two

Five months later, June

"Hey, hot stuff. Glad you made it!"

Jae stepped into his friend Mark Mannix's embrace with a smile. "Hey, yourself," he said around the quick kisses they exchanged. "Have you been waiting long?"

"Meh, you're fine." Stepping back, Mark opened the fan he was carrying with a rainbow-colored snap. "But we agreed to meet in your neighborhood to make your life easier, Jae, and you're still the last one to show. What gives?"

"You know I run late by default." Jae laughed. "And I had to stop at home after shift, because there was no goddamned way I was coming down here to party in scrubs."

"That's fair. You do clean up nice." Mark waggled his eyebrows. "And you smell *delicious*." Like Jae, he worked as a nurse specialist at Mass Eye and Ear and knew that a simple change of clothes after a long shift could do a lot to change a person's mood. His grin lengthened into a smirk as he eyed Jae's plain black tank and shorts, however, and mischief made his eyes gleam. "I'm not sure this ensemble you've got going is totally party-ready, though. Or at least not *parade*-ready."

Jae had to laugh. Mark looked sleek and sexy in dark shorts and a Harvey Milk tank that hugged his fit body. The strings of plastic rainbow beads he wore around his neck gleamed in the sun and set off his very fair skin and dark hair as he turned to a figure approaching on Jae's left.

"What do you think, Zac?" Mark asked. "Have we got anything in Owen's magic bag to give Jae's outfit a little lift?"

"Certainly. I think Jae looks perfect as he is, however, as well as very, very tall. Neither of which is unusual."

Their friend and co-worker, Zac Alvarez, stepped in for Jae's hug and kiss. He'd dressed in dark colors too, which made his beads and the temporary tattoos on his toned arms even more vibrant. A suntan warmed Zac's olive-toned skin and he looked relaxed and happy, his grin broad beneath his dark beard.

Fondness washed over Jae. He and Zac had reconnected upon his return to Boston as if no time had passed at all. It was through Zac that Jae had befriended Mark and the trio of young men who would round out their Pride party today: Aiden, Owen, and Emmett, who had moved back from Maine at the beginning of May *without* his partner, Sean, and was now very, very single.

"Ignore Mark," Zac said to Jae. "He forgets that not every gay man over forty wants to broadcast a zaddy vibe."

Jae and Mark exchanged a glance before they each cracked up laughing.

"This is not to say we don't have some festive doo-dads for you too," Zac said over their cackling. "The guys made party packs for everyone."

"Great, thanks. Less so that you just said 'doo-dads' the way my Grandma Kay used to." Jae let out a soft 'oof' as Zac elbowed him gently in the ribs.

"Smartass," Zac murmured before he looked around. "Will your man be joining us today?"

Jae aimed a mock glare at him. "Sal already had plans. Besides, you know he's not my man. Sal and I strictly friends."

"Who share a big side order of benefits," Mark chimed in, admiration written all over his face. "I remember the days when I could say words like those about myself with fondness."

Zac snickered. "Mmm, I remember those days, too. They were before you met Owen and fell head over heels in love."

"That's why I remember them with fondness and not nostalgia," Mark replied with a smile.

"Where is Owen, anyway?" Jae asked. "Out walking with my favorite dog and the guys?"

Mark shook his head. "Popcorn is hanging with my sister

today." He and his boyfriend, Owen, had found their big, white mutt at a campground last year, lost or abandoned and sweet as can be. "It's not easy wrangling a dog his size through crowds like this, and we thought he'd enjoy a play date with his aunt and uncle and new cousin instead. Popcorn is already best buddies with my nephew, Ethan, so you know they're having a fantastic day."

"As for the guys, they went off into the park to buy cold drinks," Zac said, his tone fond. "Aiden's been on an ice cream kick this summer and I'm betting they've stopped at every cart they've passed. They should be back any second."

The soft expression on Zac's face made Jae smile. In the years they'd known each other, he'd never seen Zac so gone for a man the way he was with Aiden.

"That reminds me, I meant to grab a coffee on my way down here," Jae said. "I could use the jolt."

"We've got some soda if that'll help."

Jae's whole body hummed at that voice. "I'd love some."

Turning, Jae met Emmett's dark blue gaze. He tried very hard not to stare at Emmett's shirtless torso, too, but literally stopped short as he got a look at Owen whose tight dark curls, normally tipped platinum, glowed fuchsia in the sun. "Owen, your hair is pink!"

"Yes, it is!" Owen exclaimed. He and Aiden were just as bare chested as Emmett and all three were chuckling at Jae's wide eyes. "It's supposed to be just for today, but honestly, I might keep it."

Mark cast a loving look at Owen. "Of course, you'd want to." He ran a hand over his partner's shoulders, stroking golden brown skin that shone with flecks of multi-colored glitter. "Are there any trinkets left for Jae, love?"

"Oh, yes." Handing his cup to Mark, Owen shrugged a rainbow striped drawstring bag from his shoulders. "We've got buttons, beads, and wristbands, and a visor like Emmett's if you want a break from the sun." He withdrew a second bag from his own and handed it to Jae. "There's also a fan in there, plus sunglasses, tattoos, body glitter—"

"And condoms with travel-sized lube," Mark put in. "My man does not let his friends go unprepared."

Jae laughed. "I'll remember that." Opening the bag in his hands, he peered into its depths, but looked up again as a second pair of hands came to rest by his own.

"Here—you browse while I hold." Emmett's grin was easy. "Can you grab drinks from my bag, A?" he asked over his shoulder. "Zac's water is in there, along with soda for anyone who needs one. Diet Coke for you, Jae, or do you want full sugar?"

"I'll take the sugar, thanks." Jae tried not to ogle his *stupid hot* friend, keenly aware the effort was a lost cause.

Like Owen and Aiden, Emmett's skin sparkled with glitter. He stood a few inches shorter than Jae, but he was the broadest man in their group, his chest lightly furred and muscled without being bulky, a combination Jae had always loved. Emmett radiated heat as he huddled over the bag too, his shoulders golden-pink and freckled, and he smelled of citrus and suntan lotion, a mixture Jae found endlessly appealing and a clear indication that he needed to get a fucking grip.

Jae had a good thing going here in Boston. He'd settled into his job and life with an ease that had honestly surprised him and he'd reconnected with his friends and family almost effortlessly. For the first time in years, he was able to see his parents and brother in person on a regular basis, moments that felt particularly relevant now as the Baks helped Ty and Amelia plan their wedding. A sense of groundedness had come over Jae in the last six months, too, a feeling he hadn't realized he'd missed during his time in other cities. And if he hadn't bothered to start his usual job search for the next best move to further his career? Well, there was plenty of time to do that after Ty's wedding, as well as plan wherever Jae's job might take him.

What Jae didn't have time for was the infatuation he'd developed for Emmett, an admiration that both frustrated and baffled him, because no matter how hard he tried to turn his interest off, it seemed only to deepen. Thanks to bi-weekly dinners with Ty and his groomsmen and these get-togethers with Zac and Mark, Jae saw Emmett several times a month, occasions that were no help to Jae at all in getting over his ridiculous crush.

The real problem was that Jae liked the guy very much and probably would have no matter what the circumstances. He found Emmett engaging and funny as well as whip smart and interested in everything which made him a treat to talk to. Jae liked Emmett's warm and genuine nature, too, and that even their infrequent awkward moments together were filled with a sweet charm that made him crave more. Because of course, Jae's traitorous brain made him like Emmett just as much as it made Jae lust for him.

Jae stifled a sigh. Nothing in the world was going to make him forget he was attracted to the man standing in front of him. Unfortunately, Emmett was still wrong for Jae on multiple levels. Too young, for one, at twelve years Jae's junior, and so broody over the end of his relationship with Sean that Emmett still declined to talk about it. There was also the matter of Jae's instinctive understanding that his own brother would not appreciate Jae's interest in Emmett. Ty and Emmett had grown close over the last two years and their friendship was solid, something Jae respected with all his heart.

So, he fought his impulse to touch Emmett every time they met, and the urge never waned. But with a shirtless Emmett at his side now, skin sheened with sweat and glitter, Jae wanted to do more than just touch. He was in a mood for pulling Emmett into a secluded corner and kissing the hell out of him so he finally knew what that big, toned body would feel like against his.

Get your shit together, man.

Reaching into the backpack, Jae drew out a pair of rainbow terrycloth wristbands and several strings of beads, as well as a pair of red plastic sunglasses with heart-shaped lenses. "Ooh, these are fun," he said, more to himself than anyone around him. Slipping the sunglasses on, he pivoted slightly on his feet and struck a pose, laughing when Emmett blew a teasing whistle.

Aiden laughed. "Yas, queen!" He handed Jae a can of Coke, then turned his eyes on the crowd around them, his hazel eyes bright. "Do you guys want to keep standing here or move toward City Hall Plaza?"

"Let's head over to City Hall." Mark looked at Jae. "We have tickets for the party on Lansdowne Street at nine, so Owen and I will host drinks and dinner back at our place in between. Think you're up for it? You can always crash for a while in our room if you need a power nap."

"I like the sound of that," Jae said. "Now I'm extra bummed Popcorn is with your sister, though. I look forward to lots of doggy hugs when we hang at your place."

"You're welcome to dog-sit any time, Jae," Owen said. "You know the monster dog loves you."

Amused at the thought, Jae took the backpack from Emmett and slipped it over his shoulder, so it rested against his own black crossbody bag. The group began a slow journey through the crowds already lining the sidewalks of Beacon Street, going two by two along the narrow path past revelers with Jae and Emmett in the lead and the others following behind.

"You feeling okay, Jae-seong?" Emmett asked, his eyebrows drawn slightly together when Jae turned his way. "I'd never judge anyone for needing a power nap, but Zac said you were on shift by four this morning."

"I was and I have to say, I'm feeling it." Jae cracked his soda and quickly took a slug. "It'll get better after I catch a second wind."

"Cool. I wasn't sure if maybe you needed to save up some energy for wedding talk when we meet up with your brother next week." Emmett chuckled when Jae mimed strangling himself.

"I'm not talking about seating charts today, Emmett. Or dresses or tuxedos, or why Ty has to invite my parents' mailman to the wedding reception because he was the first person in the neighborhood to offer my dad congratulations after Ty was born." Jae laughed outright when Emmett held a hand up for a high five.

"Same, dude. Same. If you think Ty is obsessed with wedding talk, you should spend time with my sister."

"You do get it from both ends, what with being the Male of Honor and a groomsman."

"Truer words have never been said. And I'd rather go with Best Man if you don't mind sharing the title. Male of Honor sounds like a stripper name and while I like to dance, that's not really my vibe." Emmett grunted. "I'm just glad my sister gave me the okay to hang out with you guys for the bachelor party weekend because I am not up for the bachelorette bash she and her posse of girlfriends have planned. Oh, hey, incoming!" he called, then lifted a grin skyward as brightly colored confetti rained down around them.

Peering up through the pieces, Jae spotted an open window in the building above them, happy faces visible through the cascade of paper bits being tossed. His diverted attention also sent him off course and crashing into Emmett and they grappled with each other for a moment to keep from tipping over while their friends reached out to steady them.

"Shit, I'm sorry," Jae said around their laughter as he got himself upright, his hands tingling where they'd touched Emmett's heated skin. "I told you I needed to wake up a bit."

Emmett squeezed Jae's arm. "You're fine. Lean on me as much as you need."

They trekked into an open space in front of the State House. The elegant brick building was closed and quiet for the weekend and its austere lines and shining gold dome were a nice contrast against the colorful chaos of the parade route and revelers.

"I don't usually catch the parade up here." Emmett said. "Aiden and I have friends who live a block from Copley Square where the whole thing kicks off. We always hang there and then walk downtown along Boylston Street to the finish. Our friends are out of town this year, though, and being up here turned out to be easier for just about everybody." He glanced around, his lips curving up. "I'm kind of liking the change."

"I haven't been to a Pride Parade in Boston in forever," Jae said, "and this is so huge in comparison to the last time I did. Seriously, it's ..." He paused, a happy ache going all through him. "It was wonderful watching it grow over the years, even though I couldn't be here myself. Knowing this city hosts one of the biggest Pride parades in the country is incredible and I am loving being here with you all." He wrinkled his nose at Emmett. "I sound like a weirdo, don't I?"

"No," Emmett said with a laugh. "I mean, you may very well be a weirdo, but all you sound like right now is someone who is proud of who he is."

"Thanks." Jae gently knocked their shoulders together and his insides turned a bit to goo when Emmett reached over and clasped Jae's hand in his, squeezing Jae's fingers before he let go again.

"I wasn't sure I'd be here for Pride this year either," Emmett said. "I was still living in Portland around the same time you blew into town—you know that—and whether or not I'd be ready to move back by summer was still up in the air."

"Well, I'm glad we both made it. I was in my twenties the last time I was here for this, you know, but the funny part is that I was with Zac that day, too, and his ex, Edward."

"May his hair fall out overnight," Emmett replied in a tone both reverent and snarky. "Zac's mom says those words every time she hears the dude's name."

"Does she really?" Jae laughed. "Sounds like something my mom would do. I was friendly with Edward back in the day and he always struck me as a decent guy. I was surprised as hell when Zac told me they'd split and why."

"People change." Emmett simply shrugged, though his face closed off ever so slightly.

Jae hummed in reply. Endless Pastabilities was thriving in Portland. During Emmett's stay in the city, he and Sean had opened three walk-up windows and launched a pair of food trucks that serviced various neighborhoods five days a week. But while the burden of increased workload and responsibilities had clearly taken a toll on Emmett's personal life, he still had little to say on the subject. That was just fine with Jae. He didn't want to talk about what had to have been a dramatic time in Emmett's life and ruin the guy's afternoon.

"Would you ever choose to live in Maine again?" he asked instead.

"I'm not sure I can answer just yet." A thoughtful air settled over Emmett. "Portland is beautiful, and its people are great. Killer food scene and the cooler weather and saner traffic are big pluses, too." He laughed. "I did miss the buzz you get in a bigger city and, frankly, Portland was not the most diverse place I've ever lived, racially or in terms of identity, which I wasn't used to.

"The city never quite felt like home, I guess. Maybe because I wasn't there long enough or because I got too caught up in working to really explore. It never occurred to me *not* to move back here once Aiden and I were sure the business would do well without me being on site." Emmett shrugged again. "So, here we are."

"Yeah." Jae breathed in deep, soaking up the vibe of what was turning out to be a gorgeous day. The sun was out and the sky cloudless, and whoops and calls of 'Happy Pride' echoed around him. Soap bubbles and laughter drifted by in the light breeze, swirling through the brightly colored flags flying everywhere and Jae heard music, of course, along with ... wait. Were those motorcycle engines? And a sudden roar of cheering?

"Hey, guys? Sounds like the parade is about to catch up to us." Emmett paused in his walking and beamed when the others stopped, too. Around them, the flow of pedestrians heading in either direction slowed. "The bikers always come first," he said, his eyes on Jae. "They're loud and attention grabbing, plus they get the leather vibe going strong."

"Excellent." Jae laughed. "That's more than fitting."

"So, what do you think?" Emmett slung an arm over Jae's shoulder, his face lighting up when Jae copied the gesture. "Do we keep walking?"

"Nah. I say we stay right here and cheer our heads off," Jae said with a smile. "I like the sound of that a lot."

Chapter Three

"You and Emmett were looking pretty friendly on Saturday."
Jae smirked. "We are pretty friendly. He's a good guy, Zac, and
I like hanging out with him."

"Yeah, I know you do." Zac fell silent as the train they were
riding jerked to a stop, then aimed a sour look at the tunnel visible
through the windows. "I swore there was some flirting going on
there, if you don't mind me saying. I mean, you guys were up and
dancing for ages at the parties on Lansdowne."

"Sure, we flirted a little, but it was just for fun. You know I've
always liked shaking my ass."

"I do. I never realized Emmett liked to as well."

Jae cocked an eyebrow at his friend. "Really?" he asked. He and
Emmett had spent a *lot* of time dancing at the Pride parties, packed
into a succession of clubs with their friends and thousands of other
revelers riding high on shared energy, cocktails, and who knew
what else. Jae had enjoyed every second and would have sworn
Emmett had too. "Emmett was the one who suggested we all get
up and dance in the first place."

"I know. I was honestly surprised." Zac ran his fingers over his
beard. "Granted, I don't go out to clubs with Emmett often but on
the occasions I have, he didn't do much dancing. Where the hell
are we, anyway?" he asked with another glance out the train's
window. "I haven't been paying attention to the stops."

"Just past Park Street." Jae pulled his phone from his pocket.
"I'm late every time I meet up with these guys, no matter what time

17

I leave." He tapped out a quick message to his brother, then slid the phone back into his pocket. "I reserved a room in the hotel for the weekend of the wedding, you know. So I'd be on time for the ceremony."

"Get out."

"It's true." He grinned when Zac tipped his head back and laughed.

"Jae, you can walk to the hotel from your apartment!"

"In a half hour, sure. But with my luck, I'd oversleep and end up hauling ass across town in my tux."

Zac's brown eyes gleamed behind his glasses. "I find this image very appealing."

"You would."

"Not many people would inconvenience themselves just to keep their brother happy." Zac sat up straight as the train jerked back into motion, crawling its way through the tunnel at a snail's pace. "You're a good man, Jae-seong."

"I'm the Best Man." Jae made a goofy face at Zac's groan. "Though so is Emmett. But you've missed a critical point, my friend. I'll have a five-minute commute, at the hotel, not to mention the housekeeping service *and* in-room dining. Not one of those things is an inconvenience."

"Okay, I see the method to your madness."

"I'm glad someone does." Jae adjusted the strap of his bag on his shoulder as they finally pulled into the station. "This is me."

"I'm coming with you. Aiden and I are meeting at South Station and I'll get there faster on my feet." Zac eyed Jae's white t-shirt and black jeans. "You look sharp. Where are you guys meeting up tonight?"

"Malay Kitchen on Washington Street."

"Ooh, Aiden loves that place. He eats there every chance he gets when left to his own devices."

"Well, now I'm really looking forward to trying the food," Jae said. "Emmett says there's plenty that's safe on the menu for someone like me."

"I'm surprised you haven't been already." Zac followed him through the train's door and onto the subway platform. "I thought you were getting out of the apartment more with Sal."

"Yeah, that hasn't happened. We usually order in. But yes, I should get out and explore more. Not to mention grocery shop.

I'm so low on stuff right now, I've had to make budget bibimbap twice this week. Not that I'm even complaining."

"Sounds like you haven't picked up any cooking skills that extend beyond the five Korean dishes you used to make back in the day."

"Oh, shut up." Jae laughed. "You never minded my cooking. And this is big talk coming from a guy who only knows how to make pancakes."

"I actually loved your meals, but I cook all sorts of things now." Zac's face was very smug. "Aiden's been teaching me."

"Well, good for you. I don't have a chef boyfriend to give me cooking lessons, but I *am* better at putting food together than I was when we were at school."

"Are Sloppy Joes still one of your signature dishes?"

"My Sloppy Joe recipe is awesome. And clearly not Korean!"

Zac's laughter rang out as they climbed the stairs toward the street.

Ten minutes later, Jae made his way into Malay Kitchen, his stomach already rumbling at the delicious smells in the air and his eyes on the quartet of men whose heads were bent close in conversation.

"Hey, guys," he called and the faces that turned to meet him lit up.

"Fucking finally!" Ty rose and grabbed Jae in a one-armed hug.

"Sorry—the trains were a mess." Jae aimed a smile over Ty's shoulder at Emmett, then turned it toward Krishnan and Thom, both friends of Ty's from his undergraduate days and groomsmen.

"Don't worry about it." Emmett's grin was warm. "We haven't even gotten around to talking about what we want to order." He pulled out the empty chair beside him and gestured for Jae to sit.

"True," Krishnan said. "It is Wednesday my dude, and we have been busy sampling cocktails and gossiping."

"Oh? What about?" Jae set his bag on the floor and sat.

"Amelia's latest battle with her mom." Ty shook his head. "Apparently there was a brouhaha over the final number of invitations."

Jae leveled a look at his brother. "Please don't tell me there are going to be more than fifty guests."

"Thankfully, there are not. Margaret put up a good fight, though," Ty said. "She added a bunch of names to the list *after*

Amelia told her it was final and, honestly, I didn't even notice. Thankfully, Amelia did because I really didn't want to be the one to explain to you guys and Ma and Dad how an extra thirty guests ended up on the list without your knowledge."

As a retiree and widow, Margaret McNeil had limited means to put toward the wedding. She'd swallowed her pride when Jae and his parents had stepped in to help Ty and Amelia, but things had really gone to hell in a handbasket after Margaret had discovered that Emmett was also pitching in. Relations between Amelia and her mother had been shakier than usual ever since.

"Ugh." Jae turned to Emmett. "You don't think your mother would try to invite those people on the down-low, do you?"

"I wouldn't put it past her." Emmett let out a short laugh. "Mother is all about controlling her environment. Not that she'd talk to me about it, of course, or anything else."

Inwardly, Jae winced. While he couldn't imagine his relationship with his own mother being so damaged, he found Emmett's matter-of-fact acceptance of the estrangement even more troubling. Everything Jae knew about Emmett told him the guy was a sweetheart and kind to his core—what the hell had his parents put the poor guy through over the years to make him this blasé?

Turning his attention to the cocktail glass by Emmett's hand, he admired the rosy pink concoction. "What are you drinking and how do I get one?"

"This, my friend, is a Glinda." Emmett's expression eased. "Lychee syrup, pink grapefruit juice, and vodka, with a little salt on the rim to finish. It's so good, I swear it'll bring a tear to your eye. They make the lychee syrup fresh here, by the way, and it is delicious."

"Sounds great." Jae watched as Emmett raised a hand to a pretty young woman passing by, a black tray tucked under her arm, and the two exchanged a nod. "Let's talk food. Zac told me how much Aiden likes this place, and I'm guessing you guys do, too?"

Thom leveled a look at Jae. "How have you not eaten here before tonight?"

"Jae sticks to what he knows," Ty said. "Mostly due to that allergy of his though, frankly, I think some of it is laziness."

Under the table, Jae adjusted his leather bracelet. "Ty's not entirely wrong about the laziness. But the allergy is the main reason. Dairy and I don't get along," he said to Thom.

"We know, Jae," Ty said, his tone dry, "just like we know you've got meds in your bag in case you somehow unknowingly ingest a piece of pizza." He fell silent, a teasing light in his eyes as Jae lifted a finger in warning.

"Shut it, you." Jae turned back to Thom. "I've found a few places around my apartment I like, but I've been lax about going farther afield."

"Makes sense to me," Emmett said. "You should be safe to eat *here*, by the way. I double-checked the menu when we sat down just to be sure."

Pleasure made it easy for Jae to ignore Ty's unsubtle eyeroll. "Thanks, Emmett. That was thoughtful."

"No problem." Emmett moved his shoulders up and down. "But you should talk to Farah about your order, so there are no surprises."

Jae blinked. "Farah?"

"That would be me." The young woman with the black tray stepped up to the table.

Ty raised his eyebrows at Jae. "Emmett's on a first name basis with everyone in the restaurant."

"And definitely with me." Farah aimed a wink Emmett's way. "Em and I go way back."

"Oh, yeah?" Jae watched the tips of Emmett's ears redden. *Interesting.* "Just how often do you come in here?"

"At least twice a week," Emmett replied in an airy tone. "You'll know why once you've actually tried the food."

Farah focused her dark eyes on Jae again, the silver hoops in her ears swaying gently. "Can I start you off with a drink?"

"Yes, please." Jae tipped his head toward Emmett's glass. "I'll take a Glinda, please, with the salted rim."

To Jae's surprise, Farah beamed at Emmett. "Honey, you didn't tell me you'd named it."

"The name is official as of tonight." Emmett raised his glass, his face smug as he regarded its contents. "Pink and sweet, with the right amount of salt to keep things interesting. Just like the Good Witch from the Wizard of Oz."

Jae laughed as the others groaned in unison. "You have got to get the recipe out to the gay bars around town," he said after Farah had headed off. "It's more perfect than any cocktail has a right to be."

"But how the hell are you naming drinks in a restaurant that isn't yours?" Krishnan asked. "Is this a moonlighting gig I'm not aware of?"

"Nah. I already told you I come in here sometimes after I get off work at EP." Emmett sipped his cocktail. "I usually sit at the bar and talk with the staff. Sometimes we plot out potions and try them out on each other to make sure they're actually safe to drink."

"Is that how you and Farah hooked up?" Krishnan smirked as the amusement in Emmett's eyes faded. "What? I've known you long enough to recognize when you're in flirt mode, dude. I don't blame you, either, because the girl's phasers are set to stunning."

"Hey, be nice—Farah's cool." A hint of glower crossed Emmett's face though it was clear he was trying not to laugh. "Yes, we hooked up and no, it was not over cocktail mixing here in the restaurant. I've known Farah for … shit, it's got to be eight years at this point. We met through mutuals and figured out pretty quick that we work better as friends. That's been the case for ages now."

"I knew it!" Krishnan practically crowed but Ty made a quelling gesture with his hand.

"Okay, boys, take it down a notch before you scare my brother off." Ty shot a grin in Jae's direction. "The guy hasn't had a chance to check out the menu yet."

Jae turned his focus on the cardboard list on the table before him. "Heck, you're right. I haven't even looked at the thing."

Plucking it up, Jae tried to ignore the questions whirling around his brain. So … Emmett was bi? Why hadn't he said anything before? Like, say, during Pride, when they'd been surrounded by people who represented every letter in LGBTQIA+?

At least Jae had never asked Emmett about his dating life and used the wrong gender. Or had he? Jae frowned. Was there even such a thing as 'right' or 'wrong' when speaking to a person who rejected the gender binary to begin with? Jae and Emmett had done a lot of talking and cocktail sipping last Saturday night, and they'd definitely touched on their dating habits. But what did it matter? What difference did it make to Jae who Emmett did or didn't date?

Shoving his questions aside, Jae studied the menu. He settled on mango chicken and rice but was soon distracted once more by Ty and Krishnan, who each had surprisingly strong feelings about whether they should order rice or noodles for the table.

Jae set his menu down. "I thought it was just me Ty liked to argue with," he said to Emmett.

"Pretty sure either one of them could talk the paint off a wall, but I suppose that's what comes from being a teacher," Emmett replied, his tone dry. "My sister is the same way, which may work in Ty's favor."

"Or against."

"Indeed." Emmett shifted in his chair and faced Jae almost head on. "Can I ask you a question?"

Jae frowned at his somber expression. "Sure. What's up?"

"You've had a question on your face for a while now." Emmett tipped his head toward the back of the restaurant. "Are you worried about the food? Or is my being pansexual a problem?"

"Uh." Jae gave a slow blink. "I might be a little wary about the food. But I don't have any kind of problem with you being pan, Emmett. I'm sorry if you thought I might."

Emmett sighed. "Shit. I don't know why I came at you like that."

"Don't worry about it." Jae licked his lips before he spoke again. "Honestly, I assumed you were gay until about five minutes ago, so I should probably be apologizing to you."

"What? No, man, it's fine." A furrow worked its way between Emmett's eyebrows. "I know Ty told you that Sean and I broke up."

Jae glanced across the table at Ty, who, like Krishnan and Thom, was clearly following his conversation with Emmett, though none of them said a word.

"Yes, he did. In my defense, you've never mentioned being anything other than gay before, not even when we were partying for Pride." Jae smiled. "I don't know, Emmett, but it seems to me that day was *the* time to talk about sexual identity."

"Fair." Emmett chuckled. "I guess I've become more guarded about my identity than I realized. I don't talk about it to just anyone. Not that you're just anyone!" he added in a rush that made Jae laugh over the momentary sting.

"You're fine. It's none of my business unless you want it to be." Jae set his glass down. "You said you've gotten guarded—do people give you shit about being pan?"

"Sometimes, yes," Emmett said. "I'm more often drawn to men and it gets awkward when I stray outside of someone's

23

preconceived box. Especially with anyone who's even remotely biphobic."

"I'm not, you know. Biphobic."

"I think I knew that, but thanks for saying it anyway." Emmett ran a hand over his head, tousling his curls. "Sean was never particularly supportive of my being pan."

Ty leaned forward at last. "Which is why breaking up with him was a good move on your part, Emmett," he said. "Sean is a douche, and you deserve better. Our focus should now be on finding you a better partner."

"Hear, hear." Krishnan picked up his highball glass with a flourish and toasted Emmett. "You do you, babe. As a single man myself, I am happy to act as your wingman, at least when it comes to straight bars since they're all I know. Maybe Jae could do the same when you're out with the gays?"

"Guys, no." Emmett made a slashing motion at his throat with one hand. "Jae has better things to do than worry about my dating life which, I'll remind you once again, is not a project. My plan is to stay single for a good long while, if not forever, and Ty over here is the one we should be celebrating, just in case everyone's forgotten."

"I certainly haven't," Ty said. Holding out his glass, he beamed as the others clinked their drinks against his. Laughter went up as Thom somehow fumbled his and half of his cocktail ended up on the table.

Eventually, talk turned to the bachelor party which, in turn, meant all eyes turned to Jae.

"I don't have much of an update tonight, but I made reservations."

"For where?" Krishnan asked.

"A place I'll tell you about next week when I send out the plan," Jae replied. He frowned at the concern he read on his brother's face. "What?"

"Bro, do you need help?"

"No, I'm good," Jae said. "I'm working days this week which means I'll have more time for getting stuff done. I swear, we'll be ready to go by the twenty-ninth."

If anything, Ty's manner grew more serious "Are you sure? I know how crazy your schedule can be, Jae, and that weekend is literally two weeks from now. Emmett volunteered to help out if

24

you need it."

Of course, he did. Because that's just what I need, alone time with a guy who is as hot as he is unavailable.

"I'd be happy to help," Emmett was saying, "but only if you want it, Jae. I don't want to step on your Best Man toes."

Jae couldn't hold back his scoff. "I think you're forgetting that you and I share the title and I'm pretty sure you'd never step on my toes. I've seen your dance moves, after all." He smiled at Emmett's chuckling. "It'd help to have someone to bounce things off, honestly, *if* you're sure you have the time. You're already handling the rehearsal dinner, Emmett, and your schedule has to be packed even before that."

"I'll make it work," Emmett said. "Aiden and I have always covered for each other when things in life come up. Like the many, *many* smaller events that keep cropping up along the way to my sister's wedding." He shot Ty a wink before glancing back to Jae. "I'm happy to pitch in however you need me to."

A nice feeling unfurled inside Jae. Why shouldn't he take the help? He could use it, whether or not he wanted to admit it, even to himself. Emmett was also closer to Ty right now than Jae was, and no wonder considering Jae had been living anywhere but Boston for years. If anyone could gauge how Ty might react to the plan Jae had cooked up, Jae thought Emmett seemed most likely. Another thing Jae didn't feel ready to cop to, especially to himself.

"Okay, yes," he said. "And thank you, really. Have you got time to talk about stuff on Friday?"

"I do." Emmett's eyes gleamed. "I'll even be in your neighborhood. I'm on the food truck outside of the hospital this week until three, then over at the walk-up window on Beacon Hill."

"Perfect. I should be off by three-thirty."

"Excellent." Emmett rubbed his hands together. "I like it when a plan comes together."

Silently, Jae agreed. And he basked in the warmth of Emmett's smile, sure that the man seated beside him looked more content than he had all evening.

Chapter Four

Despite his best efforts, Jae's plan to leave the hospital by three-thirty on Friday simply didn't pan out. He walked out just after five o'clock and though he gained a bit of energy on the trip to Beacon Hill, Emmett still eyed him askance through the Endless Pastabilities walk-up window on Charles Street.

"Dang," Emmett said. "Tough day?"

Jae pursed his lips against a smile. "You look nice too, dear."

"Sorry." Emmett laughed. "My mouth got ahead of my brain yet again. How are you, Jae-seong?"

"Very well, thank you, Emmett." Jae bobbed his head. "I'll be even better once I get a little coffee in me."

Emmett's face brightened. "Now that I can help with. You take it black, no sugar?"

"That works, yup."

"Cool. I'll be right out."

Emmett emerged from the window only minutes later, a paper go-cup of coffee in one hand and a black cloth bag bulging with takeout containers in the other. He carefully handed Jae the cup.

"Double espresso ground and brewed fresh," he said, then nodded at the bag. "I also packed dinner. Sandwiches, salads, antipasto, rustic bread we make on site. Oh, *arancini* too. Made with vegan risotto, so no cheese."

"Sounds fantastic, thank you. And again, for this." Jae popped the top on his cup and inhaled the luscious smell of fresh coffee, his eyes fluttering closed. "Mmm. I really appreciate it."

"No problem." Emmett chuckled when Jae peeled one eye open and peered at him. "I'm around food all day, Jae—it was literally no big deal. You want to take this over to the park?"

"How about we go back to my apartment?" Jae sipped his coffee. "Plenty of seating there. And I could use a shower."

"Sure." Emmett gestured with one hand. "Lead the way."

Chatting, they turned left onto Pinckney Street and climbed the steep hill that took them deeper into the neighborhood, caffeine clearing the cobwebs from Jae's head as he moved. He felt much more human as he let Emmett into his apartment and capable of reasonably intelligent conversation at last.

"I've got soda, water, and IPA in the fridge," he said on their way up the stairs that led into his unit. "There's also a bottle of red wine on the counter but I opened it last Friday and I'm not sure how it'll taste at this point." He held a hand out for the bag of takeout.

"Beer sounds great." After passing over the bag, Emmett glanced around the big, open room. "Nice place. Are you planning on staying?"

"For now, yes. Why?"

"No reason. I don't know many people who keep a stack of moving boxes by their TV, though, and these walls, Jae—they're totally naked. You need some plants or something to liven up the place."

Jae snickered. "I couldn't keep a cactus alive if you paid me. I do have some art to go on the walls, but I haven't gotten around to hanging it. As for the boxes, well, they're loaded with books. I don't usually unpack them unless I've committed to staying in a city for more than a year."

"Which you still haven't done?" Emmett crossed the room to a set of glass patio doors that looked out past a narrow, wrought iron Juliet balcony onto the building's small back garden.

"Not quite." Jae carried the takeout bag to the counter. "I probably will because the job at the hospital is fantastic, but I like to take my time and get to know a place before I make a decision. Of course, I grew up here and have a bit of a head start with the getting-to-know-all-about-you phase. Maybe that's why I'm dragging my feet about deciding."

"Or maybe you feel like you have more time to make that decision." Emmett turned his eyes on the garden below. "I like your view."

"It is nice, yes. There's no real space to stand on the balcony but the doors let in a lot of light."

Jae stared around at the apartment, trying to see it as Emmett might. Apart from the stack of moving boxes, it was tidy and spartan, which was how Jae had liked things for a long time. His frequent moves over the years led him to decorate in simple palettes of blacks, dark blues, grays, and whites so anything he bought worked reasonably well, regardless of the style of apartment he rented.

A guy your age might want to consider sticking around one city for more than a couple of years.

"It's a good place," Jae said over that annoying little voice. "Quiet neighborhood and the residents are nice. Plus, hot water is included in the rent."

"Heck, I'd never get out of the shower." Turning, Emmett caught Jae's eye. "Speaking of which, go do that while I unpack."

"Thanks. I won't be long."

"Take your time. I'm going to change too, actually." Emmett wiped a hand across his chest. "I stink like garlic and cheese, and no one needs that, especially you."

Chuckling, Jae told the smart speaker on the counter to play a chill house mix, then grabbed a change of clothes from his bedroom. He hadn't noticed food smells on Emmett as they'd walked but rather a combination of clean sweat, soap, and those traces of citrus that always seemed to surround Emmett. Jae had also noticed the enjoyment in Emmett's eyes and the flush in his cheeks, and the way his body filled out his black jeans and EP t-shirt very nicely.

Stop.

Jae shut himself in the bathroom. Turning on the shower, he stared at his reflection in the mirror while he waited for the water to heat. God, he needed to get past his interest in his friend. The guy was going to be a part of Jae's extended family in just a matter of weeks.

So? the voice in Jae's head asked. *It's not like Emmett's the one marrying your brother—you won't even truly be related.*

Jae stepped into the shower with a sigh. While true, the sensible side of his brain still warned him away. Emmett was young, hot, and single for the first time in several years, and he had a whole city at his feet. Even if he'd been a better match for Jae, he clearly wasn't interested and why should he be?

Unfortunately, all of Jae's practical thinking went up in smoke when he returned to the kitchen and found Emmett bustling about, dressed in a dark blue t-shirt and camo shorts that hugged his body just right.

Ugh, he's cute.

"Well, hey." Emmett gave him a grin. "You look a hundred percent more awake."

"The wonders of caffeine and a hot shower."

Jae noticed then that Emmett had not only opened the glass patio doors, he'd moved Jae's dining table in front of them, too, and transformed the room with those simple changes. As the warm evening air poured in, Jae felt almost as if they'd be sitting outside, and he couldn't help his wide-eyed delight.

"Wow, this is nice. I feel like a guest in my own place!"

"You did say to make myself at home." Emmett's smile turned teasing. "You ready to eat, Jae-seong?"

Jae chuckled. "So ready. You're one of only a few people who use my generation name outside of the hospital, you know."

"I noticed that, yeah. Your brother used his on the wedding invitations but doesn't anywhere else, which made me wonder about how and when you'd use the generation name." Emmett picked up a platter loaded with sandwiches. "Siblings share a name, right?"

"Not every family uses them at all, but my Dad's family always has. His generation name is Bae, while Ty's and mine is Seong," Jae said as they sat. "I don't mind if people call me Jae. It's shorter and probably feels more familiar, whereas the generation name carries a more formal weight. I've never been concerned as long as people get the spelling right." He picked up half of the sandwich closest to him, then nodded when Emmett gestured to Jae's plate with a spoonful of salad. "Yes, please. Even my parents go back and forth, though I will say that if they tack on the Seong, it probably means someone's pissed."

"I get it." Emmett helped himself to half of a different sandwich. "Any time 'Emmett Adam McNeil' came out of my father's mouth, I knew I was in for it. He wasn't a fan of nicknames, either."

"He never called you Em?"

"Nope. Not many people do. And my parents thought it was foolishness to mess with a person's given name."

Jae hummed. "Mine didn't love it when my brother decided he'd go by Ty instead of Tae-seong. My dad grew up here and he's the first one to admit that we're a very American family, but he took it as a sign that Ty wanted to distance himself from being part Korean. Ty never saw it the same way, however, because he was just being himself. It was hard for him to see my dad's perspective." Jae bit into his sandwich again. "What exactly am I eating?" he asked around the mouthful. "It's so good I want to make out with it."

Emmett laughed. "It's rotisserie pork and marinated eggplant with fried, sliced onions. The roll is called *michetta* and it's one of my favorites for building sandwiches because the inside is slightly hollow and perfect for stuffing." He pointed to the sandwich half on his own plate. "This is chicken Milanese with spicy vinegar peppers. I used zucchini cheese instead of provolone."

Emmett wiped his lips with his napkin, and Jae pretended not to notice the way they'd pinked up from eating the spicy peppers. "Does it bother you that Ty changed his name?"

"No," Jae said. "We were close growing up, but he started wanting to set himself apart from an early age—he's always been really headstrong. The funny part is that I didn't think Ty needed to try so hard." Jae cut a risotto ball in half with his fork. "I mean, I'm eight years older than him and, physically, I take more after my dad. My features are more Korean and my skin more brown, whereas Ty is fair and has my ma's big eyes and lighter hair. People didn't always guess he was mixed when we were growing up."

"He's also two inches shorter than you. Likes to complain about it when he's half in the bag."

"He's been giving me crap about it for years! That and the food allergy."

"Yeah, and why?" Emmett wrinkled his nose. "Ty knows it's a real thing, right?"

"He does, but there are times I'm almost sure he believes I'm playing it up. It's a holdover from when he was just a kid." Jae pursed his lips. "My parents didn't want Ty to be frightened if I was struggling with symptoms, so they shielded him from it as much as possible. They'd divide and conquer when they had to, my dad with me while Ma stayed with Ty. Ty got it into his head that I was using the allergy to get my dad's attention and by the time I figured it out, we had a hell of a time convincing him that my body really does hate animal milk."

Emmett nodded. "Did you inherit the allergy from your dad?"

"No. Dairy allergies are more common among Asian populations, but my Mom's genes make me more Asian adjacent." Jae had to laugh. "Also, my dad eats more cheese than anyone I've ever met."

Emmett laughed too. "Oh, man."

"Anyway, not even the allergy mattered after I outed myself during my first year of college. From then on, Ty was the straight Bak and I was the gay. He was great about it, too—never wavered in his support." Jae set his fork down. "And as long as we're speaking of Ty, we *need* to talk about the bachelor party. My brother is going to demote me as Best Man if I don't have a plan for him next week and I don't want to let him down."

"You won't. And a demotion is never going to happen, Jae—Ty loves you, even if you are a weirdo." Emmett grinned at Jae's laughter. "How about you tell me what you've got so far, and we can go from there?"

"Okay. I know Ty's talked about a weekend in Providence going on pub crawls, but I had an idea we'd go north instead. As in a campground by Goose Rocks Beach, just outside of Kennebunkport in Maine." He bit his lip at the way Emmett's mouth fell just slightly open. "Is this a terrible idea?"

"No! Camping sounds fantastic." Emmett nodded vigorously. "I'm not sure I'd peg Ty as a tent kind of guy, but maybe that's part of the appeal. Tell me more."

Quickly, Jae did, taking care to note that they'd bunk in tiny A-frame cabins instead of tents, and that the weekend of revelry would involve lots of activities, including axe-throwing, lawn games, and as many games of beach volleyball as anyone felt the need to play. Emmett warmed to the idea at once, his eyes growing brighter the more that he heard.

"I *love* this plan, Jae," he said with a laugh, "and I know Ty will too. The best part is that we can be totally out of the city in just a couple of hours."

"Right!" Jae pulled his phone from his pocket. Flipping through his photos, he pulled one up and set the device down in front of Emmett, then pointed at the map of the campgrounds he'd downloaded the week before. "We're here, and there's a lodge located about a half-mile away. It's not visible from the A-frames so, for all intents and purposes, no one will be around to bother us."

"I'm not worried about being bothered. I worry we'd be the ones bothering everyone else," Emmett said, his tone joking though Jae thought he made a very good point. "What can I do to help? Maybe arrange for people to drive? I'm happy to help you get the food supplies together and cook, too."

You've talked more with this guy in the last two hours than you have on all of your so-called dates with Sal combined.

Jae nearly groaned. That wasn't fair to Sal or even really true. Emmett wasn't here on a date—he was here to help Jae dig himself out of what could have turned into a bachelor party-sized hole. And as far as Sal was concerned, Jae didn't meet up with him to chat. They hooked up for sex and to share food and drink after they'd washed the sweat and cum from their bodies. They *did* talk, though, and share a lot of laughs. Jae didn't see why they *couldn't* get together outside their hookups. Like at Ty and Amelia's wedding, for instance.

"Jae?"

"Hmm?" Jae looked up and caught a puzzled expression on Emmett's face. "Sorry. I had an errant thought about this guy I've been seeing. Sort of."

Emmett raised an eyebrow. "Sort of meaning you don't see the guy very often? Or that you're not sure you're seeing him?"

"A little bit of both but neither."

"Sounds complicated."

"It's not." Jae pushed his now empty plate away. "I've got a casual thing with this guy, Sal—we hang out sometimes when I'm not working nights, but we're not dating by any stretch of the imagination. It occurred to me I could invite Sal to the wedding because my ma's been keen on me to bring someone and that'd get her off my back."

"I hear you," Emmett said. "Amelia was making noise about me going stag for a while, but she's been doing it less in the last few weeks—I'm hoping she forgets completely by the time the actual date rolls around."

"I'll cross my fingers for you." Jae got to his feet. "Do you have time for dessert? I've got a pint of cherry almond milk ice cream that I happen to know goes beautifully with the IPA you're drinking."

"Oh, do you now? I like the sound of that." Emmett grinned. "Will you be indulging in a beer, too, Jae, or am I still drinking alone?"

"I believe I will join you, thank you very much." Jae started stacking plates. "Let me just load the dishwasher and I'll grab the stuff from the fridge. I liked your idea about arranging rides for the bachelor party, by the way, but we should split up the cooking duties for that weekend—you deserve some time off, too."

An hour later, he and Emmett were seated side by side on Jae's leather sofa watching *Westworld*, ice cream bowls scraped clean and beer bottles half empty. Jae's long day had crept back over him, leaving his head pleasantly muzzy, but he was enjoying himself too much to make an excuse to go to bed.

"Now I know why Aiden has been telling me to watch this show," Emmett said. "This is so off the wall!"

"It really is. And it seems a crime for anyone to miss out on all of this killer robot hotness."

"Some of the humans aren't too bad, either." Emmett chuckled. "Hey, what are you doing tomorrow around dinner time?"

"No plans that I know of. Why?"

"Amelia and Ty requested seafood and fish options for the rehearsal dinner, and I want to be sure my ideas are on the right track." Emmett sat up straighter. "I thought maybe I'd cook and you'd tell me what you think. Also, I can give you ideas about plants you won't kill."

"Yeah, good luck with that—there is not a houseplant out there I haven't already destroyed." Jae licked his lips. "So, you're cooking at your place? Or do you want to meet up at the EP Test Kitchen instead?"

Emmett shook his head. "It'll turn into a cooking class if we meet at the restaurant. There is no way Aiden won't want to get in on it, along with anyone else on staff who might still be around, and that's not what I had in mind. So yeah, dinner at my place, if you're up for it?"

"Sounds great." Jae thought for a moment. "But … shouldn't the bride and groom be the ones doing the tasting?"

"They will. I'd rather get a more unbiased opinion first. My sister's inner Bridezilla has started to show and I'm afraid she'll eat my face if I make dishes she doesn't like."

"Oh, God." Jae's laughter echoed around the room. "You're such a weirdo."

"And you love it, right?"

"Honestly, I kind of do."

Turning his head on the cushion, Jae found Emmett's gaze on him, eyes glittering in the shifting light of the TV. Jae's skin prickled with sudden awareness. *Damn.* If this man had been anyone else, Jae would have climbed onto him without a second thought and kissed him until neither of them could breathe. Jae made himself smile instead.

"I'm glad you had time to hang out," he said, then hauled in a deep breath as the corners of Emmett's lips lifted too.

"Me too." Emmett gently knocked his shoulder into Jae's. "And I'm glad you have time to do it again tomorrow."

Chapter Five

Though Jae had grown up in Boston, the city had changed during his years living out of state and flourished in ways that never failed to delight him. He sometimes felt pleasantly lost when he ventured outside of the neighborhoods he knew best, and he gave himself over to that feeling now as he walked deep into Chinatown in search of Emmett's apartment building.

He nearly passed it by before realizing his mistake and paused a moment on the sidewalk to stare up at the big concrete block, its somber gray facade broken only by what might be larger than typical windows. Emmett himself appeared anything but plain when he answered the door, however, his eyes shining and his cheeks rosy as he gestured for Jae to come in.

"Hey there. Did you have any trouble finding the place?"

"A little," Jae said as he stepped inside, his stomach turning a goofy little flip as Emmett grabbed him in a quick bro hug. "But only because it's been a million years since I was even in this part of town." His cheeks were hot when Emmett stepped back, but the sight of the apartment beyond provided just the distraction Jae needed. "Oh, wow."

The studio was laid out in a long rectangle with soaring ceilings and a single massive window on the far wall that flooded the room with light. Every inch had been fashioned to maximize space, and the stark white walls were warmed by furniture made from blond woods and copper-hued metals. Potted house plants were everywhere, including the windowsill, injecting the place with splashes of green life. What Jae had first thought was a blue and white carpet turned out to be a painted parquet floor and he smiled as he spotted a sleeping loft located high in one corner, accessible by a short, steep staircase set by the kitchen.

"This is beautiful. Not at all what I expected. And look at all these plants! No wonder Amelia put you in charge of coordinating flowers for the wedding."

"It's a hobby gone wild."

"I think you mean grown wild."

Emmett laughed. "And I think you're a nerd." He pointed at the bottle in Jae's hand. "Is that for us?"

"Oh! For you, really," Jae handed him the wine. "I wasn't sure what you had in mind to cook tonight, but I figured you could enjoy a bottle of red anytime. Sal—the guy I mentioned yesterday—is big on wine and I remember him saying once that Pinot Noir goes well with summer foods. This is one I've had before."

Holy rambling idiot, Batman.

Jae shut up, but Emmett just nodded, seemingly at a loss as to how to process the babbling.

"Thank you," Emmett said as he looked over the bottle's label. "I have a bottle of burgundy, but we can save this for another time. If you'd like, I mean."

The hesitation in his voice and face punched right through Jae's nerves. "I would."

"Yeah? Well, good." Emmett's expression relaxed immediately. "I'm basically finished cooking, too, so you're just in time."

Jae glanced toward the corner that held the kitchen and raised his eyebrows at the array of ingredients on the counter and pans on the stove. "It smells great in here. Anything you need me to do?"

"You can pour the wine, but what I really need is your honest opinion on the food." Steely-eyed focus replaced Emmett's cheer as they moved toward the counter. "We'll have non-fish choices for anyone who wants them, of course, but I want to be sure I'm hitting the right notes all the way around with these dishes. Both of the courses we're sampling tonight are Sicilian recipes with no cream sauce and definitely no cheese."

"Works for me." Jae pulled the strap of his bag over his head. "Where do you keep your wine glasses?"

Emmett's eyes went wide. "Right!" He chuckled and set the

unopened bottle of wine aside. "Glasses are in the cabinet on your right and the burgundy's on the counter."

"Got it." Jae busied himself with pouring while Emmett stepped back up to the stove. "Not that it matters, but is that an Italian thing? No cheese on fish?"

"It is in a lot of people's minds. Including Aiden's, or at least when it comes to the food at EP." Emmett picked up a set of metal tongs. "The guy is slutty for fish tacos with crema and Cotija cheese, though, so clearly the rules are less strict outside of his own kitchens."

Together, they brought everything to a cafe table set against the wall.

"We'll have antipasti and courses at the actual dinner, but I figured we'd just concentrate on the first and second plates and salad tonight and serve it all at the same time." Emmett set his hand beside a long platter. "The *primo,* or first plate, is spaghetti *ai ricci di mare,* which is sea urchin." He smiled at Jae's soft 'ooh.' "Have you had urchin before?"

"Not with Italian food but this smells delicious."

"I have a feeling you'll like it. Our *secondo* is seared tuna steaks with a tomato, caper, and olive sauce, and the salad is a sliced beet *carpaccio* with lemon, crushed pistachio, aged balsamic, and some very good vegan goat cheese. Everything but the pasta and bread are from scratch, but I brought them both from EP, so I know what's in them."

Jae cast his gaze over the table, a tender feeling running through him. Emmett had clearly gone out of his way to serve something Jae could eat without worrying. "Everything looks gorgeous" he said, "though it occurs to me now that this is twice you've made me dinner just this week." Jae wagged a finger. "Next time is my treat."

Emmett beamed. "Sounds great."

"Just give me a chance to go food shopping first," Jae said with a laugh. "You've seen the contents of my refrigerator and you know I need to stock up if I'm going to cook food more complicated than fried eggs, chorizo, and rice."

"Dude, I would eat the hell out of that."

"It is pretty tasty, if I say so myself. I dated a Filipino guy when I lived in San Francisco and he made this amazing Spanish sausage called *longanzia.* He'd serve it with fried eggs and rice and the whole thing was called *longsilog*. Chorizo is a fine substitute in a pinch."

"You wanna cook for me tomorrow?" Emmett asked as they served themselves. "I'm free if you are."

"Perfect. My shift ends at three," Jae said. He tucked into his food and literally groaned as the succulent, meaty flavor of tuna hit his taste buds, mixing beautifully with the salty-sweet acid notes of the sauce. "*Damn*."

"Yeah?"

"Heck, yeah. This is fantastic. I can't wait to try the rest."

"Technically, you should have had the pasta first." Emmett made a tsking noise with his tongue. Using a pair of tongs, he scooped spaghetti onto Jae's plate. "I won't tell anyone you got your plates mixed up."

"You said we weren't doing dishes in order!" Jae exclaimed, though he knew from the gleam in Emmett's eye that he was just teasing. Someday, this guy was going to make some lucky person very happy. "You know, I'm surprised you don't have any plans tonight," he said. "It being Saturday and you being you."

"Thank you, I think. I've been out on a bunch of dates since Sean, but I haven't really been feeling it. And I'm *really* not in the right frame of mind for anything more than casual, so that works."

"Not looking for love, huh?"

"Love can eat my ass." Emmett grinned as Jae's laughter rang out. "You don't feel the same?"

"No." Jae stifled another laugh with his hand. "I'm fine with the idea of love, but I can't say I've ever been there myself. I've been damned fond of a few of the men I've dated, but love? No."

"Count yourself lucky, Jae, because feelings are fucking complicated. My new motto is 'down with love.'" Emmett said, his tone musing. "Are you seeing anyone besides your boy, Sal?"

"Sal is forty years old and he'd probably die laughing knowing that someone called him 'my boy.' But no, I'm not seeing anyone else right now. Hell, I'm hardly seeing Sal."

"Where'd you meet him?"

"In line buying beer." Jae met the surprise in Emmett's gaze head on. "He asked me about the brand of IPA I'd picked up and one thing led to another."

"Sounds like a rom-com meet cute," Emmett said, his lips turning up at the corners.

"It does! We're just friends, though. Sal's not looking for a boyfriend and I'm too busy with work to get into anything serious." Jae shrugged.

"Is that why you're still single?" Emmett asked. "Too focused on your career to settle down?"

"I suppose so, though I've never looked at it that way." Jae set his fork down. "I've been lucky and found a lot of opportunities as a NA, but the men I date are just as focused on their own careers. What we have works fine until it doesn't." He paused, then licked his lips. "Sometimes, the allergy gets in the way."

"Seriously?" Emmett furrowed his brow. "As in a guy you're dating can't hack life without cheese?"

Jae laughed. "That's a gross simplification but yes. And, to be fair, being forced to adhere to a lifestyle not of your choosing can be tough."

"Huh. I get what you're saying. Ultimately, it sounds a lot like whining, though. And like maybe you need to date different men."

"I'll keep that in mind."

"As far as being career obsessed, I've definitely been guilty too," Emmett said. "I didn't always realize it was making my personal life not great, but it's sort of an occupational hazard when you run your own business, you know?"

"Is that what happened with Sean?"

"Yup." The furrow on Emmett's forehead deepened. "I work a lot and I'm the first person to admit it. But, because Sean and I worked together all day, I thought that would be enough to keep things between us strong. Turns out, I was wrong. Sean needed more from me. I just didn't know it until it was too late. Hell, I don't think Sean knew it either."

"What happened anyway? I mean, I know you broke it off, but we've never really talked about your ex."

"Yeah, he's not my favorite subject. Sean cheated on me." Emmett's expression darkened. "The weekend you and I met, I was in town for Amelia and Ty's engagement party, remember?

"Sure, I do. You said Sean opted to stay in Portland and keep an eye on EP."

"Turns he opted to stay in Portland to keep an eye on a bartender from my favorite tavern. They spent the whole time screwing, and in my Shasta no less." Emmett shook his head. "They got so damned comfortable playing house, I almost walked in on them doing the deed."

Jae grimaced. "Oh, hell."

"Exactly." Emmett gave a short, hard laugh. "The irony is that Sean always gave me crap for even talking to pretty people because, of course, it meant I was thinking of cheating on him. Everyone knows a pan guy can't keep it in his pants, right?"

"Yeah, no. I think your ex was projecting."

"Meaning ... Sean was the one who was thinking of cheating and assumed I'd do the same?"

"I think it's a possibility." Jae's almost winced at the anger that flitted across his friend's face. "But I shouldn't have said anything, Emmett."

"No, I'm glad you did. I think you have a point. No one's ever said it in quite those words before, but it makes sense." Emmett huffed softly. "I always wondered why Sean was so suspicious of me. Because sure, I'm flirty, but I'm not a cheater. I'd never put a partner through that."

Jae nodded. "I believe you. Also, Ty's assessment of your ex was spot on—Sean is a douche."

"He could be when he wanted to, sure. But eh, that's in the past and so is he." Emmett drew in a deep breath. "After the blow up, I took a hard look at what was going on in my life and decided to make some changes. I moved back to Boston, obviously, and sold Sean the trailer. I didn't cut him a deal," he added with a cocky air that made Jae laugh. "I've also been shifting some of my priorities around so I can focus less on work and more on my life outside of EP. I'm tired of being too scattered and busy to go after things I want."

"Yeah? Like what?"

Emmett's gaze didn't waver as he set down his glass. He reached up and pushed back the hair that had fallen onto Jae's forehead with his fingers, and though neither of them spoke, the emotions Jae glimpsed in Emmett's gaze made his heart ache. Jae saw desire, yes, but tenderness too, along with a healthy dose of nerves. The world around them went still as Emmett leaned in and kissed Jae, his lips soft and sweet with the taste of burgundy wine.

Oh.

Goosebumps rose on Jae's arms. This man had *just* unloaded about his ex in a very major way, and fuck if that didn't stick in Jae's head like a burr. Could either of them really trust Emmett's current frame of mind? And what about Jae's? Despite his spinning thoughts, Jae leaned into the kiss, unable to resist the sensations washing over him. He'd wanted this moment for months, pined for it really, like a schoolboy with a crush, and God, kissing Emmett was so good. Jae felt truly breathless as Emmett finally broke away.

"Emmett," he whispered. "What are you—"

"I know." Eyes still closed, Emmett pressed his forehead to Jae's and sighed. "You have no idea how long I've wanted to do that. I'm sorry if—"

"I'm not sorry at all," Jae said at once, and meant it. He raised a hand and covered Emmett's where it rested against the side of Jae's neck. "I've thought about kissing you since the first time we met and I'm going to do it again."

And he did, raising both hands and sliding them deep into Emmett's soft curls. Jae's insides flipped as Emmett turned into him, moving an arm around Jae's waist so he could get closer. His breath hitched when Jae slid his tongue against Emmett's, and Emmett groaned low in his throat.

"Really glad it wasn't just me," Emmett murmured when they came back up for air. He stared at Jae, wonder in his eyes, as if he couldn't believe what was happening. He got to his feet and quickly tugged Jae up with him. "Acting like I don't want you when we hang out is torture, you know."

Jae chuckled. "I do." He slipped his arms around Emmett's shoulders, his body buzzing as their kisses grew hotter and then Emmett was pulling away, his expression intent.

"Can we … I need to touch you," he said, his tone hungry, and even if Jae hadn't already been on the same page, he'd have gotten there just looking at the heat in Emmett's eyes. "But only if you want to. Because you can say 'when' anytime you want and this stops, okay?"

"Yeah, okay." Jae licked his lips. "I don't want to stop," he said, "and no way in hell do I want to say 'when.'"

He kissed Emmett again, sweet and deep, losing himself in those touches. Somehow, Emmett got them to the staircase that led to the sleeping loft and they climbed it, hands clasped tightly together. Standing beside the bed in its alcove, they pulled at one another's clothes, mouths meeting again and again.

Jae tugged his t-shirt up and over his head, then watched in silence as Emmett did the same, once more revealing miles of fair, freckled skin, free of beads and glitter this time. Jae ran his palms over Emmett's torso, petting and stroking as they kissed, the sounds of their breaths growing louder. Emmett looked almost dazed as he reached for the fly on Jae's black jeans, his pupils blown and lips kiss-swollen.

"This is okay, right?" Jae made himself ask, then grinned at Emmett's breathless laugh.

"So, totally okay. I meant it when I said I've wanted this for a long time."

"Good." Jae kissed him some more, luxuriating in the way Emmett stroked his back, and fire sizzled under his skin when those hands landed on his ass.

Gently, he pushed Emmett down onto the mattress and together they moved until they were spread over the center of the bed. Jae settled on top of Emmett, his cock throbbing at Emmett's low moan. Splaying his hands across Jae's lower back, Emmett squirmed when Jae ground their bodies together. He was hard against Jae, and everywhere their bodies met was hot. Emmett had plenty to say too, his words a low murmur that got right inside Jae's head.

"Need more," he said. "Want you so fucking much, Jae. Feel you on me. Mmm." He tugged at the waistband on Jae's jeans, his breaths coming faster, and oh yeah, Jae was so with the program.

Pushing himself up, he straddled Emmett's waist and smirked as Emmett let out a hoarse curse. Jae unzipped Emmett's shorts, then bent forward over Emmett once more. Emmett met him with a hungry kiss. They tussled and tugged until they'd gotten each other's pants and boxers out of the way enough so they could touch skin, but Emmett gasped when Jae palmed his cock, a great shudder wracking his frame.

"Jesus, Jae."

Jae let out a groan. "Fuck, you're hot." Lifting his hand, he licked his palm and reached between them again, wrapping Emmett's cock up with his own in his fist.

"Holy shit." Emmett whined as Jae pumped them both, his hold on Jae bruising. "There's ... oh, *fuck*. Stuff's in the drawer on the right."

"Now he tells me."

Emmett's laughter in his ears, Jae boosted himself over to the nightstand, movements hasty as he plucked a bottle of lube from the drawer. He slicked his palms, then took Emmett and himself in hand again, grunting at the increased sensation brought by the lube and the hard, silky flesh against his. Emmett's hold on Jae tightened even more.

"I'm clear," Jae said in between kisses, "in case you were wondering. But we can use condoms if you want."

"Mmm, no. Don't you stop." Emmett gave another breathless laugh. "I'm clear, too. And I wanna feel you Jae, just you."

Jae set his forehead on Emmett's. He fought to keep his eyes open as he brought them off, the lust barreling through him almost too much to bear. Emmett's expressions enraptured him, as did the fire in his gaze. Jae's breath caught when Emmett's eyes went wide.

"Oh, fuck. Fuck. I …" Emmett clutched at him, his voice broken. "Gonna come."

Awe swept over Jae. "Show me," he whispered and worked them both as Emmett fell apart, his chest thrust up and cock pulsing, cum slicking their cocks and bellies, his mouth falling open in a silent scream.

A roar filled Jae's ears. Groaning, he thrust over and over into that sticky heat until he soared too. Eyes screwed shut, Jae came on a gasp, helpless to do anything but ride the waves of pleasure until he melted, boneless and dizzy onto Emmett's body.

"Damn," he whispered against Emmett's neck, his voice rough, and wanted to smile when a low chuckle answered him. "Am I crushing you?"

"Nah." Emmett's breath puffed against Jae's cheek. "Feels good."

They lay still for a time, Jae coasting on the afterglow as he soaked up the heat of Emmett's body. He felt centered. Relaxed. Very fucking good. And like he would absolutely fall asleep if he didn't peel himself up and off of the human furnace lying beneath him. The way Emmett's breaths had already evened out told Jae he was dozy, too.

"Okay if I use your shower?" Jae got out past a yawn.

"Absolutely. There's room in there for two if you don't mind some company."

Jae swore he heard a thread of tension in Emmett's tone. Sitting up, he straddled Emmett's waist once more. "I definitely don't mind."

"Good," Emmett said, his manner lazy now. "We could finish eating dinner and move on to dessert first, if you like. I bought a tub of that almond milk cherry ice cream you love."

"Mmm, I knew I liked you for a reason."

Jae leaned in and kissed the hollow of Emmett's throat, but the softness that fell over Emmett's face when Jae sat back up tugged at his heart. Emmett appeared wistful. Almost sad. And shit, that look right there was the reason Jae was supposed to stay away from Emmett McNeill.

Jae laid a hand on Emmett's chest. "You okay?"

"Yeah." Emmett covered Jae's hand with his own, then levered himself upright until his chest met Jae's. They shared another kiss. "I'm great actually," he said. "Just wondering, you know? Like … what do we do now?"

Good question, said the voice in Jae's head. *Things can only get weird from here.*

They didn't *have* to get weird, though. Not if Jae was careful and honest with Emmett. Honest with himself too. Like about how what they had just done was simply chemistry and fun and nothing that needed a lot of deep thought. And that was exactly what they both wanted.

Drawing a deep breath, Jae met Emmett's eyes. "How about we eat and shower, then sleep, and we can share some granola in the morning? If you're okay with me staying, I mean. It's cool if you'd rather be alone."

"I like your plan better. Though …" Emmett grimaced. "This is probably a good time to tell you I need to be up before five."

"Oh, fucking hell." Jae let out a laugh. "I'll warn you now, I'm not much of a talker at that hour of the morning."

"I won't take your silence personally." Emmett ran a hand over Jae's sternum, his touch raising goosebumps. "I don't suppose I could bribe you to talk to me, say with another double-espresso and something fancier than granola?"

"You might."

"I knew it." A chuckle rumbled low in Emmett's chest. "Who knew you were such a soft touch?"

"No one. Because I'm not."

Except that was just the problem. Jae *was* a soft touch when it came to Emmett, and he was going to have to work very, very hard to keep himself from getting into trouble. Tonight was proof of that.

Chapter Six

"This isn't real cheese?"

Jae smiled as Mark stared at the sandwich in his hand. After walking back to Beacon Hill with Emmett that morning, Jae had gone to his own apartment and changed for work. Then he'd stopped by the EP food truck on his way into the hospital, only to walk away with another cup of Emmett's delicious coffee and a bag filled with enough food to feed a crowd lunch, much to his friends' delight.

"Who says zucchini cheese *isn't* real cheese?" Jae asked.

"Science." Mark cocked an eyebrow at him. "Plant-based cheese is an analogue, man, just like Kraft Singles."

"You know I can't eat those things." Jae shrugged at Mark and Zac's laughter. "But if what I've heard is true, I'm not missing much anyway."

"Hey now, processed cheese tastes just fine when you eat it with the right things," Mark replied. "It's all about mouth feel."

"The flavor has to be good, though." Zac scooped up grilled vegetables with his fork. "Aiden makes plant-based cheese at home."

"Emmett claims it's easy," Jae said. "He even gave me a recipe. I'm not sure I'm brave enough to try making it myself but he offered to help."

Zac held up a finger. "I'd think twice before you give that man free rein in your kitchen, Jae-seong. You could end up with arugula spaghetti or oysters dressed in passion fruit foam." His eyes danced at Mark's grimace. "He and Aiden can be diabolical when it comes to molecular cooking. I'm the first to admit I've got food hang ups but plant-jello noodles just didn't do it for me. Ironic, given they're low in calories and you'd think I'd *want* to eat the stuff."

"Yes, but you're spoiled for pasta in general," Mark said. "How could you not be when your man whips up handmade spaghetti every night?"

Zac scoffed. "He does no such thing. I wouldn't be able to fit through the front door if that was actually true. Aiden makes pasta by hand maybe once every two weeks, or if we're having people over to dinner. Speaking of which, how about a meal at our place in a couple of weeks? I'm thinking Wednesday, the twenty-seventh."

"Heck, yes." Mark rubbed his hands together. "I'm working days that week."

"I'm not." Jae pouted. "I'm on the graveyard shift Sunday through Wednesday."

Zac's face fell. "Ugh. What about Thursday the twenty-eighth, then? I'm pretty sure Emmett's free that night."

Jae's brain stuttered over Emmett's name and his words right along with it. "I ... err ... Thursday?"

"Thursday's fine too," Mark said, "and I'm glad you got Emmett to come. Outside of the goddamned food truck and Pride, I feel like I never see the big lug, even though I know Owen has drinks with him and Aiden regularly."

"Yeah, Emmett's been MIA a lot since things went bad with his ex." Zac pulled a small glassine paper bag across the table and carefully extracted a light golden cookie studded with pignoli nuts. He took a small bite and made a happy noise as he chewed. "He's never said so, but I think he feels like the odd man out when he's socializing with couples."

Down with love, Jae imagined Emmett saying. "Possibly, yes," he said. "He hasn't missed any of the groomsman nights my brother has set up and he didn't even hesitate to pitch in when I asked for help with the bachelor party planning."

Zac's expression lightened. "That's good to hear."

"But don't change your dinner plans for me," Jae said. "Wednesday the twenty-seventh works and it'll give me something to look forward to. Just leave out some vegan cheese so I can snack while you guys drown yourselves in cream sauce and parmesan."

"Roast some chickens," Mark said over Zac's snort of laughter. "Or hell, a side of beef!"

"Okay, cowboy." Zac got to his feet. "Feel free to hit me up with suggestions and I'll pass them on to Aiden."

Jae extracted a cookie from the bag for himself as Zac walked off. "I have zero ideas of what Aiden could cook."

"Mmm, they can ask Emmett if worse comes to worst. He seems to have a good handle on things you can and can't eat."

While he could do nothing about the sudden heat crawling up his cheeks, Jae made sure his voice sounded light. "I'm sure Aiden does as well—the two of them feed people for a living, after all."

"Did Emmett feed you breakfast this morning?" A sly smile blossomed on Mark's face. "Or was it your turn to scramble the eggs?"

What the fuck?

Jae blinked twice before he forced himself to answer. "We had smoothies, actually. Em made these fancy bowls with dragon fruit and raspberries and a coconut custard that tasted like crème brûlée."

"Holy shit, that sounds fantastic."

"They were. Better than anything I'd have been able to make at five o'clock in the morning." Jae bit into his cookie and chewed. "Don't tell anyone, okay?"

Mark cocked his head. "About you and Emmett? Okay. Can I ask why not?"

"Because we've only hooked up once and it's complicated, what with our connections to Ty." Jae pursed his lips. "Em's also younger than me and clearly not over Sean. This is a fling, if we can even call it that."

"I like how you say the word 'fling' like it's not a fun thing." Mark rolled his eyes. "I'm the last person who'll tell you that dating a younger man doesn't work, too. I wouldn't be with Owen if that was really true, and Aiden wouldn't be with Zac."

"Yeah, but what's going on with Em and me isn't a thing we have to make work—we're just having fun. We haven't even talked about what happened last night, at least not properly."

"Because you were too busy screwing around on top of the remains of your breakfast?"

"No!" Jae let out a laugh. "Because I wasn't in the right frame of mind at five a.m. for a deep conversation about hooking up."

"That's fair." Mark took a huge bite of the last cookie, then reached over and helped as Jae started cleaning up the remains of their meal. "Are you going to have a deep conversation or take the easy route and pretend it never happened?" he asked through his chewing.

Jae's mood dipped a little. The idea of acting like last night had never happened around Emmett left him queasy. Emmett might feel differently, though, especially now in the cold light of day. And that troubled Jae more than he liked. "We're going to talk."

"Of course, you are. Both of you are very mature." Mark's gaze was kind. "When is that happening?"

"Tonight. It's my turn to make Emmett dinner. It's only fair now that he's fed me twice in a week." He frowned at the bag of empty containers in front of him. "Shit, three times now." Mark's laughter caught his attention. "What?"

"Honey, if Emmett just wanted to talk, he'd make you a meal at the EP Test Kitchen. Whatever else you do at your apartment tonight, there's going to be more than talking."

Jae could get down with that plan. He and Emmett really did need to talk, however. Particularly if a single hookup had made it obvious to Mark, of all people, that things between Emmett and Jae had changed.

"How did you know?" Jae asked as he and Mark walked toward the exit. "About Em and me, I mean."

"That." Mark tipped his head toward Jae. "You've never called Emmett by his nickname until today. The only other people I know who do it consistently are Aiden and Sean, both of whom were Emmett's boyfriends at one time."

"I guess I'll have to watch what I say." Jae grimaced. "And you're not going to tell anyone, are you?"

"I said I wouldn't. Except Owen—I'll tell him if he asks me straight out. I've never lied to him and I'm not going to start now." Mark watched Jae for a moment, his eyebrows drawn together. "Are you sure you want to do this secret boyfriends thing?"

Jae grimaced. "We're not boyfriends, secret or otherwise. This is just chemistry, Mark, and it'll run its course in a couple of weeks."

"If you say so." Mark shrugged. "And while I won't tell anyone, I won't need to. Your ears will do it for you."

"My ..." Jae raised his right hand and fingered his ear lobe. "What do my ears have to do with anything?"

"They turned a truly violent shade of red when I teased you about Emmett," Mark said. "You're going to have to watch those, too. Or wear a hat." He shot Jae a grin. "Good luck with that now that the weather has warmed up."

* * * *

"I brought cookies." Emmett held up a bakery box tied with blue twine. "Assorted macarons made with vegan love."

"Thank you." Jae turned his stare on the thing Emmett held in his other hand, namely a small white pot out of which sprouted a crown of thick, fleshy green leaves, each serrated with small, pointed teeth. "That's not for me too, is it? Because I've already told you, I am hopeless with plants and—"

"This is an aloe plant," Emmett said over Jae's babbling. His lips curved up in a smile. "They're very easy to care for and don't need direct sunlight, which makes that big window beyond those patio doors of yours perfect. It'll only need water once every three weeks."

"Which means I'll forget to do it altogether!" Jae worried his bottom lip between his teeth. "I really appreciate the thought behind the gesture, Em, but the poor thing deserves a better life than I can give it."

"I'll help you." Emmett's face turned coaxing. "We'll set some alarms on your phone to help you remember and if you have any questions you can call me, day or night."

"You're going to be sorry you said that," Jae muttered. Holding his hands out for the pot, he cradled it gently as he carried it to the end of the table that sat nearest to the window. "Is this close enough to get good light?"

At Emmett's silence, Jae glanced back, aware only then that Emmett hadn't moved from the spot where Jae had left him.

"Something wrong?"

"No. Just surprised," Emmett said. "You left the table by the window."

"Ah. I decided I liked it here." Jae set the little aloe vera plant on the tabletop then turned his gaze on the open doors and reddening sky beyond. "I never understood the purpose of a Juliet balcony before. There's no room to sit or even really stand on them, and they always seemed like a wasted feature to me.

"I get it now, though." He looked toward Emmett. "When you open the doors up, it's like bringing the outdoors *in* and suddenly, I have a patio inside my apartment."

"Exactly." Emmett smiled, but still didn't move.

Jae knew then that Emmett would give him an out if Jae wanted it. They could go back to being just friends and put the hookup behind them. Emmett would be nice about it, too. Not that Jae was surprised—he'd known from their first meeting that a gentleman inhabited the frame of the man who stood watching him.

Jae didn't want to put the hookup behind him. He wanted more from his friendship with Emmett, and to explore the connection he'd sensed between them last night, even knowing that the connection likely had a short shelf life. So, he crossed the room to Emmett's side and angled his face down, taking Emmett's lips with his own.

Emmett's eyes slipped closed. Sliding an arm around Jae's waist, he leaned in and hummed as Jae brought a hand to the back of Emmett's neck.

Mmm.

Jae gathered Emmett close, his brain already racing ahead to the part where clothes started coming off. Then Emmett dropped the box of cookies on the floor and swore, prompting laughter from them both.

"I'm sorry."

Jae kissed the apology off Emmett's lips. "Don't be. That was nice."

"It was."

"Why do you sound surprised?"

"You didn't really say hi when I came in." Emmett's cheeks turned pink. "Wasn't sure if you were just waiting for the right time to tell me to fuck off or if we were going to pretend the other night never happened."

"My bad." Jae made sure his tone was gentle. "You distracted me with your Emmett-ness and made a t-shirt and shorts look criminally hot. Plus, you gave me a *plant.*" He reveled in Emmett's chuckling. "I apologize for being rude."

"It's okay."

"No, it's not. So, hi, weirdo." Jae pressed his lips to Emmett's again and lingered for a beat before he pulled back. "Thanks for coming over."

"Thanks for inviting me."

The pleasure that stole across Emmett's face made Jae feel lighter too. "Come on over here and I'll pour you a drink. I opened a bottle of Grenache to go with the *bulgogi* I'm making, but there's beer if you'd prefer."

Emmett scooped the box of cookies off the floor. "Wine sounds great."

"Okay." Jae waited until Emmett was at his side and the cookie box safe on the counter before he spoke again. "Did you really think I'd want to pretend the other night never happened?"

"I shouldn't have assumed anything." The flush on Emmett's cheeks deepened. "At least not before we'd talked."

"Well, I probably shouldn't have kissed you either, *especially* not before we'd talked. But I don't want to pretend last night didn't happen, Em."

"Neither do I. Not when I'm with you, anyway."

"Okay." Jae handed Emmett a glass of wine as he considered those words. "Does that mean you don't want anyone else to know we hooked up?"

Emmett wrinkled his nose. "That sounds bad when you say it like that."

"I'm not sure how else to say it. I'd like to hear your reasons, though." Jae lit the burner on the stove, then met Emmett's gaze head on. "Particularly if you want to hook up again."

"I'm very okay with a repeat." Emmett's quick grin turned rueful in a heartbeat. "But you and I going public would stir up more drama than anyone needs, and I don't want that. Take Ty, for example. He won't be jazzed to know I messed around with you."

Jae didn't reply. Emmett likely had a point. Jae believed he was also mistaken, however, because Ty was far more likely to be pissed at *Jae* for doing the messing around than Emmett, especially if he and Emmett were going to do it on the sly. And that wasn't a thing Jae needed in his life, especially with Ty and Amelia's wedding so close.

So yeah, Jae was on board with continuing to keep whatever this thing was between Emmett and himself quiet. He just wasn't sure what had changed in the last ten minutes to make him sort of hate the idea.

"Hey, I'm sorry."

Emmett's voice pulled Jae out of his swirling thoughts. "What about?"

"For asking you to keep it on the down-low." A familiar worried crease had worked its way back between Emmett's eyebrows. "I shouldn't have assumed—"

"It's fine. I get what you're asking, Em. I just got stuck in my head there for a sec." Jae flashed him a smile and took the easiest route back to lightening the mood. "Come help me cook?"

Emmett's whole person brightened. "I'd love it."

They chatted about Jae's marinade and his mother's homemade kimchi, and Jae showed Emmett his technique for getting the best sear on the slices of beef without overcooking them. Emmett dished up plain boiled rice and washed red lettuce leaves, and the genuine delight in his face as they sat down to eat made Jae happy.

"I considered cooking *jjigae*," he said, "which is a spicy stew you can make with all kinds of things, including pork belly and tofu, which is my favorite type. I'm not sure either of us would have been able to truly enjoy it on a hot evening like this, though, so that'll have to wait for another time. But I'll warn you now that the kimchi is spicy, because my ma doesn't fool around when it comes to the chili powder."

"Neither do I." Emmett wasted no time picking up a wrap he'd made with a lettuce leaf and the beef. "This all smells amazing."

"Thanks. I don't have a ton of range when it comes to cooking, but I know this recipe is solid."

"More than," Emmett said around his first bite. "This is so good, dude. And *damn*, the kimchi. I think my face is on fire!"

Jae bit back a laugh. "Told you."

"It hurts so good. Is the recipe a family secret?"

"It's a family heirloom, that's for sure. My granddad passed it down to Dad and Ma and she fiddles some with the ingredients to keep the allergens out when I'm going to be eating it. I wouldn't say the recipe is a secret, though. Ma's probably already shared it with your sister, and I know she'd share it with you, too." Jae set his chopsticks down.

"Nice." Emmett's manner turned serious. "Speaking of secrets … are you really okay with not telling anyone we hooked up? Because I have fun with you, Jae, and I'd like to keep hanging out."

"I would too. Keeping it just between us could be tricky given we'll be around our families a lot over the next few weeks, but I don't think it needs to be a big deal." Jae frowned. "Are you sure *you're* okay with it, Em?"

"Honestly, hiding things about myself is not my favorite thing, even when it's the easiest way to keep the peace." Emmett huffed out a breath, sounding frustrated. "You'd think I'd be used to it after all this time."

Jae waited for more but, when Emmett stayed silent, shook his head. "I'm sorry. I don't know what you mean."

"My family. Well, my mother, specifically" Emmett turned his attention back on his food. "We don't talk about me being pan."

For several beats, Jae simply stared at him. "But she knows, right?" he asked at last.

"My sister does, of course. I really don't know if my mother knows. There was never any real discussion about my sexuality with my parents before my father died and my mother still refuses to talk about it."

Jae reached over and set his hand on Emmett's forearm. "I had no idea."

"I know you didn't." Emmett patted Jae's hand. "Mother believes my attraction to men is just a fluke and that I'm still 'finding myself.'" He wrinkled his nose. "Kind of ridiculous considering I'm thirty-one-years old. But she's convinced herself that one day I'll find the right girl who will change everything and make me magically straight. Just goes to show that denial can be addictive as any drug."

"So, your identity is the reason you and your mom aren't close?"

Emmett shook his head. "The trouble with my parents started over school. I had a football scholarship to Boston College and my coaches thought I might have a chance in the pros if I played my cards right. But I decided to switch out of the business program after my second year and that was when everything went to hell. Fred and Margaret McNeil did not approve of their only son working a blue-collar job, even if it came with a Culinary Arts degree and a tall, white hat."

Fuck. The flat quality of Emmett's voice pained Jae almost more than his words.

"The bitch of it is that while I liked playing football, I loved cooking more." Emmett's bleak expression and the way his shoulders slumped ever so slightly made it clear that the pain of his parents' rejection was still fresh, despite the passage of time. "I couldn't imagine not doing it," he said, "even after my parents told me they wouldn't support me if I decided to pursue cooking as a career."

Jae shook his head. He couldn't picture Emmett in any other profession either. He'd also had no idea how much turmoil his friend hid behind that sunny exterior.

"I'm sorry, Em. That must have been so hard."

"It was not a good time to be me. I lost the scholarship when I switched schools, of course, so student loans were the new norm and my father acted like I went out of my way to hurt him personally." Emmett carved out quotes with his voice as he spoke. "Said a career in cooking was a 'ridiculous waste of a man' which I always interpreted as code for 'too gay.' I came out around the same time, see, and the timing just seemed too perfect. The old man liked to remind me of his disappointment every time we got together."

Pushing his chair back, Jae stood and rounded the table until he was behind Emmett, then leaned over and wrapped him up in a hug. He rested his chest against Emmett's broad back and his cheek against Emmett's ear, his heart squeezing a little when Emmett reached up and clasped Jae's forearms in his hands, his temple against Jae's. For several moments, neither spoke and Jae simply breathed Emmett in.

Finally, Emmett sighed. "What is it about you that makes me want to spill all my secrets, Jae?"

"I don't know," Jae said with a soft laugh. "I'm happy to listen whenever you want to talk."

"Thank you." Dipping his head, Emmett rubbed his lips softly against Jae's wrist.

"Can I ask what your dad thought of EP? He had to have seen that cooking was what you were meant to do then, right?"

"I'm not sure what he made of it. My father got sick just as the business was getting off the ground and I don't know how much of the real world filtered in around his meds. I like to think EP's success changed his mind." Emmett leaned back into Jae's hold. "He seemed … really okay with Aiden the few times they met. They talked about baseball a lot and the best spots around the city to grab a burger, and even though it hurt Aiden pretending he and I were just friends around my parents, he never gave me a hard time. My father died not knowing who Aiden really was in my life and once he was gone, I lost interest in talking to Mother about anything, especially people I cared about."

"I think I get it." Jae held Emmett tighter. "She hurt you and you don't trust her not to do it again, even if it means hiding parts of yourself."

"It's not like I'm really hiding. I'm more presenting an edited version of reality." Emmett shrugged. "Everyone outside of my mother's circle knows I'm pan, including your ma and dad. We just don't talk about it around her."

Despite the heavy vibe, the impulse to make Emmett smile that came over Jae proved too much to resist.

"I'll remember not to grab your ass the next time we're around your mother's circle then." He bussed Emmett's cheek with a smacking kiss. "Pretty sure not even she'd be able to ignore that."

Emmett's laugh lifted the energy in the room instantly. "I'm sure you're right. And fuck, it doesn't matter anyway. You know my mother lives in Virginia with my Aunt Irene and they'll only be in town for a couple of weeks around the wedding. We can play grab-ass in front of her all we want."

"Slow down there, big guy," Jae said with a chuckle. He gave Emmett a final squeeze before straightening back up. "There's still my brother and Amelia to consider. As much as I hate the idea of lying to them—and my parents by association—I agree it's the easiest way to stay drama free. Ty's already half-annoyed with me on any given day and I don't think it'll take much to push him over the edge."

"As much as I love your bro, I think he needs to get over some shit." Emmett tracked Jae with his gaze as Jae headed back to his seat. "Being a kid who's annoyed by a sibling's food allergies is understandable but carrying it into adulthood seems more than a little ridiculous."

Sitting once more, Jae frowned at his plate. "Some of it's on me. Ty's and my roles in our family dynamics don't seem to have changed much over time. He's still playing the brat and I'm still trying to please everybody. We don't *have* to act out those roles if we don't want to."

"No, you don't." A thoughtful look filtered over Emmett's face. "But I'm not going to judge you or Ty, as long as you and I can keep doing this."

"You and I can always do this, Em, whether we're hooking up

or not—we'll just keep the hooking up part to ourselves." Jae picked up his chopsticks again, then winced as his mind went back to the conversation he'd had with Mark. "Ah. We may have a smallish problem."

"Oh?"

"I kind of already let the cat out of the bag with Mark." Jae fiddled with the chopsticks when Emmett raised his eyebrows high. "He called me out today and it just didn't feel right to lie. I know I should have checked with you first, but Mark said he wouldn't tell anyone other than Owen."

"Yeah, well, Aiden guessed too." Emmett's voice quavered with laughter. "Said I was too goddamned smiley and it was about time I got my shit together and told you how much I wanted you. Not that I could have lied to him, either."

"Okay, our friends know." Jae was sure he had to be beaming and goddamn if he could help it. "Clearly, we need to get better at the down-low part of our fooling around. But dinner at Aiden and Zac's in a couple of weeks should be two-hundred percent less awkward for both of us and I choose to count that as a good thing."

"Definitely. And it's not like that social circle intersects with our families much, so I think we can keep that cat corralled."

Now Jae was laughing. "God, you're weird. I like the way you think, though."

Emmett shot a smirk in Jae's direction. "Good. Speaking of thinking, I have ideas about the menu for the bachelor party weekend that I want to run by you."

They'd finished eating and were working together to clean up before Jae couldn't take it anymore. Crowding Emmett up against the counter, he kissed him, all teeth and tongue and grabby hands, and Emmett pulled him close, blue fire in his eyes when they came back up for air.

"Shit. I want you, Jae."

Jae pulled him into the bedroom, his cock hard in his too tight jeans. He kept busy kissing Emmett as they undressed one another, his hands in constant motion over Emmett's skin. He felt drunk as they stretched out on his bed and he sank onto that beautiful, strong body.

Emmett gripped Jae in a way that punched every one of his buttons. "Love this."

"Me, too. Wanna suck you," Jae murmured, his cock twitching at Emmett's soft moan, then kissed his way along Emmett's jaw to his throat. He licked and teased and bit as he worked his way lower, Emmett's hands buried in Jae's hair.

"Oh, *fuck*." Emmett groaned, low and forlorn. "No, I ... Need you in me."

Jae had to close his eyes and work very hard to keep from losing it right there. Goddamn, this man was going to kill him. "Okay."

Body thrumming, he took hold of Emmett's wrists, pulling Emmett's hands from his hair. He pushed up on to his knees and stared at the man laid out before him, chest flushed as it rose and fell with Emmett's breaths, his skin marked by Jae's teeth and lips.

"Look at you, Em."

"I'm looking at you," Emmett whispered, his eyes at half-mast. "You're gorgeous. And your *voice*. Think I could come just listening to you." The raw honesty in his face set a fire inside Jae.

Reaching for the nightstand, Jae quickly pulled out supplies. He sheathed and slicked himself, his cock rigid against his abdomen as he bent over Emmett. Emmett hummed as Jae skated his palms along Emmett's groin.

"Want you, Jae," he murmured. "Want you so much."

"I've got you."

Jae wrapped a hand around Emmett and slowly pumped him, desire coiling deep in his gut. Emmett hummed into Jae's kiss, so beautifully responsive, clinging while Jae fucked Emmett's mouth with his tongue. Jae only pulled back when a shudder shook Emmett's whole frame.

"No, wait," Emmett whined, his gaze wild as Jae cupped his cheek.

"Easy." Jae kissed him again, gentling his motions until Emmett seemed calmer.

Using touch, Jae urged Emmett onto his belly, and he moaned at the sight of Emmett's gorgeous ass. Emmett sighed when Jae spread his thighs but didn't make a sound as Jae teased him open. Instead, he pressed his face into the pillow.

Stretching out beside Emmett, Jae slipped his free arm under Emmett's chest. Emmett turned into the hold immediately, grasping Jae's arm with his hands, his forehead against Jae's throat. His breath moved hot over Jae's skin, wavering every so often as

Jae worked him open. Emmett swore when Jae slipped a finger inside and it was like a floodgate had opened. Rutting into the mattress, Emmett pushed back against Jae's fingers, pleas and broken phrases tumbling out of his mouth.

"Need it, Jae. I—uhh, God. Don't stop." His voice wavered. "Just ... more. Fuck!"

Jae slipped a second finger inside and teased a little longer, until he heard a sob under Emmett's words. Emmett muffled a cry with the pillow when Jae drew his fingers out.

Easing himself up, Jae spread Emmett's ass with his hands. He traced Emmett's rim with the head of his cock, then pushed, one hand wide over the small of Emmett's back. For a moment, Emmett's body tensed, but he relaxed as Jae slowly pressed forward, and the heat and pressure of the body surrounding Jae threatened to crush his control.

"Okay, Em?" he asked, his voice pulled thin.

Emmett turned his head on the pillow, his face flushed and sweaty and so beautiful Jae's whole chest squeezed. "Okay," he said, his voice a bare whisper that called to Jae.

Bending forward, Jae dropped a kiss against Emmett's shoulder and Emmett groaned, the last of the tension in his frame melting away as Jae bottomed out.

Jesus Christ.

Jae couldn't remember the last time he'd felt this alive. He fucked into Emmett, going harder and faster when Emmett started pushing back into the thrusts. The words Emmett seemed unable to hold back became moans and gasps for more, and every sound went straight to Jae's dick. He pressed his mouth against Emmett's cheek, licking at the salty skin.

Sliding an arm under Emmett's body, Jae took him in hand, matching the strokes with his own thrusts. A sweet ache built in his core, and he had to close his eyes against it when Emmett keened.

"Feels so good," Jae muttered against Emmett's ear. "So good Em, like I could fuck you forever."

"*Yes.*"

With a gasp, Emmett arched back into Jae. He craned his neck, searching for Jae, who took Emmett's mouth in a scorching kiss. Emmett's body went tight. He jerked hard and lost it, his cum pulsing over Jae's fist and onto the sheets. His moans became soft as his body relaxed and seconds later Jae's world splintered.

Pleasure crashed into him and wrung out his cells until he lay panting and wrecked against Emmett's back.

Slowly, Jae came back to himself. Carefully pulling out, he soothed Emmett's plaintive noise, then turned Emmett onto his side. Jae used the corner of the sheet to clean them both off then removed the condom, Emmett watching him the whole time, his face soft and dazed. He looked almost shy when Jae stretched out beside him once more, but his gaze never wavered, almost as if he was studying Jae. After a moment, he set a hand on Jae's belly.

"Jae? What does your name mean? I meant to ask you the other night 'n forgot."

Jae ran a hand over Emmett's damp hair, then wound a curl around his index finger. "In Korean, a name's meaning changes depending on the *hanja* used."

"And *hanja* are the written characters, right?"

"Yes. In my case, Jae is 'cultivate' and Seong is 'brightness of jade.'"

"Mmm. That's nice." Emmett's soft smile turned impish. "Bet you can't guess what Emmett means."

Jae didn't even pretend to give it some thought. "Tell me."

"'Universal.' Pretty sure my parents wouldn't have named me that if they'd known I'd one day come out as pan."

Jae laughed so hard his eyes teared. "That's fucking amazing."

"It really is," Emmett replied with another snicker, then closed his eyes under Jae's continued petting.

"You want to stay?" Jae asked.

"I do want." Snuggling closer, Emmett moved his hand to Jae's hip. "Think you broke me though. Just … gimme me a second to put myself back together."

Jae had to smile. "Sure, Em." Reaching down, he pulled the sheet up and over them both. "Take all the time you need."

Chapter Seven

Following the Korean BBQ dinner, Jae and Emmett hooked up nearly every night for a week. Jae's turn at working graveyard the next week put those fiery evenings on hold, however, because he knew his upside-down schedule would upend Emmett's too. Emmett kept in touch with messages and phone calls, however, many so NSFW they nearly set Jae's ears on fire, despite his sleep deprived state. That disrupted cycle was the last thing on Jae's mind as he climbed the stairs of Zac and Aiden's building in Fort Point Channel though, because Emmett and their friends were upstairs and that was enough to make him feel a whole lot better.

Fuck.

Closing his eyes, Jae hauled in a breath. He hadn't actually missed Emmett, had he? After just a couple of weeks of fooling around? What the hell was he thinking?

"Jae!"

Jumping a little, Jae opened his eyes and quickly spied Mark and his boyfriend jogging along the sidewalk, their hands entwined.

"I was just about to ring," he called back, "no need to run."

"Thank fuck." Mark smirked at Owen's laughter. "These shoes are not made for running," he said as they climbed the steps, too. "I'd rather not start my evening by falling on my ass."

"Serves you right for wearing boat shoes in the middle of the city," Jae teased. "What have you guys been up to today?"

"I was at work," Owen replied. The vibrant pink he'd worn in his hair at Pride had mellowed to a lovely rose gold. "Mr. Freckles over here went to the pool."

"It was my day off, after all," Mark said.

He looked suntanned and, yes, freckled, and both he and Owen were so elegant in their stylish summer clothes. Nothing at all like Jae, who'd been half asleep when he'd pulled on yet another pair of black jeans and white t-shirt and who really just wanted to lie down all over again.

"How're you doing, Jae?" Owen asked. Sympathy softened his face when Jae met his gaze. "Mark told me you've been working graveyard this week and I know how much you guys hate it."

Jae punched the doorbell. "I really, really do. But I'm good, thanks. Should be back to semi-coherent in a couple of days." He pulled at the door when the locks buzzed open and held it for Owen and Mark as they passed through.

"You've got the bachelor party this weekend, right?" Mark asked.

"Yes." Jae's groan made his friends laugh. "I'll bet I can guess what you're about to say, Mark."

"If you guessed it sounds like 'no driving for you, Jae-seong,' then yes, that's what I was about to say."

"I'm not fond of driving even when I'm well rested," Jae said to Owen, "never mind when my body clock is all screwed up. So, Ty and I are riding with Emmett up and back and I am totally okay with that."

Greetings rang out over hugs and kisses as Zac and Aiden welcomed them into their home. Jae lost himself for a moment in the comforting vibe of friendly touches and words, but a true flush of pleasure went through him when he spotted Emmett in the kitchen. Emmett's big, open smile as he crossed the floor to Jae immediately lifted Jae's energy and Jae was floored by how fucking nice it was to wrap his arms around the guy again.

"Hi, weirdo," Emmett murmured against his ear. "This may sound nuts, but it's nice to see you."

Jae chuckled. "Yeah, it's nice to see you, too." He pulled back enough to get a good look at Emmett, then pressed a quick kiss to his mouth. "Hi, back. I hope you're ready to be stuck with me all weekend."

"So ready. And if you think I'm sharing a tent with anyone other than you, you're out of your mind."

"Tent?" Aiden asked from his place by the stove. "But you said you were staying in cabins!"

Jae noticed then that their friends were watching him and Emmett, all of them grinning, and *wow*, Jae's whole head was on fire.

"We are staying in cabins." Gently, he nudged Emmett in the ribs with an elbow. "Five little A-frames surrounded by trees on three sides and just a short bike ride to the beach."

"Um, I love this idea?" Owen turned big eyes on Mark who simply laughed.

"It looked really nice when I viewed it online," Jae said, even though Emmett was already shaking his head.

"The bathhouse and kitchen are communal," Emmett said, his hand at the small of Jae's back as they joined the others at the kitchen island. "As in I have to leave the room where all my stuff is just to take a leak. That's camping, Jae."

"Not even close," Jae shot back. "That is *glamping*, my friend. As in queen-sized bed, linens, and towels provided in each cabin, along with a picture window looking out onto the woods. The kitchen you were just bitching about is specifically for our use plus, there's a goddamned doughnut delivery every morning." Jae gently poked Emmett again as laughter went up around the room.

"Okay, I'm coming around to this idea, too," Mark said. "You said there's a beach?"

Jae nodded. "Plus, activities at the campsite and two towns full of restaurants and shopping inside a ten-mile radius. Oh, and a Wi-Fi router in every cabin in case it rains or, you know, we get really bored."

"You mean in case you want to stream porn." Mark's dry tone drew more laughs, including Jae's, though he grimaced a bit too.

"Pretty sure the porn my brother and his friends like to watch isn't going to do a single thing for me," he said.

"Nor me," Emmett said. "I'm into dudes when I watch porn. I wouldn't be averse to going to a burlesque club."

"Unlikely in Kennebunkport, buddy, but if you did find one, I'd gladly act as a designated driver even though I hate being behind the wheel," Jae promised.

Deciding against sitting down, Jae leaned against the counter with a glass of water and Emmett parked on his left, grazing from the platter of grilled vegetables and various vegan dips before them as the others chatted and Aiden finished cooking. He felt pretty good when they sat down to a dinner of skirt steak and creamy polenta and more awake than he had all evening. Still, he couldn't help noticing the crease on Emmett's brow and the way his lips kept turning down at the corners.

"Something wrong?" Jae asked as he and Emmett carried the emptied plates into the kitchen. He nodded to Aiden who passed by with a cake box in his hands.

Emmett opened his eyes wider. "I think I should be the one asking you that."

"What do you mean?"

"It's like you're only half there, Jae, and you are clearly wiped."

Jae set the plates down with a thump. "Okay, I know I look like crap right now, but you're not supposed to *say* so."

"I didn't say you look like crap." Emmett pursed his lips against what Jae knew was a laugh. "I wouldn't be surprised if you keeled over though—"

"Dude."

"—and I wondered if maybe you weren't feeling well!"

"That's ... really sweet, actually." Jae rubbed a hand over his head. "And also the reason I suggested we skip getting together this week—working graveyard always fucks me up. I'm good, though, and after tonight I'll get caught up on sleep and be good as new for the weekend."

"If you say so." Emmett set his hands on his hips. "I can't believe you still have another night of this craptastic shift."

Jae barked out a laugh. "Neither can I. I'm off for five days starting tomorrow, so I'm not going to complain." He tapped one of Emmett's hands with his fingers. "C'mon, I have time for a coffee before I have to leave and we both know I need it."

"Okay. I'm leaving when you do, too."

"Why? It's not even nine, and Aiden bought a blackberry Pavlova from the bakery over on Tremont Street that you love."

"Girl, I bought that cake and I'm going to eat at least two pieces." Emmett laughed and patted his flat belly. "Leaving with you means we get to hang out a little longer."

While Jae made a big show of sighing, inwardly, he felt pleased. "Suit yourself," he said. "I'm planning to walk to the hospital, though, because the exercise will wake me up."

"Now he tells me." Emmett laughed. "Well, I'm not going to change my mind, but I may cheat and grab a Lyft for the trip back to Chinatown."

* * * *

"You can crash at my place, you know," Jae said when they hit the sidewalk forty minutes later. For a second, he wondered at the words that had come out of his mouth. Then he shrugged, both at himself and Emmett, who was looking at him askance. "What? I won't be home until nine tomorrow morning and you already know my apartment is good for sleeping. You can keep Sparky company."

Emmett cocked his head. "Who the hell is Sparky?"

"The aloe vera plant you insisted on gifting me," Jae said as Emmett tilted his head back and laughed. "I thought if I named her it'd help me remember to take better care of her."

Emmett slipped his arm around Jae's waist and laughed some more. "And how's that working out?"

"She looks good! Green and thick and ... aloe-y," Jae said. "She'd tell you my spare keys are on the hook by the door if she could talk. Just stick them through the mail slot on your way out."

"I can be there to let you in," Emmett replied. "I'm not on until noon tomorrow. I'll even make you breakfast *and* suck your dick if you think you can stay awake, Bak."

"Oh, I'll stay awake." Jae gave him what he knew was a wolfish grin. "I'll mainline a jumbo coffee if I have to."

He managed a single goofy fist pump before a laughing Emmett swept him into a hug and kissed him, right there on the street. Jae grabbed hold of Emmett's nape and kissed him back, then shot the finger at a car that honked as it drove past, all without opening his eyes.

The blaring horn brought Jae back to his senses, however. There were still idiots in the world, even in liberal and LGBTQ-friendly cities like Boston. Jae knew better than to lay one on a man in a neighborhood that wasn't his even if Emmett pouted when Jae took a step back.

"No, no," Jae said. "Save the face for someone who doesn't need to be at work in forty-five minutes."

"We could grab a ride instead of walking and kiss some more."

"Uh-huh. We could also get the heck out of here so I'm not late." Jae hooked his elbow through Emmett's and tugged him along. "C'mon. Plenty of time for kissing tomorrow, in between working and sleeping."

* * * *

"Easier said than done," Jae muttered to himself nearly twelve hours later.

He'd been in good shape when he'd gotten home. He'd tucked into the fried eggs and toast Emmett had whipped up and they'd exchanged a number of increasingly heated kisses. But Jae had been caught off guard by a sudden crash, one deep enough he wondered if he'd have made it past the couch if he'd been alone in the apartment.

Didn't mean he had to like it, though. Or that Emmett had a hand on Jae's elbow as they walked into the bedroom, as if he was afraid Jae was going to fall over. And grumbling about it didn't work at all when Jae yawned so wide his jaw cracked.

"Jeez, Jae."

"Ugh, I know." He weaved drunkenly as he headed for the bathroom. "Sorry."

"Don't worry about it." Emmett was drawing the blackout curtains in the windows closed when Jae looked back, and while his smile was small it was sweet and real. "You're beat. I get it."

Fuck, he sounded so reasonable. Jae squinted at his reflection in the mirror as he brushed his teeth, fully aware he looked like crap. His eyelids were heavy and his color was off, making him appear pale. Jae knew he needed sleep if he was going to be of any use for the upcoming weekend, but he still wanted the make out time he'd promised Emmett, too.

"C'mere," he said after he'd re-emerged. He grabbed Emmett's hand and pulled him toward the bed. "Lie down with me and kiss me stupid before you have to go to work, huh?"

"All right." Emmett chuckled. "I like it when you're bossy."

He waited for Jae to crawl under the sheets then stretched out beside him so they could wrap each other up in a hug. The soft sound Emmett made when Jae kissed him made Jae feel wonderfully cozy inside. They kissed and petted as Jae's bones slowly melted and even though his dick was rock hard, he couldn't peel his eyes open at all. He grumbled a little as Emmett ran a hand over his hair, sure he wouldn't be awake much longer.

"Would it be weird if I came back tonight after work?" Emmett asked.

"Only 'cause you're weird. Probl'y boring … You'll see a lot more of this." Jae hauled in a deep breath. He tried to focus, but the earth slid around beneath him and the soft velvet weight of sleep pushed him down and down and down, making his words sound garbled when he spoke. "Won't be more awake until tomorrow."

"Okay." Jae heard the smile in Emmett's voice. "I guess I'll see you then. Ty and I will pick you up around two, okay? That way we can get ahead of the traffic and make it to the campground before dark."

Jae might have said okay but, chances were, he didn't. He was already coasting into a dream, lulled by Emmett's deep voice and the solid weight against him.

* * * *

Jae was alone when his alarm woke him at five that evening and his very first thought was that he wished he weren't. He alternated between dozing and slowly jerking himself off for a while, until his body decided it really wanted to get off. Of course, chasing his pleasure in earnest meant someone would choose that moment to knock on his door, but Jae was grinning as he hauled himself out of bed, a sheet wrapped around his hips.

Bless Emmett and his stubborn ass.

Jae found his keys on the floor just inside the door but not the man he expected on his front step. Sal stood there instead of Emmett, a wry smirk on his face as he moved his gaze over Jae's bare chest.

"Well, damn," Sal said, dragging the word out in a drawl. "Happy Thursday to me. It's been a while, huh, Jae?"

"Yeah, it has." A strangely empty feeling came over Jae, stronger than disappointment. But he ran a hand through his hair, sure it was a spectacular mess and hoped to God his erection wasn't obvious through the bedsheet. "Let me guess—you were just in the neighborhood?"

"You are correct." Sal held up a brown paper bag. "I was also in the mood for the magic that is sashimi from Eastern Roe and figured I'd drop by. You look like you just woke up, though."

"That's because I did, but it was time for me to get up anyway." Jae waved Sal in, his brain still coming online as they climbed the stairs. "There's, uh, beer in the fridge if you want to help yourself," he called back. "I've been on overnight shifts this week, so just give me a sec to wake up."

"I have no idea how you stay sane working those hours."

"I'm used to it by now," Jae yelled from the bedroom. "Besides, I've never claimed to be entirely sane."

As a researcher for a biochem firm in central Cambridge, Sal's job was a world away from Jae's. While the work could be intense, his days were very regimented, and Sal rarely stayed at the office past six.

Quickly pulling on a t-shirt and sleep pants, Jae made a quick trip to the bathroom to wash up and tame his hair, though there was nothing to be done about the pillowcase crease on his cheek. He'd already stepped back out into the kitchen before the thought struck him that he should have started the shower. That's what Jae always did after sleeping off a long shift and he'd never hesitated to pull Sal under the spray with him in the past.

So why hadn't he done it tonight?

The question in Sal's face told Jae he'd been wondering the same thing. He'd seated himself at the table with the unopened bag of takeout but hadn't helped himself to a drink. Sal hadn't even taken off his light summer jacket and, if anything, he was giving Jae the side-eye.

"You want me to head out?" he asked.

"No." Jae crossed the kitchen to his side. "I'm sorry about that," he said with a wave toward the bedroom. "I was still in bed when you knocked, and it feels like I left my brain in there."

The corners of Sal's lips lifted slightly. "I should have called, but I'm an entitled ass as you know. I figured I'd take a chance you were home. I like the table here, by the way," he said.

"Me too. It's really nice with the air coming in." Stepping forward, Jae unlocked the patio doors, then paused as he noticed Sal shoot a glance toward the bedroom. "What?"

"Is there someone else here?"

"No, I'm alone. I thought you might have been someone else when you knocked, but there's no reason I should have."

Sal folded his hands on top of the table. "I'm afraid you're not making a whole lot of sense, babe."

"I know." After he'd pulled the doors open, Jae eased himself into the chair opposite Sal's. "I'm not fully awake, which isn't helping. Not to mention I'm ... I don't know. Confused, I guess."

"You wanna talk about it?" Sal gestured to the bag of takeout between them. "Dinner is already taken care of. And while we mostly get horizontal when we see each other, I *am* capable of conversation, you know."

"I do. We don't usually talk prior to getting off, though."

"Ouch. You're making me sound shallow."

"Sorry." Jae wrinkled his nose. "I don't mean to, but I think you'll admit I have a point."

"Yes, you do. Still a bit rude, but I'll let you make it up to me if you like." Sal cocked his head a bit. "Is your offer for a beer still open?"

"For you?" Jae smiled. "Of course. I even have the IPA you favor."

"Excellent." Sal rubbed his hands together and stood. "I'll get our dinner sorted out while you tell me about the guy you've been seeing."

How is it the men in my life have suddenly become psychic?

Jae rubbed his eyes with one hand. "What makes you say there's a guy?"

"Just a feeling, I guess." Sal took a pair of beer bottles out of the fridge, then went to the drawer where Jae kept his opener. "The table by the window, for one. And the *plant*, God. You're not a particularly whimsical guy, Jae, and that's something I've always liked about you. But this set up sort of screams romance. Plus, at the risk of sounding conceited, you haven't wanted a hookup in weeks, and I choose to believe there was more going on here than you being kind of a lousy friend."

Jae winced. Despite Sal's light tone, his rebuke was clear and, Jae knew, totally justified. "You're right." He waited until Sal met his gaze. "I haven't been a good friend and for that I apologize."

"Apology accepted." Sal pulled a sushi set from one of the cabinets. "If there is a guy—and I know I'm right about that—I can't blame you for ghosting. I might have been guilty of doing the same. Assuming you'd been around enough to notice my absence."

Sal's obvious pleasure in his own words surprised Jae as much as it amused him. "Yeah? Did you get yourself a boyfriend, Sal?"

"Mmm, we're nowhere near a label stage yet. We're not

exclusive either, and I'm not sure that's the direction either of us wants to go." Sal set the dishes down on the table and turned his attention to the bag of take out. "I'm having fun though."

"Well, good for you, man." Jae got to his feet and pulled his friend into a hug, laughing when Sal planted a noisy kiss on his cheek. He immediately returned the favor.

"Ugh, no." Sal gave Jae a playful shove.

"You started it." Jae rubbed Sal's back. "You know, this kind of fucks up some of my plans."

"Oh, yeah? What kind of plans?" Sal asked. "Something kinky?"

"Hah, I guess that depends on your definition of kink. I was going to ask you to be my date for my brother's wedding."

"Shit, really?" Sal's face shone. "I can do that! Like I said, I'm not exclusive with the guy I'm seeing, and he knows all about you and that we're friends. Just give me the date and time."

Something inside Jae felt off even as he smiled. "Thanks. How'd you and the not-boyfriend meet?"

"I met Brett through a friend of a friend of a friend. He's a lot of fun, actually, and I know you'd like him. However, *my* sex life is not what I want to talk about, Jae." Sal aimed an arch look in Jae's direction. "Let's talk about yours."

Jae opened his mouth to reply and found he couldn't. Not because he didn't have a sex life, because he absolutely did. Except … Jae wasn't sure he was free to talk about it. Outside of the small circle of friends he and Emmett happened to share, Jae had said he wouldn't talk about their hookups. Did that promise count with someone like Sal, who didn't know Emmett or Ty, or anyone among the Baks and McNeils? Jae didn't know. And that uncertainty left a bitter taste in his mouth he didn't like.

"Hey." Sal took the seat beside him. "Everything okay? You don't look so good."

Jae sniffed. He didn't feel so good, either. And that wasn't Sal's fault. "Don't be mean," he said, aiming for light. "What is it with everyone telling me I look bad?"

Sal scoffed. "Stop. You know you're gorgeous, even with the bedhead and your shirt on inside out, not to mention the sheet marks on your stupid face."

Jae peeked down at himself just long enough to confirm his shirt was indeed on wrong, then covered his eyes with one hand and laughed. "You're such a dick."

"I know." The glee in Sal's voice made Jae lower his hand, but he found only kindness in his friend's face. "How about you tell me what's got you tied up in knots? You don't have to, of course, because I'm not here to give you crap for keeping secrets. But you might feel better if you talk, Jae, and you're welcome to do it with me."

Jae pulled the beer bottle Sal had set in front of him closer. He knew Sal was right. Because keeping this thing between Emmett and himself a secret really did have Jae tied up in knots and he didn't know what to do about that at all.

Chapter Eight

"Oh, wow. This place looks fantastic, dude."

Jae chuckled as his brother almost scrambled out of Emmett's Ford Explorer. When he knew Ty wasn't watching, he breathed a quiet sigh of relief.

As planned, they'd made the trek out of the city slightly ahead of rush hour, three cars filled with Ty's friends, their gear, and a fuckton of food and drink. They'd arrived at the White Pines Camp at just past five o'clock and though Ty and his friends had been energized for the trip, Jae was glad the campgrounds appeared even nicer than the photos he'd seen online. Lush green trees grew on three sides of the site while the fourth granted a picturesque view down to the ocean over a salt marsh. With the car engines off, Jae imagined he heard the surf from the beach beyond and even after they'd stopped at the lodge for firewood and other supplies, the atmosphere surrounding the campsite was one of near solitude.

At least as far as Jae could tell from the back seat of the car anyway, since he hadn't even gotten around to stepping outside yet. Neither had Emmett, who was watching Jae from the driver's seat, a tiny smile on his lips.

"Hey, weirdo. You ready for this?"

"Yeah." Jae put his hands behind his head and stretched as best as he could. Still tired from the long nights he'd been working, he'd dropped off as soon as the car had passed the Boston city limits and slept through nearly the entire ride. "Sorry you had to manage the drive alone," he said, his voice as creaky as his body.

"Pfft. Like I couldn't handle a trip with these bozos."

Emmett shot Jae a wink before he faced forward and opened his car door. Jae still didn't move, though, his body and brain warm and mellow from sleep. He wasn't at all surprised when Emmett appeared on the other side of his window, but he did roll his eyes, and Emmett was chuckling as he popped the door open.

"I'm not letting you nap here."

"Why not? I've been doing that for the last two hours, Em, what's a while longer?"

"There are perfectly good beds right over there." Emmett gestured at the cabins set among the trees. "And, if you don't get a move on it, one of your brother's friends might steal your spot and you'll have to bunk with someone who isn't me." He lowered his voice, blue eyes gleaming with such promise that Jae's cheeks went hot. "It'd be a crying shame if that happened, Jae-seong, because I have plans for you."

Yeah, Jae had plans for Emmett too, most of them centered around keeping him quiet while Jae drove him out of his ever-loving mind. Emmett was a talker during sex, after all, and Jae himself had never been a particularly silent participant. The cabin they'd share had a door, but its walls were no doubt thin and the campsite itself wasn't large, so if they were going to fool around, they'd need to get creative.

"Fi-i-i-ne." Jae made a show of grumbling as he unlocked the seatbelt and swung his legs out of the car. He was too tall to stay curled up in such a confined space for much longer and everything about him complained as he got to his feet. Moving felt good, even if his head went a bit swimmy.

"I'll take everybody's keys, guys," Jae said as he and Emmett approached the group, who were clustered beside a fire pit. He smiled as three sets of car keys were thrust his way. "Go on and grab your cabins and once that's out of the way, we can figure out what to do for dinner."

"Oh, shit, is that a bar?" Krishnan's expression turned gleeful as he eyed a clump of nearby trees where a makeshift bar had been set up using the trunks as supports for the bar top.

Emmett brought his hands together with a clap. "Heck yes, it is. The folks at the lodge will keep us stocked up over the weekend—Jae-seong made sure of that even before we left the city." He turned to Jae. "How about I take charge of getting the food put away while you guys do some exploring?"

"I'll help you." Jae shoved the car keys in his pocket, then turned to Ty. "Can you get our gear into one of the cabins before you start looking around?"

"Sure." Ty walked to the back of Emmett's SUV and popped the hatch. "You said you guys are bunking together, right?"

"Yep," Jae stretched again. "We'll haul the food over to the kitchen in the meantime."

"Cool. Let's stash the extra beer and snacks we brought in the kitchen, too," Ty said to his friends. "And for God's sake, someone grab the cooler of beer from Krishnan's car!"

"You Bak boys are bossy." Emmett grinned as Ty walked off, duffle bags and backpacks over both arms. "You know how much I like that, Jae."

"I do." Jae knocked his shoulder against Emmett's, and they bent over the stacks of plastic crates of food. "I'm also a planner. I made some stuff ahead for tonight's dinner."

"Of course, you did." Emmett hefted two crates with a grunt. "Are you making the mystical Sloppy Joes Zac told me about?"

A laugh escaped Jae. "Uh-huh. I wouldn't call them mystical, but he was a big fan of them back when we shared an apartment."

Together, they hauled the supplies into the kitchen, chatting amiably as they worked. The rest of the crew quickly joined in and many hands made the work light, but the sun hung lower as Jae and Emmett headed for the cabin where Ty had stowed their stuff. By then, someone had started a fire and several of the guys were playing a game that involved tossing red and green balls back and forth along the length of a long, shallow pit near the bar.

"That's bocce," Emmett said in answer to the question Jae hadn't gotten around to asking. "It's basically Italian lawn bowling and pretty fun if you have the right partner. I can show you how to play, if you like."

"I would." Jae cast another backward glance at the fire pit before he stepped inside. "I hope I reserved enough firewood. I've never considered such a thing before, so I was kind of flying blind. Oh."

He gazed around the little cabin's interior, instantly captivated by its simple charm. The few pieces of furniture were mismatched in a pleasing way and they and the bedding were composed in shades of black, white, and navy, and stood out nicely against the natural wood floor and walls. The large skylights cut into the cabin's roof bathed the room with golden light, and made the trees beyond the gigantic, wall-sized window at the far end of the cabin all the more green.

"This is nice," Jae said, almost to himself.

"Really nice. I love this, Jae."

Though Emmett's back was turned, Jae heard his smile. Emmett had approached the bed under the big window and walked past it, then come to a standstill just inches from the glass. Framed in stark relief against the woods outside, he made a lovely, lonesome figure, his curls shining in the light and the lines of his body strong.

Beautiful.

Struck by the thought and the sight of the man before him, Jae found himself unable to look away. He moved to stand at Emmett's side, and his chest pulled tight when Emmett wordlessly reached for Jae's hand. His eyes shone when he turned his focus on Jae and they stood without speaking, fingers entwined, until a voice beyond the cabin door broke the spell.

"Hey, guys?" Ty called. "I mixed you a couple of drinks. Figured you'd want to chill out for a bit before you get dinner started."

Emmett let go of Jae's hand. A lopsided grin crossed his face as he turned for the door, his voice raised in cheerful greeting, and that odd, empty feeling filtered over Jae again, even more intense than the night before when he'd opened his front door and seen Sal on the step. This weekend would be the first time since Jae's friendship with Emmett had turned sexual that they'd spend time together with Ty. And while he and Emmett had agreed that hiding their connection made sense, Jae didn't like doing it. Especially around Ty.

"Jae?"

Jae turned away from the window. "Hmm?"

"Ty was asking if we wanted to hang by the fire for a bit," Emmett said. "Sounds pretty nice after being cooped up in the car."

"Sure." Jae shrugged. Reaching into his pocket, he withdrew the three sets of car keys, then moved toward his duffle bag on the foot of the bed. "I'll be right out."

"Cool." Stepping forward, Ty offered him an aluminum

tumbler. "Krishnan mixed up a Planter's Punch. It's actually pretty tasty. We have no idea if it goes with whatever you're planning to make for dinner, though, and he's open to suggestions."

"Nice." Jae took the cup and gently swirled its contents. "Dinner's not fancy. Hot sandwiches and a potato salad, so punch or beer or whatever you like is perfect."

Ty's grin got wider. "All right then. You need some help in here?"

"No, I'm good." Jae nodded at his bag. "Just, um, deciding if I want to change my shirt. You guys go on and I'll be out in a minute."

"Okay, bro." Ty turned, his hand already on Emmett's arm, but then paused and refocused his attention on his brother. "Hey, Jae? This place is great. Really."

Jae smiled. "I'm glad you like it," he said. "Emmett gave me a ton of help. And, for what it's worth, I hope you're not mad that axe throwing is only allowed during daylight hours."

Ty's laughter filled the air. "I think that's for the best. The last thing I want is to have to tell Amelia that someone ended up with an axe wound during a bachelor weekend in the freaking woods."

Turning for the door again, he headed out with Emmett on his heels. Emmett caught Jae's eye just before he stepped outside, however, and the concern on his face sent a guilty flush through Jae.

He had no right shoving his mixed-up state of mind onto Emmett. Hell, Emmett might be feeling weirded out right now, too, and the least Jae could do was be there for his friend.

Quickly stowing the car keys in his bag, Jae rejoined the group out by the pit, glad when Emmett didn't hesitate to return his smile. As the next hour passed, new drinks were made and the sky above them slowly darkened, and Jae felt easier as he and Emmett went to the kitchen to start dinner.

They couldn't really talk, of course, because the rest of the crew were constantly in and out, some with offers to help and others simply curious about what they were cooking. Emmett fended them off with a skillet of campfire nachos, all while quizzing Jae about his Sloppy Joe recipe. He chopped a bundle of dill for the potato salad and kept Jae's punch cup full, and even dashed outside to greet the camp owners when they stopped by with ingredients for s'mores and an itinerary of the next day's activities.

The atmosphere was merry as the party settled down to eat and, for a while, Jae was able to mostly ignore the odd twists and turns his personal life had taken. It wasn't entirely possible, of course, not with Emmett there by his side, his eyes glowing with laughter and his thigh just brushing against Jae's beneath the table. On several occasions, Jae found himself about to touch Emmett and though he caught himself each time, the moments held a dull sting that made him reach for his cup.

Consequently, he felt somewhat tipsy as he carried a stack of tin plates back to the kitchen and quickly poured himself a cup of water. He startled when a sudden noise sounded behind him, then swore quietly as the water soaked into the front of his shirt. Emmett was there in an eyeblink, dabbing at Jae with a tea towel, his face screwed up in a frown.

"Shit. I'm sorry."

"It's fine. It's only water." Jae took hold of Emmett's wrists and swallowed a sigh. Moving back to the sink and the plates he'd stacked there, he turned on the faucet. "But I might need to put a bell on you—you're really light on your feet."

"I've heard that before," Emmett said over the water's gurgle. He stood beside Jae, scraping the odd bit of food from the tin plates into the compost bucket before handing them off to Jae for rinsing. "Dinner was great."

"Thanks. I was a lot hungrier than I realized, so it's likely anything would have tasted just fine to me. Think I've had enough to drink, though, and Ty always takes that as a challenge. He'll give me crap for being too old to keep up with his crew."

"He wouldn't do that."

"Yes, he would. He wouldn't be wrong, exactly." Jae said, his gaze on the plates in the sink. "At my age, I know better than to guzzle rum punch like it's water."

Not to mention screw a guy who's over a decade younger than you.

"You look younger than half the guys out there," Emmett said in that oh-so-reasonable tone. "Age is just a number, right?"

Jae rolled his eyes. "Not once you hit forty. At that point, clichés start to sound like what they are—bullshit."

"That's not fair."

Now Emmett sounded grumpy. His eyebrows were drawn together when Jae looked his way and his mouth turned down at the corners. But Thom and a young man named Jaime sauntered through the door then, the remaining empty platters and bowls in hand.

"Jae!" Thom set the dishes on the counter, his eyes shiny with liquor and excitement. "There's stuff to make s'mores, right? And didn't you say you brought some kind of cake?"

"I did, yep." Drying his hands on the towel, Jae strode to the counter and plucked up a cloth bag. "The applesauce cake is already cut into squares and there should be roasting sticks for the marshmallows by the fire pit." He handed the bag to Thom, then paused and set his hands on his hips. "You know how to make s'mores, right?"

"Umm ... I think I do?" Thom glanced at Jaime and the two shared a laugh before turning on Emmett. "We may need your kitchen expertise."

Emmett cocked an eyebrow. "Seriously? What kind of person doesn't know how to make s'mores?"

"Oh, check your privilege, man." Thom snorted out a laugh. "My family are city people and I haven't done a lot of camping. So, how about you guys come out and show us some strategies while Ty mixes up shots? He's already over at the bar getting everything ready."

Jae grimaced. This bunch was going to be a mess in the morning.

"I'll finish up here and be out in a few," he said, but caught Emmett by the elbow as the other two started back outside. "Can you keep an eye on things until I can get out there? Ty's always had a good head on his shoulders, but this may be the weekend his inner dumbass shows itself. I'm sorry to have to ask, but—"

Emmett spoke over Jae, his tone easy. "It's cool. I told you I'd help you this weekend and I meant it."

"I appreciate that. But I want *you* to have a good time, too." Jae gave Emmett's arm a squeeze, then quickly dropped his hand when a chorus of voices calling their names filled the air. "Jesus. You'd better get out there before they start lobbing marshmallows through the door."

"They're so needy," Emmett muttered. "You sure you don't want my help cleaning up?"

"I'm good. Go on and have fun with your friends. Oh, and save me a piece of cake, if you can." Jae flashed him a grin, then turned back to the sink. "It's the only sweet thing out right now that I can eat besides the marshmallows and graham crackers."

Thirty minutes later, a more grounded Jae made his way outside. He found a spot between Emmett and Krishnan amongst the s'mores making and shot drinking and cheered softly when Emmett revealed the two pieces of applesauce cake he'd put aside. They ate while the stories being told grew louder and funnier and Jae pretended all the while like he wasn't drinking water. As the night wore on, talk eventually turned to Ty's wedding and, more specifically, who among the group would be attending the reception without a date.

"I'm not even going to bother asking anyone," Krishnan said with a scoff. "I'll be too busy doing groomsman shit to pay attention anyway."

"You're not wrong," a guy named Lowell put in. "I was my brother's Best Man when he got married and the girl I brought as my date took off before the reception even started because she was bored." He gave an enormous eye roll. "We were having photos taken, for fuck's sake, and what was I supposed to do?"

Krishnan jabbed a finger in Lowell's direction. "That right there, yes. I figure it's better not to waste anyone's time, including my own, just to have a dance partner." He focused his attention on Ty. "You and Amelia don't care if all your groomsmen go stag, right?"

Ty just laughed. "I'm not sure I could care less. My mom, however, has definite ideas about my big brother's singleton status."

"Like this is a new thing," Jae said over a chorus of 'ooohs' echoing out over the campsite. "She's stopped complaining about it to me, though."

"Because she talks to Amelia and *me*, thank you very much," Ty shot back, his nose wrinkling as he made a face. "I don't even know what she expects me to do about it."

"I certainly don't expect you to do anything." Jae shrugged. "But the next time Ma asks, just tell her I'm bringing my friend Sal. That'll make her happy."

Ty gave his brother a big smile. "You're the best, dude."

"I didn't know you asked Sal to be your date," Emmett said to Jae as the conversation veered off and landed on Ty and Amelia's efforts to find a new apartment.

"We talked about it, yeah, and he said he was up to the task."

Jae stared down at his cup. "It's funny. Sal and I haven't seen each other much for the last couple of weeks and it was nice to catch up." He lifted his gaze to meet Emmett's. "He really likes my kitchen table in front of the patio doors, too."

"Jae!" Ty was actually glaring when Jae met his gaze. "Are you drinking water?!"

"Ummm. Yes." Jae laughed. "Rum always goes to my head and you know I'm not a big fan of shots."

"Goddamn, you're a sneaky party pooper." Ty groaned. "But I'll get you, my pretty. You are doing shots with us tomorrow if I have to hand feed you the booze myself, Jae-seong."

Emmett let out a snicker. "Oop. You're in trouble now."

"No more of this old man aesthetic you're always throwing around," Ty continued. "That's just boring and I am not having it!" He gestured to a guy on Jae's right. "Mason even brought special stuff just for you and Em!"

Emmett narrowed his eyes, his suspicion obvious. "What kind of special stuff?"

"Irish cream liqueur *and* whipped cream made from almond milk and therefore dairy free," Mason said with a grin. "That means I can mix up all the Blow Jobs you and Jae might want, and you don't have to share with anyone!"

Emmett's laugh got caught on a mouthful of beer and the group erupted as he was forced to spray it into the fire. His eyes watering with laughter, Jae took that moment as his cue to bow out for the night and got to his feet, exchanging high fives with the guys sitting closest before he walked off, Ty's protests ringing out behind him.

The conversation and laughter were audible inside the cabin, even through the closed door, and Jae kept his ears pricked as he got ready for bed, in case Ty and his friends decided to do something silly like bust in on him. He'd stripped down to his boxers when the cabin door actually did swing open and Jae laughed at himself when he saw it was only Emmett.

"What are you doing here?" he asked. "I figured you and the boy wonders out there would be up until the wee hours."

"Eh, they'll be up for a while." Emmett shut the door behind him. "Thom found a cache of dominoes and cards under the bar and I know they're determined to finish off the cooler of beer before the ice melts."

He crossed the room to Jae, mischief making his eyes sparkle in the low light of the camp lantern. "I'm good with drinks for tonight, though," he said. "Especially since kissing you makes me feel twice as drunk."

"You're such a cheeseball," Jae murmured over the swoop in his belly, and he didn't move as Emmett took his hand. The air between them hummed.

"Maybe," Emmett said, his voice gone just as low. "Doesn't mean I haven't been dying to kiss you all day."

Jae said nothing for several moments, then gently dropped Emmett's hand. "Me too. There's powdered toothpaste on top of my bag if you want to use it," he said as he turned toward the bed. "It'll save you the trip of going back out to the bathhouse if you're ready to turn down the lights."

"Damn, you're so smart, Jae. That's one of my favorite things about you."

Emmett's smug tone made him smile. However, Jae said nothing and simply went about turning down the quilt before he drew the half shades on the big window. Taking the brushing powder and his toothbrush with a bottle of water, Emmett stepped outside. He wasn't gone long and the lock's click when he came back in sounded loud, even over the conversation from the fire pit.

Pulling a travel-sized lube from his bag, Jae moved to the camping lantern on his side of the bed and turned it down, leaving half the room in shadows. Immediately, he bit back a curse. The wavering light of the remaining lantern on Emmett's side cast an unmistakably romantic vibe over the room, splashing the walls and ceiling with a lovely, warm glow. Unfortunately for Jae, romance wasn't what Emmett had signed up for, no matter how much the idea of hooking up in a cabin tucked away in the woods appealed. Jae shoved the flutter in his chest away with all his might.

"You have to be quiet," he whispered as Emmett peeled off his clothes. But then Emmett leaned in and Jae's warning words were lost in a kiss that turned him inside-out.

Touching Emmett felt so good. Better every time they did this in fact, and Jae just craved it more and more.

"Got a condom?" Emmett asked, his disappointment plain at Jae's headshake. "But—"

"I brought some," Jae said over him. "Enough for the whole weekend provided we get time like this again." Gently, he pushed,

herding Emmett backward until he lay flat against the mattress. "I
want to try something first, though and I think you're going to like
it. I want to make you feel good, Em, the way you do me."

"Mmm, Jae." Emmett ran his hands over Jae's shoulders and
back. "You always do, every time. I just ... just wanna feel you,
okay?"

"Okay."

After he'd dropped another kiss onto Emmett's lips, Jae sat
back and reached for the lube. Wetting his fingers, he handed the
bottle to Emmett, who moaned softly when Jae took himself in
hand. Emmett was quick to slick his own hands, but a near growl
built in Jae's chest when Emmett spread his legs and started
stroking, his head thrown back against the pillow, eyes glittering in
the half light.

"God, Emmett."

Leaning forward, Jae guided Emmett onto his side, then quickly
slid in between his thighs, lining up their cocks as he took Emmett
in his arms. Emmett's mouth fell open as Jae ground into him and
it was only by luck Jae caught his moan with a kiss.

Jae reveled in the bare skin against his own. Winding himself
around Emmett, he rutted slowly, the sensation of their cocks
rubbing together made even more delicious when Emmett
wrapped a long, muscled leg around Jae's waist. Emmett clung to
Jae and their kisses deepened in intensity, becoming almost
drugging in a way Jae had very rarely known.

Despite the cool night air, heat built between them and made
their bodies damp with sweat. Desire wound low in Jae's groin, a
need to see Emmett's face overcoming him from nowhere, and
when he tried to pull back, Emmett chased after the kiss. He went
still when Jae raised a hand to Emmett's lips. A shiver shook
Emmett's frame as Jae pressed his fingertips into that hot mouth,
and when Emmett started sucking, he made a soft, tender noise
that pierced Jae through.

Enraptured by the way Emmett gave himself over so
completely to pleasure, Jae simply watched him for a while, unable
to look away. Emmett's eyes were closed and his eyebrows drawn
together, every part of him straining to get closer as he suckled at
Jae's fingers like he couldn't get enough. A shiver ran through
Emmett as Jae rocked into him harder.

Turning his attention to Emmett's throat, Jae feasted on the contrast of delicate skin and the rasp of beard stubble, aware of Emmett's steady moans, quieted only by Jae's fingers against his tongue. Jae's need burned hotter and higher, until he swore on everything holy that he was about to go up in actual flames. He pulled his hand free and slid his mouth over Emmett's once more, kissing him deeply, his core abuzz when Emmett seemed to melt against him.

Jae moved his hand to Emmett's nipple and swallowed Emmett's gasp. Pinching hard, he held onto Emmett as a shudder wracked Emmett's body, his grip like iron around Jae as his cum spread over their bellies. Jae ground down harder, his core aching with the need to soar. Pleasure broke over him in a wave so intense it almost hurt. He curled into Emmett, muffling a shaky moan against his neck. With anyone else, Jae might have been embarrassed by his loss of control, but he wasn't with Emmett, who simply held him close.

It was a few minutes before either of them stirred and each stayed silent when Jae finally rolled away. Emmett's eyes were almost closed as he watched Jae fumble for a shirt to wipe them both down.

"Never got off like that before," Emmett said, his voice low and sleepy. He kept a hand on Jae any time he was close enough for Emmett to touch, often on the wrist where Jae wore his leather bracelet. "And you were right. I liked it."

Jae let out a soft laugh. "Good."

He took a minute to set the lube on the old steamer trunk that served as his nightstand, then got out of bed and turned out the lamp on Emmett's side of bed too. Emmett's eyes were shut as Jae drew the quilt up over him, but he snuggled in close as Jae climbed back into bed, one arm around Jae and his lips warm against the hollow of Jae's throat.

"Want you to fuck me like that," Emmett whispered. "I wanna watch your face when you come."

Heat spread through Jae's core. "You keep talking like that and it'll happen sooner than you think," he said, and smothered his amusement against Emmett's curls when a low grumble reached his ears.

"Promises, promises."

Chapter Nine

Jae made good on his promise first thing the next morning.

He could have slept longer—the thin, gray light coming through the skylights and window told Jae it was still early, and the campsite was quiet save for the sound of bird noises. But Emmett was asleep on his belly when Jae woke up and just looking at the shape of his ass under the sheet proved too tempting to resist.

Jae loved every second.

Loved driving Emmett higher and higher until he could barely string two words together. Holding him as he unraveled at the seams. Coming deep inside Emmett, their fingers entwined on top of the mattress.

And Jae loved this hazy time after orgasm too, lying sweaty and loose limbed together as the thunder of his heart gradually calmed. Though they'd just woken, Emmett was drowsy and greedy for touch, like he was every time he came, and Jae would have laughed as the big guy rolled Jae onto his back and sprawled on top of him *if* Emmett hadn't been so heavy.

"Guh." He squirmed until Emmett shifted more onto his side.

"Mmm. Sorry."

"You're fine." Jae ran a hand over Emmett's muscled shoulder. "How often do you work out?"

Emmett laughed. "You calling me big, Jae-seong?"

"Good God, no. I'm calling you solid," Jae replied. "Your body is gorgeous and you know it."

"Yeah, I do. There's a gym in my building, and I work out most days. But I've always been kind of brawny, unlike you, all tall and rangy." Craning his head back, Emmett peeled open one eye. "You work out every day, huh? On the fancy bike in your bedroom?"

"Not every day but yes, mostly on a bike. I ride at a studio downtown when I can and do on-demand classes on the days I can't."

"You don't have an on-the-road bike, do you?"

"Afraid not." Jae tried to tame Emmett's wild bedhead with his fingers. "With all the moving I've done over the years, a stationary bike is easier. And besides, I'm a bit of a road hazard when I'm switching days to night and back and my sleep is all messed up."

"Good point. I've got an extra bike you're welcome to borrow anytime. Provided you get some sleep before we ride, of course."

"Thank you." Jae paused for a beat before asking his next question. "Was the extra bike Sean's?"

"Yeah." Emmett's shoulders moved in a tiny shrug. "It's in a storage unit over in Charlestown along with some other stuff he left behind. He keeps saying he'll come get everything but so far it hasn't happened."

"Maybe he's hoping you'll drive it up to him."

Emmett's laughter made Jae smile. "That's *exactly* what he hopes and the opposite of what's going to happen. Sean's used to getting what he wants and that's fine. I'm done going out of my way to cater to him, though."

"I get it. I was just curious, Em, and I'd never tell you what to do with your own stuff."

"I know you wouldn't. I'm curious about something too."

"Oh yeah? And what's that?"

"You mentioned seeing Sal last night but, you told me not to come over after work because you'd be too tired to hang out."

Taken off guard, Jae blinked at the ceiling. He didn't hear anything like a challenge in Emmett's tone, but fielding questions about Sal was the last thing he'd expected to do this morning. Particularly now that Emmett had rolled up on to his elbow and was watching Jae, his expression more serious than Jae knew how to interpret.

"Well, that wasn't a lie," Jae said, finding his tongue at last. "I was asleep by eight last night. Sal happened to be on Charles Street a bit earlier in the evening and he stopped by to see if I was home."

And when I answered the door, I was hoping to see you. Except I can't tell

84

you that because it might make it sound like I missed you and we both know I'm not supposed to do that.

Jae pressed his lips together hard. This weekend was doing funny things to his head. Leaving him unmoored and aware to the point of discomfort that acting like Emmett's buddy anytime they stepped out of this little room felt ... wrong. He looked forward to seeing Emmett, whether they were fucking around or not, but while Jae had come into this thing knowing it wouldn't last forever, he'd never expected to *like* the man beside him so goddamned much. Jae didn't have words to explain that to Emmett—hell, he hardly knew how to explain it to himself. Which meant keeping another secret from someone else.

God. This was really getting fucked up.

"Sal had a bag of sushi, and we had dinner and caught up," Jae said instead. "It was nice." He smiled. "He applauded your campaign to make my plant killing a thing of the past."

"Hah. Did you tell him about us?"

"Yes. That's okay, right? Sal's never met Ty or my parents."

"Should be fine. He'll meet your family now that you've asked him to the wedding, though." Emmett's last word slid into a yawn.

"True." Jae raised a hand to his own hair and raked it back with his fingers. "He won't say anything, though. And bringing a date to the wedding will please my ma. She doesn't like that I'm still unattached, even more so with Ty getting married. She views my being alone as a negative and worries that I'm lonely."

"Are you?" Emmett met Jae's gaze head on. "Lonely, I mean."

"Not usually, no. I work hard, but I have time to play and I've never had trouble finding partners when I want them. I mean, that's what Sal and I had going and ... you and I." Jae watched Emmett's quick nod.

"But your ma wants bigger and better for you, right? Like married and living in the 'burbs?"

"I'm sure she'd love it." Jae smiled. "Suburbs and a house filled with kids and pets."

A chuckle rolled through Emmett. "Sounds like the total opposite of anything you'd want, Jae. I mean, you said it yourself—your personal life takes a backseat to your career."

"It definitely has, yes. I'd be ... okay with settling down, though." Jae spoke with deliberation, as much to make sure he made himself heard as to get past the funny snarl Emmett's words had lodged in his chest. He licked his lips at the way Emmett's eyes widened. "I told you before that I'm not down on love—I've just never felt it. If I found the right man, maybe I'd feel ready to rearrange my priorities."

"Here's hoping you find him, then." Emmett pressed a kiss against Jae's chest. "You'd really be okay with staying in one place? And the pets and the kids?"

"Oh." Jae rolled onto his back, then closed his eyes. He couldn't look at Emmett right now, or the mix of amusement and fondness on his face that made Jae ... want. To stay in one place. Put down some roots. Be with someone special who was more than just a friend. "Those are big things and they'd need serious discussion. I have no idea if they're in the cards for me. I mean ... I'm still terrified of killing the aloe plant you gave me, never mind something I'd have to feed more than every three weeks."

Emmett hummed as he settled onto his pillow. "Is that why you came back to Boston, Jae? To find the right man?"

"No." Jae stayed silent a moment before he spoke again. "It felt like the right time to be back in this city. And maybe like the right time to work on finding myself."

* * * *

The light in the cabin was brighter when Jae woke for the second time and it took a few minutes before he was able to persuade Emmett to turn him loose. After dressing in sweats and knit cap to hide his bedhead, Jae made his way to the bathhouse, his gaze on the campsite around him. A couple of empty beer bottles sat by the firepit, but the place was otherwise neat, and he was pleased to note that everyone appeared to have made it into a cabin at some point the night before.

He was prepping for breakfast in the kitchen when he heard a car engine approaching outside, followed by voices that told him Emmett had emerged from their cabin to pick up the morning doughnut delivery. Emmett's grin as he stepped in with a stack of brown cardboard boxes made Jae smile too.

"These smell amazing," Emmett said as he set them on the counter. "I just want to bury my face in their sugary goodness."

Jae laughed. "I'd like to see that, and yeah, I can smell them from here. I'd join you in the face planting if I could."

"Well, you are in luck, my friend." Emmett crossed the room to the shelf that held the tin coffee cups. "This bakery makes an excellent vegan glazed cruller, as well as blueberry iced and chocolate cake, all of which you can eat."

"And how do you know that?"

"I asked the camp owner about his suppliers last night when he stopped by. Made the connection when he mentioned the bakery's name."

Emmett brought his cup to the counter. Picking the top-most box up from the stack, he set it by the cutting board and now Jae saw not only the bakery's logo but also the big 'VEGAN' scrawled in Sharpie across the box's upper-right corner.

"Eric's Baked Goods has a store in Portland, too, and it's one of a few places I truly miss." Emmett said. "I spent a fair amount of time sampling *all* of Eric's baked goods after stuff went bad with Sean, and I was lucky to escape when I did. I was definitely in danger of becoming not svelte." He patted his flat belly and smirked.

Jae's heart crumpled a little at that crooked smile. For all Emmett's cheery attitude, Jae thought the guy could have used a hug and here Jae couldn't give him one because they needed to be careful no one saw them acting as more than friends. And fuck if that didn't sting.

Turning to the pile of sweet potatoes he'd peeled, Jae picked one up and started dicing. "Somehow, I doubt that. I'll split a blueberry iced with you, if you like, because they sound fantastic."

A heavy silence followed. It lengthened, seeming to fill the room, and when Jae finally looked up, Emmett's smile had disappeared.

"What's wrong?" Emmett asked.

"Nothing." Jae picked up another potato and, when Emmett didn't respond, seized on what felt like the most obvious topic. "I know you don't like talking about Sean, yet this is the second time we've done so today."

"Ugh, you're right." Emmett grimaced. "For a while, I was so talked out on the whole topic of Sean and the big breakup. Like even thinking about it was exhausting. But I don't feel that way anymore and I … guess that's a good thing." He turned and rested his ass against the edge of the counter, his coffee cup cradled between his palms.

"After we split, everyone wanted to talk about it, even Sean, and he was never one for deep discussion. He did it though, and while it sucked at the time, it was also good, at least for me. I needed to make changes in my life and talking about why our relationship went to hell gave me some perspective."

Jae frowned. "What happened between you and Sean was not all on you, Em."

"Here, let me help." Turning back around, Emmett set his cup down and grabbed another knife. "You're right—our problems weren't all on me. Fixing my part in them was, however, and still is," he said as he diced. "Taking time for me, keeping my head out of EP when I'm not working, living and staying in the moment instead of constantly looking forward to whatever comes next—those are things I can and should do, both for me and anyone who might be in my life.

"You already know I didn't do that when I was with Sean," Emmett said. "But the ridiculous thing is that I'd already been through something way too similar with Aiden. Aiden didn't cheat—he'd never do that." Emmett sniffed. "But we were always so focused on work it was like we forgot how to be a couple and morphed back into friends. And did I learn from the experience, Jae-seong?"

"I'm guessing the answer is no." Jae considered the man before him for a moment. "You're being a bit hard on yourself, don't you think?" he asked. "I mean, maybe the universe is trying to tell you not to date your coworkers, but it's not like you can help who you love."

Emmett laughed. "Oh, fuck love. And fuck dating too, while we're at it, and all its complications."

"Dudes, please tell me there's more coffee."

Glancing over his shoulder, Jae breathed past the burn in his chest. Ty stood in the doorway, clad in a t-shirt and sleep pants and looking somewhat worse for wear.

"Help yourself." Jae tipped his head at the pot on the stove. "Eggs and hash'll be ready in a bit and there are doughnuts to tide you over until then."

"Oh, yes," Ty said, his tone fervent as he headed for the stove. "Krishnan's mixing up Bloody Marys, but I really need some caffeine in my brain. What kind of hash are you making?"

"Sweet potato and chorizo," Jae replied. "You can add Gouda

and feta to your own plate, too."

"Because God forbid you get too close to cheese." Ty wrinkled his nose at his brother. "I don't suppose there's any kind of creamer for the coffee, right? Or am I supposed to be all manly and drink it black like you?"

"You're supposed to stick a doughnut in your mouth and quit giving me crap," Jae replied, then turned back to his work over the sound of Emmett's laughter.

The bickering continued as Ty fixed himself coffee, and Emmett's expression grew more and more amused the longer the brothers sniped back and forth. He was the one who rescued the box of vegan doughnuts after Ty spotted it and told him in no uncertain terms to fuck off outside with the rest of the boxes if he didn't want to get thumped for bitching about Jae's eating habits.

"He's going to be like this all day," Jae muttered as he sautéed the sweet potatoes with slices of green onion, though his warning just made Emmett laugh some more.

Thankfully, some food evened out Ty's mood and he was cheerful again by the time everyone squeezed into two of the cars for a trip to Gooseneck Beach. The party played volleyball and swam in the surf under the cloudless sky, and Krishnan manned an effort to build a sandcastle large enough that kids who were playing on the beach flocked to help. Talk turned to axe throwing as the bachelor party gathered for a picnic lunch.

"Did you say we need to do that while it's still light out?" Ty asked around a mouthful of turkey sandwich.

"Yes," Jae said, "otherwise we'll just be flinging axes into the woods."

Emmett shook the water in his hair at Jae. "That sounds surprisingly fun."

"And you look decidedly sunburned." Jae picked up a t-shirt from the towel beside him and handed it to Emmett. "You need shade, white boy."

"I do too," said a young man named Kal. He'd draped his towel over his red hair like a hood, using it to shield his fair, freckled skin. "I'm slicked up with SPF 50 but there's only so much sun this Irish skin can handle."

"Then back to the woods we'll go." Ty clapped his hands together. "We're about out of beer anyway and Jae's due for some shots. Especially as he and Emmett volunteered to stay sober today so they could drive us all back to camp." He caught Jae's eye. "I know you hate driving."

Jae snorted. "I really do. And I *am* up for drinks. I'll just blame you if I end up too tipsy to help cook dinner."

"Yeah, same," Emmett said. "How about you and I make another round of sandwiches when we get back, Jae, just in case we get too wrecked to be trusted around flames?"

The comments drew laughter from the others, but Jae noticed a thoughtful air about Ty that lingered as they packed up.

Shit. Jae racked his brain. He and Emmett hadn't acted too friendly towards one another, had they? Touched or smiled in a way that might have caught Ty's attention? Jae couldn't imagine they had. He'd hardly been near Emmett since they'd left the campsite until everyone had sat down to eat. They'd all been too busy playing in the sand and surf like kids. Yet Ty continued to appear almost distracted, even as the group headed for the cars.

Jae caught up with his brother while the others were still deciding who would ride with whom.

"You okay, Ty?"

Ty met Jae's gaze, his eyebrows raised almost comically high. "Me? I'm great. Why?"

"You've got your sulky face on." Jae injected a teasing note into his tone to make sure Ty knew his words were meant to be joking and sure enough, Ty's manner turned droll.

"I'm not sulking—I'm thinking," he said, "something I've been known to do from time to time. But seriously, I'm fantastic." Ty leaned against the side of Krishnan's Toyota RAV4. "I was a little leery when you said we'd be camping this weekend, but this has been fucking amazing, Jae. Way better than pub crawls in the city. Thanks for talking me out of that."

"You're welcome. And hey, we can do pub crawls for your birthday if Amelia says it's okay."

"Oh, fuck you." Ty tipped his head back and laughed. He glanced down the road apiece to where Emmett and the other guys were clustered around his Explorer. "You and Emmett ... you're having fun, right?"

"Of course." Jae swore his heart missed a beat. "Why do you ask?"

"Well, you both got thrown together into this out of nowhere and I can tell it's been a ton of work keeping everyone happy. Like the cooking and staying sober to drive us around ... Hell, you're even bunking together."

"It's not like it's a hardship. Em and I have mutual friends and we hang out on the regular."

Ty walked around the front end of the car to the passenger side. "Okay, sure. But what time did you guys wake up just to get breakfast ready?"

"It was early, but my body clock is sensitive right now." Jae ignored the heat crawling up his neck. "And, at the risk of sounding like an old man, acting as designated driver is hardly a sacrifice."

"It is if you want to party." A smile crossed Ty's face when Jae laughed. "Which is sort of my point. You guys haven't exactly been free to party yourselves."

"I haven't felt that way. I think Emmett's enjoying himself too, especially with feeding everyone. The man I saw this morning bringing in the doughnut delivery was in his element." Jae shared another laugh with his brother, but his chest went tight at Ty's next words.

"This is going to sound sappy, but I'm glad I got to know Emmett. Like, how lucky am I to have found the coolest girl in the world and her brother is Emmett-freaking-McNeil?"

"I'm happy for you, Ty. Really glad."

"Thanks." He gave Jae a soft look. "I know you're not into heteronormative crap like being married and settling down with a forever person, but I hope you don't mind me saying that I think it'd be great if you met someone like Amelia. Or fuck, like Emmett, I guess, since you're the Bak who's into dudes." Ty barked out a laugh. "Ma and Dad would love it and so would I."

Jae simply hummed.

I'm starting to think I'd love it, too. Especially with a guy like Emmett.

* * * *

Arriving back to the campsite ahead of schedule meant flowing drinks and flying axes, and though Ty made good his promise to feed Jae shots, Jae did his best to keep his head. He surprised everyone—including himself—by showing better than average skill with axe throwing, and it was through a roar of approval he was crowned that day's champ. To his surprise, no one appeared happier than Emmett when the time came to pack the axes away and Jae gave into the urge to tease as they entered the kitchen to start the evening meal.

"I thought you'd enjoy that activity more," Jae said, "particularly as I'm one-hundred percent sure you throw harder than anyone here. I'm starting to think you let me win."

"Yeah, no. You won all on your own, Jae-seong." Emmett threw him a dark look. "Watching you heave that axe around and the way your body moves ... fuck, so hot. So distracting."

"Good to know." Jae didn't bother fighting off the impulse to preen. "I'll remember if we ever go bowling so I kick your ass at that, too."

Emmett let out a loud laugh, then cast a glance at the door. The next thing Jae knew, Emmett was in his space, hands on Jae's waist and fire in his eyes. The heat pouring off Emmett's body made Jae's knees wobble.

"We can't," he murmured and forced himself to step away. "Someone will see and ... You don't want that."

"Yeah, my bad." Emmett's lips thinned and he turned his gaze toward the door. "I lost my head for a sec there."

"You're fine." Jae went to the refrigerator and pulled out a trio of big Ziploc bags filled with cubes and strips of marinated meat. "I'll get started on making kabobs if you want to check the fire. I know you wanted to do your cooking outside tonight."

"The fire can wait." Emmett stepped up beside Jae at the counter, his voice quieter, and Jae pressed his lips into a hard line when a hand settled over his.

"Emmett—"

"I don't want this to be weird for you, Jae."

The regret in Emmett's gaze when Jae looked at him rooted Jae to the spot. "I know you don't. I don't want it to be weird for you, either, but it is when we're around Ty."

It's only going to get weirder when we're around the whole family.

Emptiness filled Jae as the thought hit home. So, what the fuck was he going to do about it? Nothing tonight, that was for sure. Maybe nothing at all, considering it was nobody's business who Jae spent his time with. If he wanted to keep fucking around with Emmett he would, even if it meant keeping things from people he loved.

"C'mon." Gently, he pulled his hand out from under Emmett's.

"Let's get the crew fed before they turn on us."

They slipped back into the task of cooking and for a while Jae lost himself in routines that didn't require him to think too hard. He rolled his eyes when Ty showed up with cocktails for the cooks, though the gesture tickled him, too, especially when Ty stuck around and chatted with them instead of going back out to play bocce with his friends.

All in all, they spent a perfect evening by the fire with good food and drink and the stars overhead, the smell of salt from the ocean beyond the trees in the air and Emmett's solid form planted firmly next to Jae's. Emmett nearly swept Jae off his feet once the cabin door was locked behind them, however, and Jae was forced to kiss him just to muffle Emmett's groan.

"Shh," he whispered as Emmett kissed his way along Jae's neck. "We need to be quiet."

"I'll try," Emmett muttered against the hollow of Jae's throat. "Not sure I can though. Want you so much." He shivered and crowded a little closer. "I feel like I could blow if you even breathe on me the wrong way."

"I'll remember to breathe on you the right way then."

In the half light of one camp lantern, they stripped each other bare. Jae petted and kissed as the garments fell away, delight in his core when Emmett's skin prickled with goosebumps. Gathering him close, Jae skimmed his palm over Emmett's belly, then dipped his hand lower, and kissed Emmett some more when he gasped.

"Mmm, Jae. Wanna suck you."

"Okay. Let me play first, though." Pushing gently, Jae guided Emmett to the bed, then laid him out, heat pulsing in his groin as Emmett raised his hands up over his head.

A quiet moan went through Emmett as Jae caught Emmett's crossed wrists in one hand. He lavished attention over Emmett's neck and chest, kissing and sucking his skin, though he took care to be gentle along the places where Emmett was hot from sun exposure.

Emmett was breathing hard when Jae raised his head again, his voice rough. "Please, Jae."

Jae let go of Emmett's wrists and laughed softly when he found himself being manhandled onto his back. His skin prickled as Emmett used his greater weight to pin Jae down and they kissed, long and slow, each moment gradually turning Jae's brain to goo.

He melted into the sheets as Emmett moved lower, nuzzling and teasing with his teeth. Shocks zigged through Jae and straight to his dick when Emmett turned his attention to Jae's nipples, and he grabbed onto Emmett's curls with a hiss.

"Jesus, Em." He felt Emmett smile against his skin.

"We need lube."

Jae made a grab for the bottle they'd stashed under the pillows. He wet his fingers then passed the tube down, and he forced his eyes open wide so he could watch Emmett push up onto his knees. Even in the dim light, he saw Emmett's cock standing stiff against his abdomen. Emmett turned and faced Jae's feet, and he shot a smile over his shoulder when Jae set his hands on Emmett's hips. Emmett straddled Jae's chest, then crouched low, his amazing ass held high. Wrapping his arms around Emmett's waist, Jae pressed his face into Emmett's groin, breathing in deep as they turned on to their sides, his mouth watering at the combination of musk, smoke, and man.

Emmett wrapped a hand around Jae then took him in his mouth, and a near growl built in Jae's chest. He licked and nibbled Emmet's skin some more, reveling in salty skin and coarse curls of hair before he finally took Emmett between his lips. He sucked Emmett deep, loving the hard weight on his tongue and the bitter taste of pre-cum. Winding himself around Emmett's body, Jae held fast with his arms and thighs, his body lighting up white hot when Emmett grabbed his hips and effortlessly hauled Jae close. Fuck, Emmett was *strong*.

A feedback loop of pleasure built between them. Jae's eyes rolled behind his closed lids as desire coiled tighter inside him. He wanted to fuck the man in his arms. Make him come. Lose it so hard he forgot his own name.

Jae teased the tender skin behind Emmett's balls with his fingertips, and Emmett thrust deeper into Jae's mouth, his own moans muffled by the cock in his throat. He made a desperate noise as Jae teased his rim, arching his back and chasing after Jae's touch, even as he used Jae's mouth.

Fuck. He loves it.

Sinking a finger inside Emmett, Jae went as deep as he dared, aware Emmett's whole body was trembling. His chest squeezed at Emmett's broken sounds and he slid another finger in, fucking and sucking until Emmett's thrusts lost rhythm. He went rigid on a gasp, his cock pulsing in Jae's mouth. He twitched and jerked, and Jae fucked Emmett's face until he followed Emmett over, pleasure rolling through him in waves that made him want to scream.

Pulling off, Jae shuddered as his own dick fell from Emmett's lips, but as he shifted to unwind his legs from around Emmett's torso, Emmett tightened his grip. Jae's skin prickled at Emmett's rough whisper.

His bones still molten, Jae gently tugged himself free. He got himself turned around and pulled Emmett into his arms and Emmett pushed in close for kisses. His touch was clumsy-gentle as he stroked Jae's hair and shoulders, as if he couldn't get enough.

"Mmm. So good," Emmett murmured, his voice creaky and wrecked. "Love this with you, Jae."

I love it, too. And you. More than you'll ever know.

Jae's heart—the love that ran all through him—rose up and choked him as words he'd never said to anyone crowded onto his tongue. Dazed in a way that felt a lot like fear, he buried his face in Emmett's neck and stayed there until Emmett slowly relaxed into sleep.

Long after the rest of the campsite had gone quiet, Jae lay awake, staring up at the stars through the skylight while Emmett slumbered beside him.

What the fuck was he going to do now?

Chapter Ten

A week later, Jae was no closer to finding an answer to his question.

He hadn't changed his behavior. Hadn't put Emmett off when he called or texted, wanting to hang out around the variations in Jae's schedule. Which meant they met up most nights, regardless of how late either of them might be working. While they often screwed each other silly, they talked no matter what, even on the nights Jae was too tired to keep his eyes open for longer than a few minutes. And those were the times Jae knew he'd miss most when this thing they had going ran its course.

He'd miss mornings like this, too, waking up with Emmett curled around him, his slumbering breaths warm against Jae's neck. Even more so now that Jae had made up his mind to stay in Boston.

Carefully, he slipped out of Emmett's hold and swung his legs over the edge of the mattress. Jae hadn't said anything about his decision or about the shift in his feelings. How could he when those feelings were exactly what Emmett had said he didn't want?

Falling for Emmett—falling in *love*—was so far outside anything Jae had ever imagined, he still didn't know how to wrap his head around it. And it hurt to even think those words knowing full well they didn't matter in the end—however much Jae wanted Emmett in his life as more than a friend and fuck buddy, Emmett simply wasn't on the same page.

A hand came to rest against the small of Jae's back.

"Where ya goin'?"

"Was thinking about a shower." Jae patted the arm that looped around his waist. "We're due at Ty and Amelia's in a couple of hours and we should probably get up."

"Gah. Do we have to go?"

"I'm afraid we do. Your mom flew up here for this brunch because your sister didn't want a formal bridal shower and I think she could use your support. Amelia, I mean, not your mom."

"You're so responsible." Emmett sighed. "That's both one of my favorite and least favorite things about you."

A laugh worked its way past the burn in Jae's chest. "You grab the shower first."

"What are you gonna do?"

"I'll work out. You need to get back to your place to change clothes and waiting for me is going to make you late, so—"

"So, I'll be late." With a playful growl, Emmett shifted, then hauled Jae back onto the mattress as if he weighed nothing. Jae cackled right through his own surprise.

"Emmett, no!"

"Emmett, yes." Emmett rolled on top of him, eyes gleaming with mischief. "I'm not leaving here before you come, Jae-seong, and that either happens here in your bed or in your shower."

Jae folded like a house of cards. "Fine. Have it your way," he said, then looped his arms around Emmett's neck and pulled him down for a kiss.

* * * *

"Hello, son."

"Hey, Dad." Jae stepped inside Ty and Amelia's Charlestown place and gave his father, Kun-bae, a quick hug. "Do I want to know why you're answering the door?"

"Oh, the ladies have been busy with the entertaining, so I volunteered to act as bouncer. You are the last to arrive by the way, which means I can just hang out and chill with the rest of you now."

Jae checked his watch. "I'm not late, am I?"

"Nope. Everyone else in this family runs early, that's all." Kun-bae grinned. People often said Jae was a carbon copy of his dad with his tawny brown skin and his very dark hair. Kun-bae's smile matched Jae's exactly and seeing it never failed to make Jae smile, too.

Ty and Amelia's rented house was an old, historic structure with all sorts of nooks and crannies, and a large foyer that effectively split the ground level in half. A formal front room and library made up the first half while a mishmash of dining, living, and kitchen areas filled out the second. After leaving his bag and a gift for the happy couple in the library, Jae followed his dad through to the party where Jae was quickly enveloped in a flurry of greetings and hugs. He chatted with Amelia's aunts and neighbors and friends, every one of them pleasant and smiling and decidedly female. Even Jae's dad had vanished by the time Jae stooped down and hugged the diminutive Margaret McNeil, who quickly passed him off to his own mother, Christina.

"Hi, Ma." Jae grumbled a little as his mom fussed with his hair, but he didn't really mind the attention, especially when he glimpsed real delight in her hazel eyes.

Christina gave his arm a quick squeeze. "I know you've been responsible for your own grooming for more than half your life now, but I still feel the need to apologize for giving you my cowlicks."

"Eh, I'm mostly used to them. Besides, they give me an excuse to buy lots of hats."

"You always were very practical, even as a child." She chuckled.

"Where's Ty?" Jae asked. "Hiding out somewhere with Emmett?"

"Yes. They're outside on the deck with the rest of the men." Margaret tipped her head toward a screen door that led outside. "They'll be glad to have another Y chromosome in their midst, I'm sure."

"Speaking of men, I was hoping you'd bring your friend today," Christina said. "Your father and I wanted to meet him before the wedding."

"Friend?" Jae frowned at his mother a moment before the pieces clicked into place. "Do you mean Sal?"

Christina gave a delicate roll of her eyes. "Yes, of course, I mean Sal. You should have told me you were dating someone, Jae—I'm not sure how I feel about having to hear about new boyfriends from your brother."

Oh, shit. Jae quickly held up both hands. "Whoa, whoa, whoa,

Ma. Sal is not my boyfriend."

"He's not?" Christina furrowed her brow at Jae.

"No. Like, we're dating but not *dating* dating."

"Meaning it's not serious yet," Margaret piped in. When Jae turned her way, she gave him a look he could only describe as encouraging. Jae blinked.

"Um. Right." Still unsure what the hell was happening, Jae nodded at Margaret, then turned back to his mother. "Sal and I are more friends than boyfriends, if you get what I mean."

"I do and damn," Christina said.

Jae couldn't help laughing. "I'm sorry. Did I burst your bubble?"

"A bit, yes. Your brother said Sal was your 'friend', but I hoped he was just being coy."

"I'm not sure Ty has ever been such a thing in his whole life, Ma."

"Hah, good point! Okay, you and Sal are friends—that's fine for now." Christina gave Jae a look he found very cunning. "Friendship can easily become something more, provided you want it to."

She patted Jae's arm, oblivious of the hurt her easy words had set off inside him. "Now if you'll excuse me, I have some gifts to grab from the library. Amelia and your brother have decided they'd like to open gifts outside which is a lovely idea except for said gifts needing to be moved."

"Do you need some help?" Jae asked, even as Christina waved him off.

"Margaret and I already have the job half-done, honey, so don't fuss."

"The arthritis in my hands has been giving me trouble," Margaret said to Jae after his mother had walked off. "I really can't thank your parents enough for all the help they've given Amelia and me today. And thank you for arranging Ty's bachelor party and getting him home in one piece! Amelia was worried about the axe throwing of course, and while Ty's friends are all very nice, I'm not sure one of them has the sense that God gave a billy goat. Ty hasn't stopped talking about the trip all morning."

"I'm glad he had fun. I certainly did." Jae smiled. "Even more than I anticipated, which made the time Emmett and I spent on planning doubly worth it. Some mutual friends of ours are making a trip up there in August and invited Emmett and me, which I think will be nice. We can take a turn hanging out instead of playing cruise directors."

"Hm." Margaret frowned. "Ty mentioned that you and Amelia's brother planned the trip. But Emmett himself hasn't said a word about it, at least not to me."

Probably because you rarely address him directly or even say his name?

Jae shrugged off the thought. "Emmett's likely being modest. He's not one to toot his own horn."

"Well, I'm glad he was helpful to you at least. Please, help yourself to anything you'd like," Margaret said, and waved Jae toward a food-laden table on the far end of the room. "Everyone was instructed to bring dairy free dishes and if they weren't able, Amelia and her brother marked them as such. They were *very* thorough."

"I'm sure they were." Jae was sure his gratitude showed on his face. "Emmett and his teams do a lot of research on food intolerance for the restaurants and trucks. He probably knows more about my allergy than I."

A musing air came over Margaret. "I see. Enjoy yourself, Jae, and please tell me if you need anything." She smiled at him, then walked off toward the front of the house, no doubt to help Jae's mom.

Walking to the food table, Jae poured himself a glass of wine, then chuckled as he caught sight of wee cow-shaped stickers affixed to several of the serving bowls and platters. Clearly, Emmett's sense of whimsy was at play here, but Jae appreciated being able to clearly spot which foods he should avoid.

A burst of laughter from the deck outside drew his attention then, and as Jae looked up, he saw he had a clear view out the screen door. He glimpsed Emmett, looking summery and gorgeous in a short-sleeved madras shirt and khakis, his curls just this side of messy and a glass of something fruity-looking in one hand. Emmett hadn't shaved during the last several days and the longer beard stubble gave him a rugged and slightly untamed edge as he, Thom, and Ty chatted with a pair of pretty young women whom Jae knew were Amelia's bridesmaids.

As Jae watched, Emmett settled an arm around Kaylee's shoulders and Kaylee leaned into the loose embrace without missing a beat. Just as Jae would. Provided he and Emmett were out of sight of their families.

Jae turned his back to the screen door. Hauling a breath in through his nose, he dropped a few items from the platters without the cow stickers onto his plate but rather than go outside, he headed back to the front of the house, seeking quiet. Except that stillness seemed to seep into Jae as he settled himself on a couch in the now empty library, leaving him hollowed out and cold.

Way to be a drama queen.

Jae set his plate on the sofa cushion beside him. Emmett was probably just flirting with Kaylee, just as he did with lots of people during the course of an average day, whether those people picked up on it or not. And if Jae didn't like seeing Emmett cast his charms on someone else, well, he'd have to get used to it sometime. Because for all Emmett's claims about not wanting love or relationships in his life, he wouldn't feel that way forever—Jae knew it in his bones. Emmett was one of the most loving people he'd ever met. Someday, Emmett would be ready for a new partner, someone he could love out in the open, in full view of his family and friends to see, and damn, how much fun was that going to be for Jae to fucking watch after he'd been left behind?

"I can't keep doing this," he murmured to himself. He had to stop seeing Emmett, except as a friend. To cut that tie before someone (Jae) got hurt and get his life back into a groove that didn't involve hiding things from people he cared about.

Time to say 'when.'

Emmett would respect his wishes. He'd work hard to get them back on track as friends, too, instead of ghosting because that would be simpler. They'd hang out with Zac and Mark and the boys or with Amelia and Ty, and maybe grab dinner and drinks while they recalibrated the countless little intricacies that went into being friends. With some time, things between Jae and Emmett would ease into a thing Jae could manage. And maybe when that happened, Jae's heart wouldn't feel so wrecked.

Fat fucking chance.

A wild urge to laugh came over Jae, so his sinuses burned. But even as he rubbed his eyes with his hand, something else tugged at Jae's awareness, forcing him to shake himself and come fully alert. That's when he noticed the tingle spreading through his mouth.

Dropping his hand, Jae stared at the plate of food on the cushion beside him. Raw vegetables, rice crackers and hummus, along with a pair of deviled eggs, one already half gone. And though Jae didn't remember eating, only one thing made his tongue itch the way it did right now.

"Shit."

"Jae? Is everything all right? What are you doing in here all by yourself?"

Margaret McNeil was there when Jae looked up, her face worried and her blue eyes so familiar Jae's chest gave a sudden squeeze. His mouth went very dry.

"Um. I'm … Margaret, would you please find my father and tell him I need to speak with him?"

"Of course, I'll just—" Margaret cut herself off with a sharp inhale, her eyes going wide as she slowly placed a hand on her throat. "You're red here, Jae. There are blotches on your skin."

"Yeah." Jae grimaced, his entire torso itchy and hot, the tingle in his mouth pricking at his lips. "I ate something that isn't going to agree with me, and I need to leave. I'm fine," he added. "Please don't say anything to anyone else, especially Ty."

Or Emmett.

Jae's eyes stung with sudden tears.

For a second, he was sure Margaret would argue. But then Jae coughed into his fist and she nodded, her hands clasped tightly together. "I'll get your dad."

Jae grabbed his bag as she hurried off and quickly found the tube of antihistamine caplets he carried with him everywhere. Swallowing them dry, he looped the strap of the bag over his head, then pulled his phone from his pocket. Jae coughed around the weight slowly creeping onto his chest, adrenaline firing through his body along with an awful sense of dread that made his hands shake.

"Jae-seong."

Jae stood. "Hey, Dad." He kept his tone even, but his insides trembled when Kun-bae stepped forward and settled a hand against the back of Jae's neck. It'd been years since Jae had been through a reaction in front of his father, but that touch was enough to bring years of shared emotion roaring back. Jae's fear spiked even higher and for a second, he didn't trust himself to speak.

"Sit down, son."

Jae obeyed without question, then drew one of the bright yellow autoinjectors he carried from his bag. "Chest is heavy."

Kun-bae's mouth set in a grim line. He picked up the plate of abandoned food and handed it to Margaret, then sat beside Jae on the sofa. With his knuckles, he moved Jae's shirt collar aside, inspecting the wheals that had risen on Jae's skin without touching them. The heat and discomfort crawling through Jae intensified and, over a thicker and louder round of coughing, Jae stuck himself in the thigh with the injector, his whole focus on getting air in and out.

In the span of a heartbeat, the knot in Jae's chest started to ease. The heat and itch burrowing under his skin decreased in intensity and, despite his body's shaking, Jae could breathe again by the time he pulled the injector out. He knuckled moisture from his eyes.

"Better," he said when he was able, aware now that he was drenched with sweat. He knew from experience that the anxiety running through him would take longer to dissipate and he sighed when his father reached over to help him get the cap back on the injector. "No idea what set me off. I need to get checked out."

"Have you called 911?"

"No." Jae swallowed. "I'll call a Lyft. It's a quick ride from here to MGH."

"Absolutely not." Kun-bae squeezed Jae's shoulder. "What if you need another shot?"

"I've got more in my bag." Jae patted his father's hand. "I've been through this enough on my own to know what to do, Dad. No reason to fuck up the afternoon more than I already have."

Kun-bae cocked an eyebrow. "I'm not arguing this with you, Jae, and you're not thinking straight. I'll give you a ride or call an ambulance, you choose."

Jae swallowed against a lump that rose in his throat. "It's faster to drive. Plus, I want to be at MGH. Just give me a second to get my bearings."

"Can you stand?"

"I'll get Emmett," Margaret said, but her voice trailed away when Jae shook his head hard.

"Please don't. I don't want Emmett. Or anyone. I—" Jae cut himself off with a gulp. Even thinking Emmett's name made him want to say the kind of things he shouldn't and fuck, Jae's thoughts were *all* over the place. He drew in a shaky breath, his vision blurring with tears again. "I'm sorry," he almost croaked.

"What? Oh, Jae, no." Margaret's voice was pained. "*I'm* sorry, I really am."

"Not your fault. And I'm fine now, honest." Jae scrubbed at his eyes, then levered himself up, using his dad's arm for support. Together they walked slowly toward the front entrance.

Jae pulled out his phone once they'd made it to the sidewalk. "I'll text Zac n' Mark," he murmured. "If they're working, they might meet me at the ED."

"Okay." Kun-bae kept his hand on Jae's elbow as they approached his car. "You can call your ma next."

"Was hoping you could do that." Jae grimaced at his dad's dry laugh. "But I guess that's a no?"

Despite the worry etched on his features, Kun-bae smiled wide. "I'm going to be in the doghouse for sneaking you out of here without telling her, kid, so yeah, that's a no."

* * * *

"Still itchy?"

"A little."

Jae stared at the pewter medallion attached to the bracelet around his wrist. Bad reactions always shook him to the core, and he was beat in both body and mind, despite having dozed on and off since he'd been admitted. While it might be days before he felt truly recovered, his allergy hangover was worse than usual tonight and he badly needed an anchor. Jae didn't say any of that, however. He just hauled in a breath, smoothed the hem of his hospital gown against the legs of his pants, then lifted his gaze to meet Zac's.

"Can't believe I had to stick myself in front of Emmett's mom."

"Better that than keel over in your brother's parlor," Zac said.

"Library. And I almost did that too."

"Shit." Mark huffed out a laugh from his position by the exam room's door. "You really went all out, huh?"

"Jae's always been a 'go big or go home' kind of guy." Lifting the ear tips of his stethoscope, Zac slipped them into his ears. He pressed the diaphragm of the chest-piece to the left of Jae's sternum, listening to his lungs through the gown for several beats before moving it. A small smile crossed Zac's face as he let the chest-piece drop.

"Lung sounds are good."

"They feel it." Jae cleared his throat. "No change since I got here."

Zac hummed, then took hold of the neck of Jae's gown. He peeled it down, exposing Jae's shoulders, upper chest, and back, and the hives that still covered large sections of his skin. "Not much change here, though the redness has improved. Nothing to do but let the antihistamines and time do their thing."

Jae didn't reply. They all knew the drill. Zac had seen Jae through bad reactions in the past, as well as their aftermath, and nothing he nor Mark had done in this cubicle of the ED was out of the ordinary. Still, Jae found the rote nature of the question-and-answer routine soothing, particularly because Zac and Mark were so very measured and good at their jobs. Despite the gentle teasing, neither of them would give Jae crap for ingesting food he wasn't supposed to either, an exercise he was more than capable of doing all on his own.

"How's the anxiety?" Mark asked, his eyes kind when Jae looked his way. "Feeling more like yourself?"

Jae thought he did and said as much. He no longer felt like the sky was about to fall or that there wasn't enough air, and the stark and overwhelming sense that everything was very, very bad had faded.

"Good." Mark crossed the cubicle to Jae's side and helped Zac raise the hospital gown back up onto Jae's shoulders. "I need to go. My shift starts in ten." He pressed a quick kiss to Jae's cheek. "I'll check your refill for the EpiPen on my way past the pharmacy."

"I'll get it, Mark," Zac said. "We're about done here anyway and then I can walk Jae to his place."

"You don't need to." Jae sketched a wave at Mark as he let himself out the door, then quickly turned back to Zac. "I'm okay getting home on my own."

"Forget it, dude—you're stuck with me for the evening. We both know you need eyes on you for the next couple of hours."

"You said you had plans with Aiden."

"Plans we can reschedule for another time. C'mon." Zac fixed Jae with a look that brooked no argument, then headed for the door. "I'll grab your refill while you get dressed and then we'll get the hell out of here."

Jae had only just pulled off the gown when the door to the cubicle slid open once more. "That was fast," he said. "Did you sprint both ways?"

"Oh, Jesus."

Whipping around, Jae caught his brother's and Emmett's wide eyes, then grabbed for his shirt in a mad scramble to hide his rash. His cheeks flamed as he stuffed his arms into the shirtsleeves, but at least the wheals on his chest and neck were fewer than those covering his back.

"What are you doing here?" he bit out, working at the buttons on the shirt with clumsy fingers, his heart speeding up as Ty crossed the tiny room toward him.

"We wanted to make sure you were okay, you big, fucking idiot." Ty's voice was pained. "What the hell happened?"

"I ate something that set me off, but I handled it."

"With an EpiPen, according to Margaret."

"Yes, and you know that happens. I'm—"

"I swear to God, if you say you are fine, Jae, I am going to fucking lose it." Ty laid a hand over his forehead. "You look like a car wreck!"

"My mother said it was bad." Unlike Ty, Emmett was calm, almost somber, but there was an undercurrent in his voice that told Jae Emmett was far more stressed than he appeared. "She said you were coughing and sweating. Said she could *see* you were freaked the fuck out. You scared her, Jae."

"I know." Jae scrubbed his hands through his hair. "I'm sorry about that, Em. Your mom walked in just as it started and ..." He dropped his hands to his sides. "I shouldn't have dragged her into it. But sometimes my thoughts get weird when the symptoms start and after Margaret asked me if I was okay, I just said it. I'm sorry I scared her." Slowly, Jae ran his bottom lip between his teeth. "I'll call tomorrow and apologize again."

"That's not what I meant." Emmett narrowed his eyes and, fuck, Jae knew he was in for it. Emmett was *pissed.*

"Hi, guys." A white paper bag in his hand, Zac stepped into the room, his manner stern despite the friendly greeting. He leveled a stare first at Emmett and then Ty. "I'm sure you've got reasons for bringing this big dick energy onto my patient, but Jae isn't up for a battle right now."

Ty frowned. "I don't want a battle."

"I think you do." Carefully, Zac pushed past Ty and Emmett and positioned himself by Jae. He was shorter than Ty and not as built as Emmett, but Zac turned his body just so and forced them each back a step. He eyeballed them for several seconds longer before he handed the prescription bag to Jae. "Whatever else Jae tells you, he feels like garbage right now. He needs rest and quiet and I'd like to get him home, so I'm asking you to hold off on any immediate plans to bitch him out."

Emmett met Zac's glower with one of his own. "Fine. I'm coming with you."

"Em, no." Jae wrapped his hands around the prescription bag and squeezed. The hurt in Emmett's eyes was almost too much to bear. But even though shutting Emmett out made Jae feel like shit, he literally didn't have it in him just then to deal with anything more complicated than gathering enough energy to get himself home. "I just told you, I'm okay."

"Yeah, I heard you." Emmett crossed his arms over his chest and scowled deeper. "The problem is, I don't believe a word of it, Jae."

Jae's stomach tumbled right through the floor. The silence that followed seemed to fill the whole space and for a long, tense moment, Emmett held Jae's stare, his lips pressed thin and fire in his eyes. But then Emmett sighed, and Jae actually saw his anger break apart, leaving behind a man who looked chastened and confused, and more than a little bit sorry. That unspoken apology tugged at Jae's heart and tightened his throat, and it was all he could do to keep his hands steady as he cast his gaze down and went back to buttoning his shirt.

Chapter Eleven

Silence reigned as Jae signed himself out of care, as if no one dared break a fragile truce. Busy directing his energy toward staying upright and putting one foot in front of the other, Jae didn't feel much like talking anyway, not even when Emmett insisted they get a Lyft rather than make the short walk. That was the moment Ty decided *he* wanted a chat, of course, and Jae stifled a groan as his brother pulled him aside.

"Ty, I don't—"

"Want to talk about what happened, I know." Ty led Jae to a nearby bench. "Honestly, I'm not sure I do either."

"Then what's this about?" Settling onto a seat, Jae stared at the sky overhead, melancholy stealing over him. The sun hung low, only an hour or so from setting, and the air was hot and still. A whole afternoon had passed by as Jae sat in the Emergency Department, simply because he'd eaten the wrong thing.

"Are you really okay to go home, Jae?"

"Sure." Jae turned his gaze back to Ty's. "I've been through this before and Zac said he'd stay with me tonight. I'll be all right."

Ty nodded. "I forgot what this was like," he said after several beats. "When you moved out, you took the allergy with you and for a while, I tried to pretend it didn't exist at all."

"Good." Jae shrugged. "I would never have expected you to think about it."

"I didn't want to. The longer you were gone, the easier it got to blow it off, even when Ma or Dad mentioned it or you swung through town for a visit and oh, fuck, anything cow in the refrigerator had to go." Ty shook his head. "You were always so careful it was almost like nothing was wrong. And when things *did* go wrong, Ma and Dad were just … calm. That was all an act, huh?"

"Yes. They were scared, every time." Jae ran a hand over his head. "Once in a while, I'd have to lie on the floor because my blood pressure would nosedive and being on the ground made me feel safe. Ma would bring you upstairs and play Candyland with you while Dad waited for the EMTs with me and not once did they make me feel like I'd fucked up or that I was a burden or broken."

Ty frowned. "Did I make you feel that way?"

"Sometimes. I knew you didn't do it on purpose. You were just a kid."

"Yeah, and so were you. Why didn't you ever tell me?"

"We didn't want you to worry," Jae said when his brother grimaced. "I still don't."

Ty's expression tightened. "I do worry, even if it doesn't seem like it. When Dad told me that you were here, everything I thought I'd forgotten came back in a rush."

"I had a similar kind of feeling." Fuck, Jae was tired. He stared at his hands in his lap. "I haven't had a reaction around Dad in so long but with him there it was like being stuck in a time warp. I'm still not even sure what happened today."

Ty grunted softly. "Pretty sure it was the eggs. Amelia's friend swore up and down that she used vegan crème fraîche in her recipe, but she also made a spinach dip with full dairy products, so it's possible there was cross contamination."

"Well, that's unlucky." Jae frowned, then lifted his gaze to Ty's once more. "Who puts crème fraîche in deviled eggs?"

"People who've watched too many cooking shows? Oh, heck, she was probably trying to impress Emmett."

"Hah, I'll bet you're right. But your friend made death eggs instead of deviled."

Ty gave him a long look. "Really? You end up in the ED after being poisoned by fancy sour cream and your response is to crack a joke?"

"I'm not sure what the right response is, bro, but I'm pretty sure you just made an egg pun." A sweet buzz went through Jae as his brother laughed. "Not sure I'll ever be able to look at deviled eggs in quite the same way. Ugh."

"Yeah. I get that."

Ty sat down beside him. He appeared much younger as they watched one another, and Jae could really see the boy who'd sometimes stared up at a teenaged Jae-seong Bak with equal parts love and awe.

"Jae, do you think ...?" Ty ran his teeth over his lower lip. "Are you going to be okay for next weekend? Ma and Dad said you'd never skip out on the wedding, but I don't want you to push it if you're still feeling shitty."

"Whoa." Carefully, Jae set his hand against the nape of his brother's neck. "I'm *going* to be at your wedding, Tae-seong. I wouldn't miss it for the world."

A brilliant smile transformed Ty's face. "Okay. I know we drive each other crazy but it's really good to hear you say that. The day wouldn't be the same without you."

"And that's why I'm going to be there for you and your girl. Now c'mon, bro." Jae gave his brother's cheek a gentle pat. "I'm tired and my clothes are funky, so let's get the hell out of here."

Jae tuned out for most of the next couple of hours. He checked in with his parents, found his mother still royally pissed about being left out of the loop, then shut himself in the bathroom and soaked under a hot spray for much longer than was necessary. His eyelids were heavy enough by the time he'd toweled off that he would have gone straight to bed but for the aromas coming from beyond his bedroom door, so tantalizing and familiar they woke Jae's appetite. Ambling into the kitchen, he found Emmett and Zac at the counter and the table set for three.

"What's all this?"

"He lives!" Zac cried, his face alight as he crossed the room to muss Jae's damp hair. "I was about to come and fish you out of the shower, actually, because I believe it's time for another dose of Benadryl. It's coming up on six hours since you called me from Ty's."

"Mmm, you're right."

"Yes, I am." Hooking an elbow through Jae's, Zac turned them toward the table. "How about some food?"

"I could eat. Was just thinking that whatever you're making smells really good."

"That's because it is." Zac laughed. "I told Emmett about the cold noodle salad you used to make back in the day and, naturally, he whipped some right up."

"They won't be the same," Emmett said from behind them. "Zac didn't remember much beyond soba and sesame."

"I'm surprised I remembered that much, frankly," Zac muttered, then gently pushed Jae into a chair. "But, judging by the smell, your creation is bound to be delicious, Emmett."

"I'm sure of it." Jae cast a glance back at Emmett, who still hadn't moved from the counter. "Did you need help ransacking my pantry, Em?"

"I managed okay, thanks."

Jae heard more than saw Emmett's smile, but there was a strain around his eyes when he joined Jae and Zac at the table. Emmett seemed tired and down throughout the meal, his usual spark missing despite the good food. Jae's heart sank just watching him, even more so when Emmett insisted on staying the night with Jae but also made it clear that he didn't want to address the allergic elephant in the room just yet.

"You scared him," Zac said as he and Jae stood on the step outside Jae's front door. "A big part of me gets it, too. I was terrified the first time you had a bad reaction in front of me and I had the training to know how to deal with it. It wasn't until after I knew you were going to be okay that I let myself fall apart."

"That's why I didn't want him to know about it today." Jae leaned back against the door and tried to convince himself he was telling the truth. "Understanding the allergy is one thing but seeing it is another thing entirely. You should have seen Emmett's face when he got a look at my hives."

Zac grimaced. "Yeah, that could have gone better. But I'm pretty sure Emmett was mad before he got anywhere near the ED. I'd be ready for that talk if I were you."

"Yeah, I picked up on that already." Jae's huff of laughter turned into a shaky exhale as Zac pulled him in for a hug. "But thanks for the heads-up."

"Hey." Zac rubbed Jae's hair with one hand. "You okay, Jae-seong?"

"Yeah. Just tired, you know?" Jae closed his eyes and hung on for another beat before he forced himself to let Zac go. "This is when some guys lose interest—after the allergy goes from concept to real for the first time. Not that Em and I are dating."

"I don't know, man. You and Emmett may not be boyfriends but there's something there, I'd swear to it." A frown pulled at Zac's features as he leaned back and caught Jae's eye. "He's not going to ghost you."

"I almost wish he would."

"Meaning what?"

"I don't know." Jae glanced at the door leading upstairs to the man who'd come to mean so much to him. "This thing with Emmett has gotten complicated and you know as well as I that complicated is not what he wants in his life."

Zac gave Jae another squeeze. "Yeah, I do. But will you be okay going back to uncomplicated?"

No, I won't.

Jae made himself shrug. "Sure. Emmett and I are friends," he said. "Nothing's going to change that."

After Zac had walked off, Jae climbed the stairs again, his heart heavy as he readied himself for what might be the hardest conversation he and Emmett would ever have. His resolve wavered as he spied Emmett parked on the sofa, setting the scene for a perfect, quiet Sunday night in, then faded utterly after Emmett held out a hand. Jae swallowed down every word he'd drummed up the courage to say as Emmett pulled him into a hug.

"Fuck, Jae," Emmett said. "I'm so pissed at you right now."

"I know." Jae chuckled against Emmett's shoulder. "I'd apologize but I'm not entirely sure you'd believe me."

"Oh, shut up." Emmett sat back and pinned Jae with a hard look. "You're really okay, right? Can I touch like this or does it hurt?"

"You can touch me. I'm more tired than anything else right now."

"Your reactions aren't biphasic, right? Like symptoms popping up again out of nowhere?"

Jae swallowed hard. "I ... no, not usually."

"That's what Zac said, too," Emmett said, his lips thin. "He told me what to look out for while you were in the shower. I'd like to know why you didn't tell me yourself."

"We've talked about my allergy, Em." Jae sank back onto the sofa cushions. "You knew about the EpiPens and the stuff in my bag."

"Yeah, I did. But that's not what I meant."

Rising up over him, Emmett cupped Jae's face in his hands and kissed him, his touch like fire against Jae's skin. Both were breathing hard by the time they came back up for air.

"My mother said you didn't want my help today." Hurt flickered in Emmett's eyes, but his voice only got gentler. "That's what I want to talk about, because for the life of me, I can't figure out why you would say that. Or why would you leave without telling me what had happened."

Jae set his forehead against Emmett's and closed his eyes. "I was afraid to see you," he murmured. "Your mom was there and my dad, and I wasn't in my right mind. If you'd walked in—"

I'd have told you I love you. That I hoped you could love me too, someday.

Bringing his hands up, Jae circled Emmett's wrist with his fingers. "I'd have said the wrong thing. They'd have known, Emmett, and that's not what we wanted."

"Okay," Emmett said on a sigh. He kissed Jae again, slower and sweeter, almost lulling Jae the longer they went on.

Jae slipped his hands up under Emmett's shirt, palming his smooth skin. His chest expanded at Emmett's quiet hum. He felt floaty under the sway of those deep, drugging kisses, and his head spun as Emmett somehow guided Jae up on to his feet. Neither spoke as they walked hand in hand to Jae's room.

Slowly, they peeled away each other's clothes, though Jae shook his head when Emmett fingered the hem of Jae's t-shirt. For a second, anger flashed bright in Emmett's eyes before it faded, becoming something infinitely sadder before that too, winked out, leaving only heat.

Emmett arranged Jae on the mattress, then turned to the nightstand for supplies. After slicking his fingers, Emmett tossed the lube and a condom on the bed and took himself in hand. Jae's cock twitched as Emmett worked himself over, head lolling back and back arching on a quiet gasp.

"Jesus," Jae murmured.

Slowly, Emmett straightened back up. His eyes burned as he crawled on top of Jae then ground slowly down, the lube on his shaft easing the friction of skin against skin even as heat built between them. Emmett pressed his lips to Jae's ear and groaned.

"Jae."

Jae's stomach flipped at the wanton need in that single word. His bones turned leaden as Emmett got up on all fours. Reaching back with one hand, Emmett held his ass high in the air, then rocked back slowly, a low noise in his throat. Jae almost lost it right there as he realized Emmett was working himself open. He took Emmett's face between his hands.

"God, Em. Does that feel good?"

Emmett moved his head in a slow nod. His lids were heavy and his jaw slack, but his gaze didn't waver from Jae's, even after Jae slotted their mouths together. Jae couldn't look away either, his body and brain buzzing hard by the time Emmett pushed up on to his knees.

Without a word, Emmett found the condom he'd laid out earlier and tore the package open. He rolled it over Jae's dick, his touch sending jolts of pleasure straight to Jae's groin. Jae set his hands on Emmett's thighs as Emmett straddled him, his erection jutting up hard and red against his groin. Jae couldn't resist the urge to touch. A single stroke had Emmett curling forward and squeezing Jae's torso with his powerful thighs. His shaky breath echoed in the quiet of the room around them.

The silence between them registered in Jae's head then. Emmett was a talker in bed and they'd always shared a lot of laughter. Emmett also loved to bait and tease and urge Jae on with cocky words that devolved into begging as Jae took him apart.

Tonight, Emmett said nothing. There was no teasing or laughter, even as a shudder racked his frame, his jaw rigid and face almost pained. Jae's throat filled with rocks.

"Emmett, come here."

Levering himself up, Jae slid an arm around Emmett, his heart squeezing hard at the way Emmett grabbed him, his grip on Jae's waist bruising. Jae kissed him deep, slowly pumping Emmett's cock all the while, and the heat between them built. Jae only stopped after Emmett let loose a quiet moan.

"Need you," Jae said as he guided Emmett up and onto his cock. He repeated the words between the kisses he rained over Emmett's chest and shoulders, his voice reduced to a thready whisper as Emmett sank slowly down.

Emmett's breath hitched as Jae bottomed out. Wrapping him up in a hug, Jae held as still as he could, his body throbbing with the need to move. Only after Emmett had wound his arms around Jae's shoulders did Jae start rocking, his thrusts slow and deep. He watched the shift in Emmett's body and expression as the ache of being split in two became pleasure, and Emmett set his forehead against Jae's.

"So good," Emmett said, his voice still far too quiet. "So good, Jae. I ... fuck."

"Yes."

Jae hauled Emmett even closer, aware of Emmett's cock trapped between them. Emmett clutched at him, as if he'd crawl inside Jae given the chance, and Jae thrust up, harder and rougher. He snaked one hand down and took Emmett in his fist once more. Swallowing Emmett's cry with a kiss, Jae set a relentless pace until Emmett went rigid in his hold, back arching hard. Emmett's motions slowed as he rode out his high, until he slumped into Jae, his breath hot against the side of Jae's neck. An overwhelming tenderness stole over Jae as he held Emmett up, his insides tight with more than his own need to come.

Emmett came back to himself and wrapped Jae up in his arms, nuzzling Jae's cheek as they rocked together once more. Jae buried his face in Emmett's neck.

"Baby," Jae murmured, fire in his bones and love in his heart, so grateful for the arms around him that held him together as he began to unravel. "Oh, God."

"That's it," Emmett said, his voice hoarse. "Show me how you come, Jae."

Jae smothered a moan against Emmett's skin. He thrust over and over until the world tilted around him and when he fell, he also soared, higher and higher till he could hardly breathe.

He pulled Emmett with him as he floated back to earth. Jae knew he should get up. Peel off the shirt that was now sticky with Emmett's cum and find a towel to clean them up, but his body wouldn't obey. He snuggled in closer to Emmett instead, determined to hold the world—and the toughest decision that lay before him—at bay, at least for tonight.

In the end, he couldn't do it, even though it hurt like hell to say the words.

"I need to dial this back," he murmured. "I can't ... I can't do this anymore."

Emmett went very still before he pulled back enough to get a look at Jae's face. "What happened?" he asked with a frown. "Did my mother say something to you about us? Or Ty?"

"No." Jae closed his eyes for several seconds before he opened them again. "But … I think that's coming. Because I'm starting to forget how to pretend we're just friends and I know people are going to notice."

"I'm not sure what you mean."

"I know. But trust me when I say I need some space." Jae ran a hand over Emmett's sexed up hair. "I can't keep doing this. Keeping things from people I care about, Em. From you."

Emmett shook his head. "From me? What are you keeping from me?"

"I have feelings for you." Jae swallowed at the way Emmett's face went blank. "I didn't mean for it to happen but somewhere along the way, things changed for me. I want things you can't give me. And if we keep going the way we are, someone is going to end up hurt. I don't want that for either of us."

"Neither do I." Emmett seemed to come back to life all at once and shit, the confusion in his eyes made Jae's chest clench. "That's the last thing I'd want, Jae, but … We talked about this. And I thought we wanted the same thing. Where the hell is this coming from?"

Grabbing Emmett's hand, Jae pressed it over his heart. "From here." He covered that hand with his own. "I wanted you so badly today, but I couldn't see you. As fucked up as my thinking got in those moments, I knew I'd never be able to hide what you mean to me. Didn't matter who was in the room with us, or even that you wouldn't have wanted to hear it."

The sorrow that flickered over Emmett's face cracked Jae wide open. "I don't know what to say."

"I understand. This is why I have to stop. I need more, Em. Everything. All of you instead of pieces here and there." Jae closed his eyes. "So, this is me saying 'when,' okay?"

"Okay," Emmett whispered, soft enough Jae almost had to strain to hear it.

Jae stayed silent as Emmett rolled out of the bed, too wrung out and sad to do anything else. The space in the bed beside him yawned huge and empty, and for a breath it was as if he hung suspended, a chill creeping over him. But then Emmett was back, touch gentle as he coaxed Jae out of his shirt and wiped him down, body warm and solid when he stretched out beside Jae again. Jae knew he needed to ask him to leave. He didn't, though—couldn't really—because he knew everything would be different tomorrow.

And for just a little while longer, Jae wanted to be selfish and hold tight to the man he loved.

Chapter Twelve

"Did I hear you say you've rented a room here for this weekend too, Jae?"

"Yes, ma'am, you did." Jae met Margaret McNeil's inquisitive gaze with a smile, though his mother was also quick to chime in.

"Jae's concept of the space-time continuum has always been a bit spongy," she said, and looked past Jae to Margaret as the three stepped onto a cinder path.

Tonight, the Baks and McNeils had gathered at a massive hotel on Rowes Wharf for a run through of Ty and Amelia's wedding ceremony. Emmett had left immediately afterward for the Endless Pastabilities Test Kitchen and the rest of the party had stopped for drinks at one of the hotel's bars before following him on foot. They set a leisurely pace south, winding along a section of the Rose F. Kennedy Greenway, a linear park that snaked for more than a mile through several downtown neighborhoods, its landscaped gardens, promenades, fountains, and public art covering what had once been an elevated highway.

"What my mother isn't saying is that I have a tendency to run late," Jae said to Margaret. "I don't want to throw Ty and Amelia's wedding day into an uproar, of course, and as I'll be the one with the rings, I figured I'd make it easier on everybody and just bring myself to the hotel."

Christina tucked her hand into the crook of Jae's arm. "I was sure you were joking about staying there overnight but, the more I thought about it, the more it made sense."

"I suppose it does." Margaret chuckled. "Oddly enough, my children always ran early for everything and still do. I guess that's what comes from having grown up with a military man."

Jae nodded. Listening to Margaret talk about her family was an odd experience for him. He knew Emmett's parents had been intolerant of their son's life choices, but Margaret had been consistently nice to Jae every time they met. She'd never given him grief about being gay or his nursing career, and she'd seemed utterly unfazed when Jae had mentioned his date for the wedding would be a man. He'd called her a few days after the death egg incident and while she hadn't wanted Jae's apologies any more than Jae had wanted hers, Margaret had clearly been concerned about him.

Margaret's attitude toward her own son seemed to be thawing, too. She'd approached Emmett directly tonight rather than speaking to him through other people, and their conversations had appeared calm and even friendly to Jae's wary eye. While a long road lay ahead of the McNeils to get past years of hurt feelings and disappointment, Emmett's manner around his mother had been far less guarded tonight, and Jae found himself hoping that mother and son were close to turning a corner.

Not that Emmett's relationships were Jae's business anymore. He'd lost that privilege when he'd told Emmett he'd needed space. A request Emmett had more than filled.

Jae cast his gaze at his shoes and swallowed down his hurt while his mother and Margaret continued chatting.

Jae had woken alone in his bed on Monday morning. Though he'd expected as much, he'd lain there for a long time before he'd felt ready to start his day. He'd stayed away from the EP food truck when it was parked outside the hospital and the walk-up window on Charles Street, and though he and Emmett had exchanged text messages several times over the week, he'd begged off when Emmett had suggested they meet for a drink. A second invitation hadn't come. Jae didn't know how to feel about that, either, given the idea of seeing Emmett and pretending everything was fine made him feel sick, a sensation made worse knowing he'd be forced to do it all weekend.

It had started yesterday evening, when Jae had gathered Ty and his groomsmen together to pick up their tuxedo rentals. Emmett had been his usual friendly self of course, exchanging bro hugs with Ty and Krishnan and Thom, but he hadn't touched Jae once. There'd been a tight set to his jaw too, and dark circles under his eyes, as if Emmett hadn't been sleeping. Luckily for Jae, he'd been scheduled to work that evening, which gave him all the excuses he needed to beg off what would have been a tortuous dinner.

He bit back a sigh now. Not seeing Emmett was hard but being around him *and* relegated to the friend zone was worse. Jae hated being just like everyone else in Emmett's world, especially after having basked in the glow of his full and very personal attention. Acting as if nothing deeper had ever existed between them hurt like a motherfucker.

The only things that ever existed between Emmett and you were friendship and sex. You were the one who couldn't stay with the program and went and fell in love.

Gaze unfocused, Jae stared ahead to Amelia and Ty who were walking with Kun-bae. Keeping his distance was better in the long run if Jae wanted to avoid a broken heart. Actually doing it was proving tricky, particularly right now with the hurt still fresh.

"You wouldn't happen to know what we'll be eating tonight, would you, dear?" Margaret's voice pulled Jae out of his dark thoughts. "I asked Amelia and Ty, but they gave me different answers and Emmett simply said 'trust,' before he left for the restaurant."

"You can take him at his word," Jae said. "Emmett tried out some of the recipes he was thinking about cooking tonight and I am not exaggerating when I say everything was fantastic."

"Poor you, having to test drive food," Jae's mother said, her voice teasing.

Jae snorted. "Right? It was a real hardship."

"Honestly, it helps me to know this," Margaret said. "I'm not an adventurous eater, though Amelia has told me repeatedly her brother is quite capable."

Jae couldn't help his frown. "You've never eaten at the Test Kitchen?"

"No. I've never eaten Endless Pastabilities' food, period. I've lived away from Boston for years now and, honestly, I've never been one to eat food from a truck." Margaret winced slightly. "I'm sure that makes me sound like a terrible snob."

Jae was still trying to wrap his head about the idea that Emmett's mother had no idea what her son was capable of when

Christina gave a gentle laugh.

"It makes you sound like someone who's been missing out on a lot of good things to eat, Margaret. Street food is one of my favorite things in the world!" Christina cocked her head at Jae. "I learned to make *bindae-tteok* after our first trip to the Gwangjang Market in Seoul, remember?"

"No." Jae laughed at the outrage on her face. "I was only four years old at the time, Ma—I don't even remember the first time I tried them." He shifted his focus to Margaret. "*Bindae-tteok* are mung bean pancakes and they are amazing. I'm lucky Ma taught me to make them so I could feed myself when I started living on my own."

"Luckier than you realize," Margaret replied. "My mother didn't cook. She grew up with housekeepers as did I, and I never learned. Plants were more my thing. Much easier to feed and they never complain if a recipe doesn't come out right." She smiled, absolutely unaware of the way Jae's heart squeezed. "Anyway, after I was married, I had to teach myself to cook and I was never any good at it. I've burned more dinners than I care to recall, and had no family recipes to pass down to my daughter. Or son," she added after a beat. "Did you know that Emmett learned to cook at an after-school club?"

Jae shook his head. "I didn't."

"Two afternoons a week from grades five through twelve. He juggled the schedule around football practice." She hummed. "It amazes me now seeing how far he took that hobby. He's good, isn't he?"

"Very good," Jae said. "Emmett loves both cooking and feeding people. He also inherited your green thumb." He met Margaret's raised eyebrows with a nod. "He's got dozens of houseplants in his apartment."

They exited the park and quickly crossed over Purchase Street, heading into the tangled streets of Boston's financial district. "You may have trouble picturing the food you eat tonight being sold from a truck," Jae said, "but I assure you it is."

Margaret hummed again. "I'll keep that in mind. All this talk about food has me so hungry I might forget I had to walk on cobblestones in these shoes instead of dining back at the hotel."

"And *I* almost forgot that I wanted to ask you a question, Jae." Christina's wily smile sparked dread in his core. "Any chance your boyfriend will be joining us for dinner?"

"Ma, we've talked about this. Sal is not my boyfriend."

"Yes, yes, you've said as much." His mother waved Jae off. "I'd still have liked to have met him before tomorrow when we'll all be too busy to do much socializing."

Jae tried not to groan. He really needed to adjust his mother's expectations about the Sal situation, for everyone's sake.

Ten minutes later, they trooped into the Test Kitchen and Margaret's eyes went wide as she gazed around the bright, minimalist space. Emmett and Aiden immediately came out from the bustling, open kitchen to greet them, and both looked so dashing in their black chef's uniforms. But while Emmett was typically gracious, the crease between his eyebrows tugged at Jae.

Just be yourself, he longed to say. *Show your mom who you are and let her make up her own mind.*

"We're right over here." Emmett led the party past a long, glassed-in area that split the Test Kitchen into two large rooms, speaking over his shoulder as he moved. "Aiden wanted to seat you all in that fishbowl back there that we call his office, but I thought the banquet table would be nicer."

"You can see Emmett's point." Aiden gestured to a massive wooden table milled from a log that dominated the left side of the restaurant. "You'll have more room to move around here instead of feeling packed in on top of each other."

Emmett shared a smile with his friend, then turned to Margaret, who was watching the interplay at Jae's side.

"Can I start you off with a glass of wine, Mother?"

Before Margaret could reply, Amelia took hold of his arm. "Actually, Em, I need you for a hot second."

"Er, sure," Emmett said. "Just let me get the drink orders and—hey!"

"Nope, right now. I'm sure Aiden can manage the drinks!" Amelia called back as she practically dragged Emmett away.

Aiden stared after them a moment, his mouth slightly open, before his laughter rang through the room. "It's been a while since I witnessed the full force of the hurricane known as Amelia," he said to Ty who was snickering into his fist. "She may be teeny, but she could power a city."

"She's always been that way," Margaret put in, "and Emmett indulges her even now. Which, I suppose, is what big brothers can be expected to do under all sorts of circumstances.

"I don't suppose Emmett will have time to dine with us tonight?" she asked, her eyes going narrow as she stared Aiden down. "I'd like someone to tell me in plain terms what I'm expected to eat."

Despite Aiden's assurances, Jae guessed that keeping Emmett in one seat tonight would pose a challenge. Emmett was playing host to a party of people he cared about, after all, and no doubt felt as though his mother would be watching his every move for the first time in ages. Which, to be fair, seemed likely.

"I think I can sub in for Emmett if he's busy," Jae said to Margaret. "I told you earlier that I've had some of the dishes he has planned for us tonight and I can help figure out the rest, even if I can't eat them myself."

Emmett's mother bobbed her head. "All right then. You've got yourself a dinner partner."

That was how Jae got to watch Margaret McNeil's understanding of who her son was change forever. While sometimes tentative about ingredients she didn't recognize, she tried everything on the little plates that were served, from tender lamb skewers with pistachio-mint pesto, to spicy-sweet spaghetti puttanesca, to buttery fillet of beef with mushrooms in black garlic sauce.

She enjoyed every bite.

"I know you've told me Emmett cooks food like this on a truck, but how?" she asked Jae, her expression almost blissful as she worked her way through the sliced beet salad. "I can hardly get through boiling macaroni in a kitchen with Alexa as my guide, never mind anything even remotely complicated."

Jae waved a hand at his own plate. "I can't cook like this either, or not without a *lot* of help. These guys are pretty magical when it comes to food, though." Topping off his wine glass, he handed the bottle across the table to Krishnan and the bridesmaids. He knew Emmett had joined them when Kaylee looked past Jae with a big grin.

"What's this about magical food?" Emmett's gaze was warm as he moved it between his mother and Jae, but Jae read questions there, too.

"Jae was talking about you and Aiden and your crew," Margaret said, "and how good you are at this." Setting her fork down, she met her son's eye. "Everything is wonderful, Emmett."

Despite Emmett's easy air, he seemed to literally glow from the inside out. "Thank you, Mother. I'm glad you're enjoying it."

Jae's stupid heart melted a bit at the way Margaret's face softened. Pushing his own half-eaten salad aside, he got to his feet and met Emmett's searching look with a smile.

"Sit," he said quietly. "Talk to your mother, Em, and tell her about the food you made."

Taking his glass with him, Jae headed outside. He leaned against the building to the left of the Test Kitchen's entrance but kept an eye on the street, scanning for cops on patrol who'd no doubt issue him a hefty fine for drinking alcohol in a public place. The air outside of the restaurant was hot and damp, but Jae welcomed the relative quiet as he made a call to Sal, relief at being alone again running all through him.

His wine was gone by the time the Test Kitchen's door swung open and Jae wasn't surprised in the least when his mother stepped out.

"There you are," she said. "I was starting to think you'd snuck out here for a smoke."

Jae pushed off the wall with a snort. "Ty was the smoker, not me, but I know you remember that."

"Of course, I do." She smiled at Jae as he got closer. "Thank you for taking care of Margaret tonight."

"Oh, sure. It was just dinner, Ma."

"I know, but it was sweet of you to step in when her own children were busy." Christina gave Jae's arm a squeeze. "She'd probably deny it if asked but being here on her own hasn't been easy for Margaret. Facing Emmett after all this time has been particularly tough."

Jae met his mother's comments with a frown, the urge to protect his friend swift and strong. "Why? Because he's a success in spite of the way she treated him? Emmett's parents turned their backs on him because he chose a career he loved, Ma. A career that brings him joy *and* profit, a combination many people never know in a lifetime at work."

"You're right." A troubled expression fell over Christina's face. "I can't say I'll ever understand why Margaret and her husband treated Emmett the way they did. Your dad and I ... neither of us can imagine ever doing such a thing. All we've ever wanted is for you and Ty to feel fulfilled by what you do, even when your choices might mystify us. I honestly have no idea how you got through your anatomy courses, honey." She grimaced. "Just hearing about the things you had to dissect made me want to barf.

"I do know Margaret's thinking has changed over time, however," she said over the tail end of Jae's laughter. "And I believe she's genuinely interested in making things better between Emmett and herself, *if* Emmett will let her."

"That's nice, Ma, but this can't be on Emmett. His parents disowned him for following his dream. And for his identity," Jae added, "though neither ever bothered to tell him so directly or even acknowledge he'd come out. Can you blame him for not trusting her?"

Or me, given the things Emmett went through with the last man he'd dared to love?

God, Jae wanted to cringe at the thought. His mother simply sighed, oblivious to Jae's self-doubt.

"No, I don't blame Emmett at all. I still hope he'll find it in his heart to try. Given what your brother and Amelia have told me about him, I suspect that repairing the relationship would benefit Emmett even more than Margaret."

Jae fought the urge to cast his eyes skyward. "Emmett's one of the sweetest people I've ever met," he murmured. "Again, this can't be his sole responsibility."

"For what it's worth, I agree with you." Christina gave Jae's arm another squeeze. "My concern is not for Emmett, though, but you. Are you feeling all right, Jae? You didn't eat much at dinner and you seem ... out of sorts, for lack of a better word."

Yeah, well. It's hard to be cheerful when you feel like half of you has gone missing.

Jae patted his mother's hand on his arm. "I'm good. Working a few things through in my head while I also get ready for tomorrow."

"Is there anything your dad or I can help you with?"

"I don't think so. But do you guys have time to talk before you head back home? There's something I'd like to run by you before tomorrow."

"Of course." Christina bit her lip. "It's not about you moving away again, is it? At the risk of sounding like a selfish mom, I hoped you'd stay a little longer. I love having you only a train ride away."

Her words sent a bittersweet pain through Jae. "I promise it's not about moving." He dropped a quick kiss on his mother's cheek. "But I'm happy to talk about the plans I *have* made and anything else that might come to mind."

"Sounds great." Christina gave him a half smile, then tipped her head toward the restaurant. "I've been told we *need* to eat dessert before we leave, however, and Emmett's brewed up what smells like the best coffee in the world."

Jae drew a deep breath in through his nose. The last time he'd shared coffee with Emmett, they'd had it with breakfast in Jae's bed, not even twelve hours before everything had gone to shit. "Everything Emmett makes is good, Ma," he said, then held an arm out to his mother. "We'd better get in there before we miss the lion's share."

And if even the length of a room wasn't enough to make looking at Emmett easy, well. Jae could fake it for a while longer.

Chapter Thirteen

"Your boy's not late, is he?"

Jae looked up, his stomach flipping as he met a familiar steel blue gaze. He hadn't been prepared for the sight of Emmett McNeil in his tuxedo, curls tamed and manner grave, and wow, the man could wear a suit.

"No, Sal is not late. But what are you doing down here?"

"Same as you, I'd think. Looking for a man cave and a break from wedding talk." Emmett shot a small smile in Jae's direction then. "Mother and I finished building the altar a while ago and I decided to stop by Ty's room to see how he was holding up. He's the one who told me where you were hiding."

"I'm eating, not hiding." Jae gestured toward the plate of tuna tartare before him. "Something cheesy got all over the food Krishnan ordered up earlier, so I figured I'd grab something while there was time. Where are the ducks?"

Emmett smiled bigger. "I left them with Ty. I like the tradition of wooden ducks being present for the ceremony, but I'm not carrying them around with me. That just wouldn't end well."

Like his father and Jae, Ty Bak identified as American and the wedding he and Amelia had planned was thoroughly western. However, they'd both liked the idea of incorporating traditional Korean wedding ducks into the ceremony and commissioned a pair to be carved the day after Amelia had accepted Ty's proposal. Jae and Emmett would each present a duck to the couple immediately following their vows as blessings for peace, fidelity, and fertility.

"Smart man." Jae laid a hand over his breast pocket. "Imagine how I feel carrying around the rings. Ty doesn't need me just yet, does he? We're not scheduled to start for another hour."

"He asked me to make sure you didn't take off. And to tackle you if you tried."

Heat streaked over Jae's cheeks, and he had to look away as he laughed. Emmett's playful tone really was more than he could bear. "I've told Ty about a dozen times I'm not going anywhere, *especially* with these rings in my pocket," he said, his gaze on his cocktail glass. "Still can't seem to get it through his stubborn head."

"Maybe he's projecting."

Jae met Emmett's gaze and frowned. "Why would you say that?"

"Oh, don't get me wrong—it's not like I think Ty's going to skip out on my sister. But he is nervous. That was very clear to me when he asked Krishnan to mix up a batch of shots right before I came down here to find you."

"Lord. I guess I should get up there. I'm basically done here."

"Relax, your dad has it covered. Said he'd lock up the liquor cabinet and call in the mothers if he really needed to."

"Okay then." Another, louder laugh squeezed its way past the nerves in Jae's chest and he made himself ask the question that had been caught in his throat. "Can I buy you a drink?"

Emmett's smile faded slightly. "Thanks. I'd like that."

Neither spoke as he pulled out the chair across from Jae, the air between them nearly crackling with tension. Fuck, this was weird and awkward in ways things had never been with Emmett and that was all on Jae. He'd said they'd always be friends, whether they were having sex or not, but when push had come to shove, it'd been too hard for Jae and he'd pulled away.

Serves you right for falling in love.

Jae quelled a groan. "The Gimlet is nice," he said, then pointed at his cocktail. "Also dangerously delicious, as the lime juice is fresh."

"Sounds great. Fits in just right with this bar, too." Emmett glanced around again, admiration clear on his face. "I've always meant to have a drink here and just never made it. I tried to get Sean in here a couple of times, but he said it was too old-fangled for his tastes."

"Sean missed out, if you ask me. Granted, you already know my thoughts on your ex." Jae liked this bar, too, and its throwback feel that was classy but not stuffy, all rich mahogany walls, deep scarlet carpet, and coffered ceiling. "Then again, I'm a bit of an antique myself and maybe that's why I like it here."

Emmett frowned. "You're right, Sean did miss out. But, then again, he's nowhere near as plugged-in to the world around him as you."

He raised a hand to a passing server and Jae ate a bit more tuna while Emmett ordered a French 75.

"I owe you an apology," Jae said as soon as the server had moved on. He wasn't surprised by the uncertainty in Emmett's expression.

"What for?"

"For being MIA this past week. I haven't been a very good friend to you, Emmett, and I'm sorry."

Red stained Emmett's cheeks. "Thank you for saying that. I didn't want to push you either but ... honestly, I've missed seeing you, Jae. Sex or no sex."

"Me too." Jae huffed out a laugh. "I just need time to figure myself out. Once I'm together up here" —he tapped one finger against his temple— "I think I'll be okay going back to the way things were before."

"Good." Emmett's smile didn't quite reach his eyes, though. "Anyway, where's Sal? Still up in your room?"

"He's not here. I told him to stay home and relax."

"You did? How come?"

"Because bringing him as my date felt like a lie."

The server returned with a flute glass for Emmett. The pale yellow cocktail looked beautiful against the drama of his black suit, and if it weren't for the way Emmett's eyebrows had drawn together, Jae would have been more than happy to forget all about the topic of his now-canceled plus one.

"I don't understand," Emmett said. "Why would bringing Sal to the wedding feel like a lie?"

"My ma kept talking it up." Jae picked up his own glass and nodded when the server offered to clear the remains of his lunch. "Kept going on and on about Sal being my boyfriend and how happy it made her that I'd found someone I liked. No matter how many times I explained that Sal and I weren't dating, she just kept going in the opposite direction."

Emmett grimaced. "I told you, man, they want us all married off."

"It seems that way, yes. Anyway, last night ..." Jae licked his lips. "I started thinking about how Ma would feel if she knew I'd only asked Sal to be my date so she'd be happy. And it felt wrong. She'd be hurt, knowing I'd cooked up a plan with the main goal of putting one over on her." Emmett gave a silent nod. "So, I canceled with Sal and told Ma the truth. Or, an edited version of the truth, at least. I was okay telling her that Sal and I were casual, but I really did not want to say the words 'fuck buddy' to my mother."

Emmett made a quiet noise of assent, though his brow was still furrowed. "I'm sorry."

"No, it was good to clear the air," Jae said. "After I spilled my guts, Ma did too. She's been worried I'd be moving out of state again and hoped some guy would hook my attention and get me to stick around." He smiled. "The thing is, she wouldn't have worried about it at all if I'd been upfront about my plans to stay in Boston."

"Wait, what?" Emmett shook his head as if he was trying to clear it. "Did you really only kick me to the curb six days ago? Because you hadn't made a decision about staying in Boston the last time we talked about it."

Jae could feel his smile falter. He knew Emmett had seen it too when he quickly set his drink down.

"Shit, I'm sorry, Jae. I didn't mean that the way it sounded."

"No, it's ... I'm sorry if you thought I was rejecting you, Emmett." Jae *should* have guessed Emmett would feel that way, though; he knew what the guy had been through with Sean. Hell, Emmett's parents had set the stage even earlier on. "I just—" Jae's phone's chime cut him off. "Damn," he said with a glance at the screen. "Ty wants us upstairs."

"All righty." Emmett got to his feet and grabbed his flute glass. "Let's hope they haven't deployed the bridesmaids to do recon just yet."

Jae laughed outright. "Oh, God. At least Kaylee and Marlisa like you enough that we can safely assume they won't do us any permanent damage."

"Good point. I've known Kaylee since she and Amelia became best friends in the second grade—if anything, she and her girlfriend would lie to help us out."

Quickly, Emmett held out his glass and tapped it against Jae's. His words hadn't quite settled into Jae's brain as they bolted the rest of their drinks.

"Ugh." Jae set the cocktail glass down and gave himself a quick shake, while Emmett snickered into his hand.

"I've never met anyone who hates shots as much as you."

"Tequila with lime and salt is fine but everything else …" Jae made a face. "Anyway, did you just say Kaylee has a girlfriend?"

"Uh-huh. You'll meet her during the reception. Kaylee's bi, but that's sort of new. I'm not sure who else knows beyond Amelia, Ty, and me." Emmett set his glass down too. "Why are you looking at me like that?"

"Like what?"

"*That*." Emmett waved a hand at Jae. "With the big Bambi eyes, like you just got caught with a hand in the cookie jar."

"Oh. Heh. I wondered if maybe you were interested in Kaylee." Jae tilted his head toward the door. "C'mon."

"Uhhh … no." Emmett wrinkled his nose. "She's gorgeous and great, but I've never thought about her that way, probably because I've known her for way too long. Even thinking about it feels a bit weird. Did you really think she and I were …?"

Jae slid his hands into his pockets as they headed for a bank of elevators. "Somewhat, yes. I saw you with her at the bridal shower and it struck me that you two looked good together. I guess my brain took it from there."

Something in his voice must have caught Emmett's attention because suddenly, a hand curled around Jae's elbow.

"Hold on a sec." Emmett tugged Jae around until they were facing one another, his expression stern and, Jae thought, hurt. "Did you call things off with me because of Kaylee?"

"No, I did not. I know you, Em." Jae frowned. "You'd have told me if you wanted to be with Kaylee and you'd have stopped seeing me entirely if you had feelings for her. And that's the thing. You're down on love right now but you won't always feel that way. Someday, you'll want someone in your life, and it will hurt me when you pull away. I don't want to feel that with you."

With a long breath out, Jae lifted the arm Emmett had hold of and lightly grasped Emmett's wrist. "I don't want to look back on this summer and the time I've had with you and remember pain. I like you too much for that. Instead, I want to be able to think back and remember the way I feel right now."

He grunted as his phone chimed again, followed instantly by Emmett's, this time with text messages composed entirely in uppercase letters.

"Okay, we've got to go," Jae said. "I've never seen Ty so close to completely losing his shit."

Quickly, they hustled onto one of the elevators and Jae hit the button for Ty's floor. Facing Emmett again, Jae studied him, his heart aching a little at the faint frown that still marked his features. "Are we okay?"

"I think so, yeah." Emmett's expression smoothed out. "I didn't mean to give you a hard time."

"It's okay. I'm sure you wouldn't have if we'd been talking the last few days instead of stewing in our own juices. That's my fault. I promise I'll be better about reaching out."

"I'd like that. I'm happy you've decided to stay in Boston, you know." Emmett's lips twisted into a wry smile. "It's been nice to see you the last few days, Jae, even when it's been awkward."

"Yeah, it has," Jae said, and realized the second the words left his mouth that he meant them. "We should go shopping sometime. I'd like to buy a bookshelf and truly finish unpacking."

* * * *

Ninety minutes later, Jae stood with his brother at the far end of the hotel's domed harborside pavilion, the wooden ducks in the crook of one arm and Thom and Krishnan behind him. The sun hung just above the horizon, painting the sky with streaks of orange as the bridesmaids walked down the aisle, but every eye in the place remained fixed on the entrance as Emmett and Amelia stepped through the doors.

Jae set a hand on Ty's shoulder, unsurprised to find him trembling. "Amelia looks beautiful, man," he said over the music, and smiled at the happiness he glimpsed on Amelia's face.

"Yeah." Ty's voice was soft and reverent, and though he raised his hand to pat Jae's, his eyes never left the bride. Jae had never seen his brother so awed. "I can't believe this is finally happening."

Happiness surrounded Amelia like an aura, but Jae's attention was drawn to Emmett who looked fit to burst with pride. He escorted his sister to Ty, then exchanged a hug with the groom before he stepped back, and Jae held his breath as Emmett caught his eye. They exchanged a nod before Emmett and the bride and groom turned toward the Justice of the Peace.

"Who gives this woman to be married to this man?" the Justice asked, smiling as Amelia held her head high.

"She gives herself," Amelia replied, her voice clear and strong, "and with her family's blessing."

With one more grin for his sister and Ty, Emmett headed for the bride's side of the wedding altar they'd created from flower arrangements and fabric, where he stood with Kaylee and Marlisa. While Jae tried with all his might to keep his focus on the happy couple, he remained intensely aware of the man standing opposite him and the heat of his gaze.

Looking out at the friends and family who were seated in the chairs beyond, Jae caught sight of Margaret McNeil seated with her sisters, the joy in her face tinged with melancholy. Jae's own mother's words came back to him then and threw the absence of Fred McNeil into sharp relief.

How many times had Jae taken his own parents for granted over the years, especially living far enough away that he didn't need to see how much they might miss him? Glancing at them now, Jae glimpsed anew the fine lines on their faces and silver threads in their hair, signs of age that almost disappeared against the love in their expressions as they watched their younger son make his vows. Their love filled Jae up too, soothing the still rough patches of his heart so he could truly smile and wish Ty and Amelia well as they shared their first kiss as man and wife.

Jae felt centered and content as the bridal party and their guests moved from the pavilion into an event room on the second floor of the hotel for the cocktail hour. He did his part to look after his newly expanded family, making sure their drinks were full and the mothers had comfortable seats, and he knew Emmett was working just as hard.

"Eat up guys." Emmett set down a plate of hors d'oeuvres down beside Amelia and Ty at one corner of the large, square table where the bridal party would sit. "We've got five minutes before the photo call starts on the terrace and I swear I can hear your stomachs rumbling from here."

"God bless you, Em." Amelia fell on the tray with a groan, then passed a hand over the head of one of the wooden ducks that Jae had placed by the table's centerpiece. "I haven't had anything since breakfast, and I swear I'm hungry enough to eat my arm."

"Amelia, maybe you should wait until after the photos," Margaret said, then sighed as Amelia shoved what appeared to be smoked salmon on some kind of bread crisp into her mouth. Margaret's gaze turned arch as she focused on Emmett, but there was amusement in her face when she spoke. "You couldn't be Mr. Helpful *after* your sister finished the photos and talking to fifty people?"

Emmett hummed. "Better now than later, Mother, because a hangry Amelia is a scary thing."

"Hell yes, she is." Ty yipped under Amelia's poking finger and turned wide eyes onto the table at large. "You all know it's true. She once threatened to break up with me because I ate the last two slices of bread and finished off the peanut butter," he said to Jae, who laughed as Amelia rolled her eyes.

"Because we were stuck in the house during a blizzard, Ty, and had no idea how long it would be before we could go out." She reached toward the tray again. "For the record, he *hadn't* eaten all of the bread or peanut butter, because I'd stashed extra supplies in a hiding spot under the sink." Amelia bit into a crostino this time and hummed loudly as she chewed. "Oh, my God, yum! These are almost as good as the stuff you make, Em."

Emmett dropped a kiss on his sister's cheek. "That's what a guy likes to hear. Make sure you save some for your man, too, because I brought enough for the both of you."

Marlisa exchanged a glance with Jae and Thom. "What about the rest of us?" she asked. "Why do we have to schlep our own food around?"

The banter went on as Amelia and Ty finished their snack and both appeared newly energized as they led the party back outside for a million photographs by the harbor. But the crease had reappeared between Emmett's eyebrows by the time they'd finished, and he excused himself as the bride and groom went off to mingle with their guests. Emmett's mother frowned as she tracked his retreating figure.

"Where on earth is that boy off to now?"

Jae imagined Emmett was off to have a glass of wine in relative peace and maybe marshal his resources for what promised to be a fun but active night. Jae thought it sounded like a fine idea. He glimpsed concern in Margaret's eyes, however, and that more than anything else pushed him to linger with her for a bit longer.

"I'm sure he'll be back in no time." He smiled. "Knowing Emmett, he's probably making sure the rest of the food looks as good as the hors d'oeuvres."

"Lord, I hope you're wrong." Margaret chuckled. "A chef Emmett may be, but he deserves the odd evening off, too."

"I can work on making that happen."

"Thank you, Jae." Margaret paused as a server bearing a tray approached them, then selected a mini lobster roll. She frowned slightly when Jae passed the tray up and eyed him as the server walked off. "Is everything all right? You're not still feeling unwell after what happened last week?"

"Oh, no, I'm fine. A little nerved up about having to make a speech later and my appetite's not what it should be. It happens sometimes after I have a bad reaction." Jae moved his shoulders up and down. "It's like a part of my brain needs time to catch up with the understanding I'm okay."

"That's awful."

"Eh, it's not so bad. Better than a case of anaphylaxis in my brother's apartment."

Margaret covered a laugh with one hand. "Oh, God. Well, I'm sorry about it anyway. Even more knowing you enjoy Emmett's cooking and maybe didn't get to appreciate it last night as you should."

"Thank you." Jae waited until she'd finished chewing before he spoke again. "I'm glad you got to see Emmett at work. To know what kind of talent he has and how much enjoyment he brings to his job."

"I am too." The respect in Margaret's voice was clear. "I really had no idea. I'm sure Emmett's told you his father and I wanted something different for him. We thought ... I don't even know anymore what Fred and I were thinking." She huffed out a breath. "Neither of us was very good at listening to our children and really hearing what they were trying to tell us. And Emmett was so ... determined. So sure about what he wanted even if it meant going against us."

"Can you blame him?" Jae asked.

"Not now, no. I wish he'd tried harder to tell us back then, though. Or that I'd been better at hearing him." Margaret picked her glass up. "When Fred and I heard Emmett would be helping Aiden Marinelli with his business, neither of us knew what to think." She glanced back in the direction Emmett had walked. "We assumed things, of course. Aiden's face is the one in the magazines, after all, and he has a formidable presence. But it's obvious now that Emmett doesn't just work for Aiden. He's a part of the business and integral to it."

Jae nodded. "Endless Pastabilities was Aiden's idea, but the venture wouldn't be what it is today if Emmett hadn't been there from the start. Aiden is the first person to say so."

"I believe it." Margaret pursed her lips. "It's not always easy for me to wrap my head around the man Emmett is today," she said. "He's become a stranger to me in so many ways."

All sorts of replies filtered through Jae's head, starting with a pointed reminder that the McNeils had kicked their own son out of their lives. That they had denied a crucial piece of his identity. And, according to Emmett, that Margaret was still in denial about his being pan. Yet, saying such things—particularly here, on this night—didn't feel right to Jae, and the prospect of essentially outing Emmett all over again was a thing Jae did not want at all. He saw a chance to keep nudging Margaret toward bridging the rift between herself and her son, though, and he didn't hesitate to take it.

"It doesn't have to be that way," he said. "Work at making things right between you and Emmett. You can't go back to the way things were, but it's possible the two of you could make something good in its place."

Margaret nodded slowly. "I'd like to think you're right." She gave Jae a look he didn't know how to decipher. "Thank you for not judging me, or at least not out loud. Emmett is lucky to have you."

Jae made himself smile back. "I'm lucky to have him as a friend, too."

"That's not what I mean."

"Okay?" Jae drew his eyebrows together. "I'm not sure what you—"

"How long?" Margaret asked over him, her voice even quieter. "How long have you loved my son, Jae?"

Oh, fuck.

Jae's heart was pounding so hard, he thought for sure he'd pass out.

"I can hear it in your voice when you speak about him," Margaret said through the charged silence. "Feel it coming off you when you and he are in the same room. When you offered Emmett your seat last night, so he and I could talk? It was all over your face."

"Yeah. I suppose it was."

Jae blew out a huge breath and rubbed a hand over his eyes, head light, bracing himself for the worse when Margaret frowned. Still, her next words were not what he expected at all.

"Am I really the only person who's guessed?"

"I ... think you are, yes. But *Emmett* doesn't know. I haven't said those words to him because I don't want him to know how I feel." Jae fell silent for a beat as the ache inside grew too much to bear. His voice was thin when he continued. "He and I have mutual friends and our social circles connect pretty regularly. We got closer while we were planning the bachelor party and became really good friends." He gave her a shaky smile. "It was easy from there for me to shift from like to love. Emmett made it easy."

"Just as your mother said." Margaret's frown deepened. "Friendship becomes more, provided you want it."

"Yes and no. Emmett doesn't feel even remotely the way I do. He and I are *just* friends." Jae swallowed against that bitter half-truth, then made himself tell another. "And I'm okay with that. It's not his fault I got my wires crossed and fell for a guy who doesn't feel the same way."

"I don't know what to say."

"You don't have to say anything, Margaret. I'll get over this ... crush, I guess you could call it, and in the meantime, staying quiet means that no one feels weird or awkward."

"Except you." The wry tone in Margaret's voice made Jae laugh.

"Awkward is sort of my default," he said. "I've always been a bit of a weirdo."

This time it was Margaret who laughed. "This explains why you and Emmett get on so well, then." Still smiling, she studied Jae for a moment, then patted his arm. "You're a good man, Jae. And, whatever the case, I stand by what I said earlier—Emmett is lucky to have you."

"Thanks." He glanced around the room and frowned when he still didn't see Emmett. "I should track him down. Dinner starts in twenty and I know he'll want to be here for that."

"Oh, yes, true." Margaret gave Jae a gentle push. "Go on, then. I'll hold off the others in the meantime if need be."

Jae's thoughts spun as he headed past the long banquet tables already filling with guests. This ... alliance that had formed between Emmett's mother and himself confused him. He was sure it was a bad idea, too. And as he spotted Emmett standing at the bar closest to the exit, Jae's stomach twisted. Because if Jae was struggling to understand why Margaret McNeil seemed to like him, what would Emmett think once he'd caught on, too?

Chapter Fourteen

Emmett's attention was focused on a glass of red wine on the bar top before him, and he appeared lost in his musings as Jae sidled up beside him.

"Hey, weirdo."

Emmett's gaze snapped up. He blinked at Jae's greeting, the tips of his ears going red. "Well, hey."

"Wondered where you'd got off to. You okay?"

"Sure." Emmett gave Jae a crooked little smile. "Join me for a drink?"

"Okay. What have you got there?"

"A Gamay. It's from a vineyard I like in Côte de Brouilly." Two fingers on the foot of the glass, Emmett slid it over the bar's surface in small circles, sending its crimson contents swirling gently against the glass's sides. "Great raspberry and plum notes, and it smells like violets. Want to try?"

Jae nodded. He really did like listening to Emmett talk about food and wine and the easy confidence his knowledge lent his voice. Jae picked the glass up by its stem, then quickly cast a look back at the party.

"No one's paying any attention to us."

Emmett's gentle tone caught Jae's attention immediately and the affection in his friend's expression warmed Jae even as he shook his head at himself. It seemed they'd gotten so used to making sure no one saw them acting like a couple, Jae was still going out of his way to be cautious, even now.

"Thanks," Jae said. He sipped wine and savored it, the bright flavors bursting onto his taste buds. "Damn, that's delicious."

"I thought you'd like it." Emmett signaled to the bartender for a second glass. "Are you having fun?"

"I've never been one for weddings, but this is nice." Jae nodded. "I'm glad we could be here for Ty and Amelia. And that my ma and dad and Margaret could, too."

"Yeah. I like seeing my sister happy." Emmett's grin dimmed by several degrees. "Being around my mother is kind of a mind fuck. She seems ... different."

"Like how?"

"More open, I guess. Definitely more approachable than she has been in years. I'm used to Mother acting like I'm not in the room—freezing people out was always one of her favorite tactics. I'm not sure she's spoken to me directly more than a couple of dozen times since she and the old man kicked me out of the house."

Jae couldn't help his sigh. What kind of person acted that way toward their own kid?

"She's stopped with the big freeze this summer, though. I saw a few signs here and there during her visits over the past few months. And I really noticed it during the bridal shower." Discomfort flickered over Emmett's face as he spoke. "She was *nice* to me that day. Has been since. Wants to talk to me, asks how I am. She said she'd like to get together before she goes back to Virginia so we can talk, and I'm embarrassed to say I don't know what to make of it."

"You still don't trust her," Jae said, his tone certain rather than questioning, and felt no surprise at Emmett's quick nod.

"No, I don't. And how fucked up is that?"

"Given what you'd been through, I don't think it is at all." Jae cast a brief look back toward Margaret's table, then focused on Emmett again. "I can't imagine what you're feeling."

"I'm not sure I know myself. I'm definitely not sure what to do, either." Emmett went quiet for a beat. "It's been such a long time since I had a normal conversation with my mother," he said. "So, do I act like nothing ever happened between us and start over again from scratch?"

"Mmm. No." Jae frowned. "I think you should tell Margaret what you've told me. That you don't trust her after all this time.

Your mom needs to know, Em. To recognize that the way she and your dad treated you changed you as a person." Jae sipped from his glass and swallowed. "I also think you should hear your mother out if she wants to give her side."

Emmett's mouth tightened, something furious flickering in his eyes before he visibly reined himself in. "Her side?" he asked, voice low. "What side is that, exactly? What kind of excuses can a parent give for kicking their own son out of the family?"

"I don't know because I can't imagine what went through their heads. I do know the way your parents acted can never be excused, though, and honestly, I get the feeling Margaret is starting to understand it, too."

"Yeah, well, of course you'd know that," Emmett muttered. "Don't think I haven't noticed how much the two of you have been talking to each other."

The hurt in Emmett's voice sent prickles of shame through Jae and he cast his eyes down at his feet. "I'm sorry if it bothers you. I can't tell you why your mother started talking to me because I'm not sure myself," he said. "But Margaret's been paying attention since she came back to Boston and trying to understand what she left behind when she moved to Virginia. Trying to understand you in particular."

"Did she tell you that?"

"Yes." Jae brought his gaze back up to meet Emmett's. "I think it'd be good for you to talk with her about what happened back then."

Emmett made a disgusted noise. "I'm not sure I agree. I stopped giving a damn what my mother thinks of me years ago, Jae."

"Except you didn't," Jae said, and those three words cut through Emmett's bluster like a knife. "If you'd truly stopped giving a damn, you'd have told your mom who you really are. That you're pan. Who Aiden is to you and how much he's meant to your life. Sean, too, and the other guys you've been with since you moved out of your parents' house."

You'd have told her about me hung in the air between them, but Jae pushed past those words. This conversation wasn't about him—it was about an old scar from Emmett's past.

"Show her that side of you." Jae set his hand on Emmett's arm. "Let Margaret get to know you and your life, and maybe you'll want to know her back."

"But what if I don't?" Emmett's face was almost haunted. "What happens then, huh? I've been getting by just fine on my own for a long time now, so who says I need my mother in my life at all?"

"No one."

"You just said—"

"That I think you should talk to the woman. That's all. It's still your choice in the end." Jae gave Emmett a small smile. "Margaret's headed back to Virginia in a couple of weeks and things can go right back to the way they've been if that's what you want to happen. I'm just not sure you'll be able to truly let go of all the old hurt unless you talk to her first, though."

Emmett let out a groan. "I fucking hate this."

"I know you do." The discomfort pouring off Emmett pained Jae and oh, how badly he wanted to put his arms around his friend and squeeze. "Think about it for as long as you need," he said instead. "Whatever you decide, it'll be on *your* terms this time. You didn't have that kind of power back then, when you were just a kid trying to figure out how to make your dream work, but you damned well do now."

"Yeah." Emmett heaved a big breath. "I'll give it some thought, okay?"

Heart in his throat, Jae carefully moved his hand over Emmett's where it lay on the bar. He swallowed hard when Emmett's gaze landed on those joined hands.

"Don't make the decision for me, Em. Make it for *you*. I already know the man you are. Whichever way you decide isn't going to change the fact that I respect the hell out of you." Jae paused, then stroked his thumb over Emmett's knuckles. "And you don't have to get by all on your own anymore, you know. You have a family. Your friends, Amelia and Ty, my parents. Me. We've got your back, Emmett."

With equal care, Jae moved the hand aside again, then glanced back toward the space where the bridal party was gathering. "We should get over there," he said, his voice quiet. "We've got a dinner to eat and speeches to give, not to mention I know you want to dance with Amelia."

Emmett appeared to give himself an internal shake. "Yeah, okay," he said. "What about you? You gonna do your Best Man thing and treat your brother to a foxtrot?" He looked much more relaxed at Jae's snicker.

"Heck no. I'll be on the terrace when the dancing starts, wine in hand and Best Man duties mostly done, finally getting my chill on."

* * * *

The evening whirled by as Jae and Emmett sat down to dinner. Sitting side by side, they chatted with each other and the group as the courses were rolled out, and though Jae tried hard to relax, his nerves were strung tight about giving his goddamned speech.

Yet a near calmness fell over him when the time came at last, because Emmett was there beside him with a ready smile as soothing as any hug. They'd gone back and forth several times as they'd decided who would go first and Jae had to bite back a snort when Emmett, ever impish, pretended to steal Jae's notecards. Laughter rippled through the room as Jae took the mic in hand.

"Good evening, everyone." He smiled. "For those of you who don't know us, I'm Jae-seong and this is Emmett. Now, I'm the guy who has annoyed Ty ever since his first day on earth, so imagine my delight when he asked me to stand up for him today and declare myself Best Man." Jae grinned at the hooting that followed his comments as well as his brother's exaggerated eye roll.

"Before I tell you all about how lucky my brother is to have found *anyone* who wanted to marry him, I'd like to take a moment to thank our parents, Kun-bae and Christina, as well as Amelia's family, Emmett and Margaret, for including us all here on this special day." He paused and met Emmett's gaze for a beat as a wave of applause rolled over him.

"For a brief span of time during his childhood, Ty thought I was cool," Jae said to the crowd. "He used to follow me around and steal gum from my stash when my back was turned. He'd sneak into my room and hide under the bed with his Matchbox cars, which always ended with Ty being covered in dust bunnies the size of tumbleweeds."

"I named one of them Cleo!" Ty called through cupped hands, and beamed when the crowd erupted in laughter, Jae included.

"Although Ty is eight years younger than I, he's always been sure of himself," Jae said once the room had quieted. "He changed his name because he wanted to and decided he was going to become a teacher before he'd even finished middle school. Ty was the first person I told when I came out and even though some of his friends gave him grief for having a brother who was gay, he always had my back. I'm grateful for his support to this day." Jae sensed rather than truly saw Emmett step closer.

"As an adult, Ty has forged his own path with an ease I admire. He found a job he loves, and friends who are steadfast and, of course, he found Amelia." Jae sent a smile Amelia's way.

"I've never met anyone who makes my brother happier, Amelia, and I'm honored today to welcome you into our family," he said, his heart pounding at the sudden shine in Amelia's eyes. "I want to thank you from the bottom of my heart for bringing love into my brother's life every single day. Ty is a good brother and a good man, and to me, he's the best person you could choose to have by your side. I wish you both a lifetime of love, unity, and happiness."

Jae raised his flute glass. "To the newlyweds."

Turning, he held his glass up to Emmett, humbled by the emotion in his friend's eyes. The burst of applause from the crowd took Jae off guard, though, and he set his free hand against his chest.

"Holy shitballs," he mouthed, delight curling through him at Emmett's laugh, and a lovely, cozy feeling went through him as he handed over the mic.

"Thank you for warming up the crowd so beautifully, Jae-seong," Emmett said, "and for making me re-e-e-eally glad I practiced my own speech in the mirror six times this morning."

Emmett knocked his shoulder playfully against Jae's, clearly basking in the laughter of the people around them before he turned his head in his sister's direction.

"Amelia and I are only a year apart, so neither of us has ever known a life without the other." His expression sobered. "It's not a lie to say we've been through stuff, both together and separately, and my sister has always been strong and sure and shown me how to get things done. I'll never have words enough to thank you for just being you, sis." He pursed his lips when the tears standing in Amelia's eyes spilled over.

"I knew from the first moment you introduced me to Ty that he was someone special in your life. And I didn't feel even a hint of nervousness knowing it, because I saw right away how special you were to Ty, too. I knew even then that of all the men in the world you might meet, you'd found one who would treat you right."

Emmett licked his lips and, for just a second, brushed the knuckles of his free hand against Jae's.

"My sister is special and dear to me, Ty," Emmett said, "and I am incredibly grateful she found someone who understands how precious such things are in this world. So, congratulations, you two, and allow me to bless you with an old Irish saying bestowed on every couple in our family. 'May your troubles be less, your blessings be more, and nothing but happiness come through your door.'"

With a brilliant smile, Emmett raised his glass. "To the bride and groom," he said, toasting his sister and Ty before he turned back to Jae.

"How'd I do?" He chuckled as Jae tossed back the rest of his drink. "Oh, look at you, Mr. I Don't Like Shots."

"Yeah, well I need one," Jae said on a laugh of his own. "There's no way I could have followed an Irish goddamned blessing so thank you very much for letting me go first."

He paused then and held Emmett's gaze, but there wasn't time to tell him how beautifully he'd done before Jae was engulfed in a bear hug of epic proportions.

"You guys were amazing!" Ty said over Amelia's slightly quieter praise, her voice muffled against Emmett's broad chest as they embraced. "You didn't seem nervous at all!"

"It was Emmett's suggestion to stand up together." Jae leaned into the hug. "And I can honestly say it was the best idea either of us could have had."

"Yeah, well." Ty tilted his head back enough to capture Jae's gaze, his smile fond. "It's just like you giving the credit to someone else. And, for the record, I still think you're cool. I always have. Even when I'm busting your chops."

With the most stressful of his wedding duties behind him, time went blurry and soft for Jae. He relaxed into it with gratitude, finally getting a little more food and drink down, and he felt happy and loose by the time the DJ stepped back up to the mic.

Jae applauded and cheered through the introductions of the bride and groom and each member of the wedding party, then slipped out onto the terrace as Ty and Amelia took to the dance floor. He stood by the balustrade, his gaze on the party inside, riding a happy wave as he watched Ty and Amelia move together, their grins wide and joyful. A deep tenderness crept over Jae as he watched Ty hand his new wife off to Emmett, however, and his throat went tight as brother and sister spun around the floor in a graceful waltz.

Heart aching, Jae turned away and stared out at the darkened harbor, which was dotted with pinpoints of light from anchored seacraft and framed by the cityscape on both sides. He didn't bother turning around when the song changed, nor when the door nearest him opened, the music and conversation from within bubbling out into the air before it was muffled again as the door was closed.

"You got your chill on, Jae-seong?"

"Getting there." Jae's smile as Emmett stepped up beside him grew wider after he spied the wine bottle in Emmett's hand. "Look at you, all prepared."

"You're not the only one who was looking forward to the Best Man duties being over." Emmett topped off Jae's glass and then his own. "Not that dining and dancing with people I like is a hardship."

"True." Jae sipped his wine. "I knew you liked to dance, but I had no idea you waltzed. And here I thought I knew you."

"Oh, you do. Amelia and I danced a foxtrot, by the way." Emmett chuckled at Jae's mock groan. "Aiden taught me a bunch of different dance styles about a million years ago, just for fun. He even insisted I lead most of the time which you know went against every bossy cell in his body."

Jae tipped his head back and laughed. "I'd have liked to have seen that."

"He was surprisingly cool about the whole thing." Emmett bent and set the bottle on the ground by his feet, then turned away from the water and toward Jae. "He also taught me how to follow in the event I ever had a dance partner who wanted to lead."

Jae shifted his weight so he faced Emmett. "And have you? Had dance partners who want to lead, I mean."

"To date, no." Emmett's lips curved up. "I haven't met many people who are interested in ballroom dance. I don't suppose you ...?"

"I never learned," Jae replied. "Not properly, anyway. I'm good with the basic move around in a graceful kind of way, but I haven't met many people who are interested in ballroom dance either."

"You never will if you duck out of parties the second people start partnering up." Emmett made a tsking sound with his tongue. "But I'm happy to teach you, whether you want to lead or not." Warmth washed over Jae as Emmett carefully took his glass. Setting them on the ground beside the bottle, Emmett moved back into Jae's space, his eyes shining in the low light as he positioned his right hand on Jae's lower ribs.

"You may not know which way you prefer, of course," Emmett said, then threaded the fingers of his left hand through Jae's right. "So, we can make it up as we go."

"That sounds nice." Jae swallowed. "But—"

"But nothing," Emmett replied. "Just dance with me, Jae, and let's leave the rest for later."

The rest of what?

Jae's thoughts swirled as he moved his free hand to Emmett's shoulder but oh, it was nice, the strong arm holding him, Emmett's aftershave bright and clean as Jae breathed him in, their hands clasped as Emmett steered Jae backward. Jae closed his eyes when Emmett's cheek met his and he relaxed, trusting Emmett to lead him through the unfamiliar steps. Though they went slow, everything about that moment under the stars with the hushed lapping of water in the harbor beyond felt right and true. Magical.

"God," Jae murmured. "You really are a romantic at heart."

"You're one of very few people who have noticed."

Emmett's words settled over them just as the tempo of the music inside changed. Jae couldn't help frowning at the reminder that while he and Emmett were alone on the terrace for the moment, they wouldn't be for long. In fact, Jae wasn't sure the terrace wasn't at least partly visible from inside despite the low lighting.

"People will see us, Em."

Emmett simply hummed. His hold on Jae didn't change, and he moved them a bit faster around their makeshift dance space. "I don't mind if they do." He held on a little tighter when Jae's steps stuttered right along with his brain.

"Since when?"

Emmett's cheek pulled up in a smile against Jae's. "Since a very good friend reminded me to make decisions for myself instead of for other people and I realized he was right."

Jae held his breath as Emmett drew even closer. "Is that so?"

147

Emmett turned his head and traced his nose over Jae's cheek. "Yup."

"Well." Jae swallowed against the lump in his throat. "This friend of yours sounds like a smart guy."

"He is. Weird as hell, too," Emmett said, then held fast when Jae mock gasped. "Still, I really like him. Probably more than I should." He didn't stop Jae from pulling away this time, though Jae only moved enough to make eye contact. "I also know he's a good man and he'd never hurt me on purpose." Emmett's honeyed voice was softer and the vulnerability in his features visible in the half light.

"No, I wouldn't. I like you too much to do that." Jae's heart squeezed at the shyness in Emmett's face. "I'm just not sure what you want, Em."

"I want you." Emmett drew them both to a stop. "I don't want to lose you or what we could have together just because my ex messed up my ability to trust." He moved their joined hands to his own chest, pressing Jae's flat against the lapel of his tuxedo jacket. "So, can we start over, Jae? Because I would really like to do that with you."

"I'm not sure," Jae said, his words slow. "I think I may be too far gone to start over." His stomach dipped when Emmett brought his eyebrows together.

"What do you mean?"

Pressing his forehead to Emmett's, Jae closed his eyes. "You already know I have feelings for you. But the truth is, I've never had feelings like this for anyone, Emmett. I don't know how to go back to the person I was before, because everything changed when I fell for you." He pressed his lips together at Emmett's sharp inhale.

"Oh, Jae." Emmett's voice held such longing. "I don't want you to go back. I want you exactly the way you are right now."

Hope rose inside Jae that he couldn't squash, even though he tried. "What changed?" he asked, his skeptical side not quite ready to back down. "Not even a week ago, I told you I wanted more, and you said you weren't ready for that."

Emmett rubbed the space between Jae's shoulders. "It wasn't a lie. I wasn't on the same page as you that night and didn't want to be. To me, feelings have always meant complications, and after Sean, I just haven't wanted to go there. So, I agreed when you told me you needed space." He sighed, the sound so forlorn Jae peeled his eyes open, his heart racing at the regret he glimpsed in Emmett's face.

"It gutted me to leave you the next morning," Emmett said, "even though I knew it's what we both needed. But, Jae, I haven't felt *right* since. Seeing you this week and not being able to touch or even talk the way we used to has been fucking hard. It made me think—like, really think—about what we had together and how much you mean to me. I want you in my life. I want this thing between us to be real and not just fooling around. For us to be on the same page, more than anything."

The joy that swooped through Jae made his chest squeeze so hard it almost hurt. "I would love it," he said, "as long as you're certain it's what you really want. I'm not sure my heart can take it if you change your mind again and the last thing I want you to feel when you're around me is regret."

"I won't change my mind. I'm not even sure I could." Carefully, Emmett drew Jae back into a dance. His lead was very gentle this time and their feet moved only enough to bring them around in slow circles. "My life is better with you in it, and if there's anything I regret it's that it took me needing to walk away to figure it out."

Jae raised his hand to Emmett's cheek, his doubt melting as Emmett turned into his touch and pressed a soft kiss to Jae's palm. Using that hand, he brought Emmett to him, slotting their lips together in a sweet kiss that was both 'Hello' and 'I missed you,' and made Jae crave more. A soft noise rumbled through Emmett's chest when Jae kissed him again, slower this time, the air around them fairly buzzing with energy.

Letting go of Emmett's hand, Jae cradled Emmett's jaw in his palms, pleasure blasting through him as Emmett hugged him hard. Deepening the kiss just a bit, Jae's gut tumbled when Emmett opened immediately, his breath hitching as Jae slid his tongue against Emmett's. The kiss went from sweet to scorching in a flash.

It was a while before Jae forced himself to stop, the kisses cycling through heat and tenderness more than once, and he was giddy and grateful for Emmett's steadying touch. Emmett kept Jae close even then, as if he were loath to turn Jae loose. Jae swallowed his impulse to tease when he realized Emmett was trembling.

"Hey," he pressed a softer kiss against Emmett's cheek. "You okay?"

"Yeah." Emmett let out a shaky laugh. "I didn't realize how much I needed to kiss you until you let me. I must sound like a wreck."

"Not to me. Honestly, I was just thinking how lucky I am that you were holding me up or I'd have ended up on my ass."

Emmett chuckled, then gave Jae another kiss. "Sitting down sounds good right about now. Plus, I want to kiss you some more. You want to sneak out of here and talk or would that be in bad taste?"

"I'm not sure we need to be worried about offending people at this point. I mean, you're macking on a guy at your sister's wedding, Em, who the hell cares if we duck out for a while?"

Both went still as the door leading inside opened, music filling the air again, along with a low whistle.

"I knew it."

"Oh, good." Jae rolled his eyes at his brother's gloating tone and tightened his fingers around Emmett's. He swiveled his head toward the door where Ty and Amelia stood, both smiling widely. "What did you know?"

"That things were changing between you and Emmett, duh." Ty slipped his arm around Amelia's shoulders and the two crossed the terrace toward them. "You've been acting strange around each other for a while now. As in I noticed it during the bachelor party weekend." He waved his glass between them. "Exactly how long has this been going on?"

"Long enough for this moment to be more awkward than I anticipated." Exhaling through his nose, Jae faced his brother and Amelia fully, though he still didn't let go of Emmett's hand. "We didn't want any drama with the families. And I definitely thought we were doing a good job of hiding it."

"You were. But there were signs," Amelia said. "I noticed them the very first time you met, in fact."

Emmett's jaw went slack. "The engagement party? Seriously? That was over six months ago."

"And literally nothing was going on then." Jae shook his head. "Emmett was still with Sean."

"Yeah, but I was sure I saw *something* between you." Amelia shrugged. "Ty convinced me it was just wishful thinking on my part."

"Because Emmett had that boyfriend my brother just

mentioned," Ty reminded her before he turned his gaze to
Emmett. "After Sean was out of the picture, I wondered if maybe
you guys would hit it off."

Jae snorted on a laugh. "This is nuts. We were sure you'd be
pissed if you found out we'd hooked up."

Ty cocked an eyebrow. "Shows what you know. Why would I
be pissed?"

"Because I'm a fussy, old geezer," Jae said, and though he tried
to keep his tone gentle, Ty's face still fell.

"I don't really think that about you, Jae. Maybe ten years ago
when I was an immature little shit, but not now. I just like giving
you crap."

Jae nodded slowly. "All right. So, you're really okay with the fact
that Emmett is younger than you?"

"Amelia is younger than me," Ty replied, "and Dad is five years
younger than Ma. What difference does it make how much younger
or older you are than someone you care about? Okay, yeah—I
probably *would* have warned you off Emmett if I'd known you two
were hooking up, but more because I didn't think Emmett was in
the right headspace to be good for you than anything else."

Emmett frowned. "Dude, really?"

"'Fuck love' has been your mantra for months," Ty said to
Emmett. "I even heard you say the words to Jae when we were at
the campsite in Maine. And while I get why you'd feel that way, I
wouldn't have wanted you to shovel that shit onto my brother."
Every trace of amusement in his manner faded as he and Emmett
stared each other down. "You haven't been, right?"

"No, he hasn't," Jae answered in Emmett's place. He glanced
down at their joined hands then met Emmett's eyes again, and the
two shared a smile. "We're still working out some details but—"

"We'll get there," Emmett finished.

"Ugh, you guys are already finishing each other's sentences." Ty
sighed. "Ma is going to love this." Oblivious to the cool trickle of
dread his words sent through Jae, Ty tipped his head in the
direction of the door. "You guys ready to head back in?"

"We'll meet you in there," Emmett said, his tone just slightly
off.

The trickle of dread now a full-on stream, Jae's heart sank down
to his shoes. The little bubble that had surrounded Emmett and
himself all this time had been well and truly breached and Jae

honestly had no idea what that meant. Still, he kept his chin up as Ty led Amelia back inside.

"How do you want to play this?" Jae asked once the door had closed behind them. Gently, he dropped Emmett's hand, then headed back toward the spot by the balustrade where they'd left their glasses. "You can go in first if you like, and I can follow in five."

Emmett's chuckle came as a surprise followed by a sting that made Jae grit his teeth. But then Emmett cut in front of Jae and brought his hands up, his eyes soft as he clasped Jae's face between them.

"Uh-uh," he said, tone soothing. "I'm done sneaking around. Anyone who has a problem with the two of us together can fuck off into space." He silenced Jae's startled laugh with a kiss so sweet Jae's insides turned to mush.

"Thank you for saying that." Jae circled Emmett's wrists with his fingers. "But I'm okay with taking this slow if it's what you need. We can keep it just between us until you're ready to share, and, even then, only with the people you want to know."

Emmett kissed him some more, deeper this time, and heat rose between them again. "You're so good to me, Jae," he said when they came back up for air, his voice rough. "I want everyone here to know who you are to me, starting with your ma and dad and yes, my mother. I want to dance with you *inside* the party, not just out here, and I want to hold your hand and kiss you where everyone can see."

"That last part sounds pornographic," Jae got out through a laugh, and he hugged Emmett when he laughed too. "I'd suggest you keep the kissing on the G-Rated side before I drag you upstairs, though."

Glee made Emmett's eyes sparkle. "That sounds like a dare, Jae-seong. And we both know I'm not one to turn down a challenge."

Chapter Fifteen

"I'm sure you don't want to hear it, sweetheart, but I'm really enjoying seeing this side of you."

Heat flashed over Jae's cheeks. The expansive warmth filling his chest instantly undid any bashful feelings his mother's words might have brought on, however, and he couldn't remember the last time he'd felt so light.

A few eyebrows had gone up when he and Emmett had rejoined the party, and lots of eyes had fixed on their joined hands. There'd been some light teasing, mostly from the knot of Ty's friends who'd attended the bachelor party weekend, several of whom noted they'd seen the same chemistry Ty claimed to have witnessed. But there'd been smiles going around too, and hugs from Jae's parents, and if Emmett had skirted the table where Margaret and her sisters were seated, Jae had said nothing. Being on the receiving end of an enthusiastic high-five from Kaylee and her girlfriend had been way more fun.

Christina patted his shoulder now. "You and Emmett look wonderful together."

"Thank you, I think." Jae turned her in a half circle on the dance floor and immediately spied Emmett at the bar, drawing pictures in the air with his hands as he spoke with Kun-bae. A beat later, he'd caught Jae's eye and Emmett's smile lit him up from the inside.

Christina turned her head enough to follow Jae's line of sight, and she practically cooed when she spoke again. "I have never seen you like this before."

"Yeah, yeah, we're adorable, I know." Jae grunted. "Everything happened so fast. Emmett and I were just having fun, but I walked into this room a single man, Ma."

"You're not leaving as one," Christina said with a laugh.

"No, I'm not."

"And that makes you happy."

"Yes, it does. *Emmett* makes me happy."

"I can tell." She gave him an indulgent smile. "As far as things moving fast, I wouldn't worry too much about that. Just trust yourself, Jae. And Emmett. He's got a good head on his shoulders from what I've seen, and he is one thousand percent into you. In the meantime, I'll just adore seeing you like this."

"I hope you mean it." Jae dropped a quick kiss on her cheek. "You're bound to get tired of it now that I've decided to stay in town. Pretty sure you'll end up wishing I'd move back to L.A."

"I would never." Christina's face screwed up in a scowl. "I didn't want to tell you at the time, but I was disgustingly emotional after you told your dad and me that you'd decided to stay in town. I actually cried in the car."

"What? Why?"

"It was such a relief knowing I wouldn't have to say goodbye just yet." She winced. "Don't get me wrong, honey—you were always wonderful about staying in touch with calls and the phone apps. I often saw your face more regularly than I did your brother's and the boy lives four miles from your dad and me. When you came back early this year, I must have reminded myself a thousand times you'd probably want to leave within a year, but I still got used to you living only three train stops away. I wasn't looking forward to losing that."

Jae gave her a quick hug. "You won't. I can't promise I'll always live only three train stops away, but I have no plans to move anywhere that would involve logging hours on a plane when we want to visit."

"Just what a mother likes to hear. You misunderstood me earlier when I said I'd never seen you like this."

"Oh? What did you mean?"

"That I've never seen you in love." Christina's beaming expression softened. "You've had men in your life, of course, and even seemed content with a few of them. Nothing like this,

154

though."

Jae covered his eyes with one hand. "Oh, wow."

"What? Did I say the wrong thing?" His mother sounded amused. A second later, she had a hold of Jae's elbow and was tugging his hand down and away from his face. "Is this the moment you actually expire from embarrassment?"

"That's not even it." Jae hung his head, unable to meet his mother's gaze. "You're the second person who's said that to me tonight," he said at last.

"You act as though I accused you of terrible things." Christina's tone was chiding. "And what do you mean by the second person? Who knows you as well as your own mother?"

"Margaret, apparently. So maybe it's a mother thing."

Christina made a small 'o' with her lips. "Wow."

"Mmm-hmm. She asked me how long I'd had feelings for Emmett right before dinner. I almost choked on a baby carrot, I was so surprised." Jae made a pouty face at his mother's laughter. "It's not funny."

"It is a little. Especially since I know you're not fond of baby carrots which means you're probably just trying to get a laugh. But I understand why you were surprised—I didn't see it coming at all. Margaret has never acknowledged that Emmett is pan to me or your father. What did you say when she asked?"

"That any feelings between Emmett and me were one sided and all on me. It wasn't even a lie. I'd asked Em to give me some space and he was being noble about respecting that … if he hadn't come out to the terrace to talk to me, I'm really not sure where we'd be tonight." Jae spun them in another lazy half-circle and watched his mother's face grow somber.

"So, we might never have known about the two of you?"

"Probably not." Jae thought back to the entrance they'd made, hands clasped and stars in Emmett's eyes, and grimaced. "I'm sorry I didn't tell you guys."

Christina hummed. "I don't love that either of you felt the need to hide but I'm sure you each had your reasons for handling it the way you did. Those reasons are no one else's business."

"You're right." Jae frowned. "Hiding things from you was hard, though. Almost as hard as hiding things from Emmett."

"What do you mean?"

"I haven't said those three words to him. I flat out couldn't before and now … I don't know. Emmett knows I care about him a lot, but this is all still so new, Ma. He and I are still working to get on the same page."

More like hoping Emmett gets there. Jae bit his lip against his lurking fear.

Christina was quiet a moment. "Emmett may not be ready to say he loves you back just yet, but it's clear to me his feelings run deep. Don't hold off because you're waiting for it to 'feel right.'"

Jae breathed through the knot forming in his chest. "I don't want to scare him off."

"I'm not sure you could." Her smile was small and sad. "Emmett's parents forced him to choose between his own happiness and theirs once, but the man stood beside you tonight in front of his mother and friends and family. My opinion is that he's around to stay."

The ache inside Jae eased. "I'll keep that in mind."

They were headed for the bar when the song changed again, and were quickly intercepted by Jae's dad, who grinned as he led his wife back out onto the floor. Their shared laughter seemed far away to Jae, however, because his gaze was on his man. Emmett stood with his back to the bar, elbows propped on its top, his posture easy and elegant, as if he hadn't a worry in the world. His eyes heated as he watched Jae's approach and he reached for Jae's hand as soon as Jae drew close enough.

Jae didn't hesitate to wind their fingers together. Stepping up close, he set his forehead on Emmett's, his heart expanding in his chest when Emmett's eyes fluttered closed. "Hey, weirdo."

"Hey." Emmett laughed softly, then opened his eyes again. "You and your ma looked pretty good out there."

"I tried." Jae stepped back enough to meet Emmett's gaze. "Managed not to step on her feet, which I'll count as a win."

Emmett heaved a sigh but there was a playful air about him. "We'll have to work on that."

"We can use my apartment for lessons." Jae made his eyes wide. "I have less furniture and fewer houseplants to knock over."

"Dude, I'm buying you more plants," Emmett said with a snort. "We need to warm up that glorified dorm room of yours now that you're staying in town and make it feel more lived in. Besides, Sparky needs company."

Jae wrinkled his brow. "She's only still alive because of you,

Em. I still have to track the days she needs watering on my phone."

"You say that like it's a bad thing." Emmett chuckled. "There are other plants out there that are hard to kill, Jae—I know we can find some for you."

"Aloe is a good choice," Margaret said, "or jade if you think the room is bright enough."

Emmett's whole body tensed and, for a beat, he didn't move. The laughter in his voice was gone as he shifted his attention to his mother. "Jae has a pot of aloe already, but jade is a good suggestion. Maybe some golden pothos, too. There is a big, east-facing window in Jae's apartment that gets a big hit of light first thing in the morning."

Despite the mild tone, Jae heard a challenge in Emmett's words. Something fierce rose inside him, curling just beneath the surface and coiled to spring at the weariness that crossed his lover's face. It was all Jae could to keep himself calm. Breathing deep, he reined himself in and faced Margaret too, determined not to add more stress to Emmett's evening.

"I've always been hopeless with houseplants," Jae said. "I was so sure Emmett's were fake the first time I saw them. Not that I told him so."

"I knew." Emmett's lips twitched at the corners when Jae looked his way. "You freaked so hard when you brushed up against the touch-me-not and its leaves folded up."

"Because moving plants are *weird*. It probably listens to your conversations, too."

"Says the guy with the robot smart speaker in his apartment."

"Okay, that's fair."

The laughter bubbling out of Jae brought a real grin to Emmett's face, but it quickly faded against Margaret's small, equally genuine smile. Jae gripped Emmett's hand harder.

"Anyway, this guy has convinced himself that I can be reformed and make my plant killing days a thing of the past. I figure I'll give it a shot." Jae shrugged. "You know what Em is like when he gets something in his head."

"Yes, I do. You always were a very determined soul," Margaret said to Emmett. "But you were consistently kind, too, even when the people around you were not. I'm glad to know you haven't changed."

The crease worked its way between Emmett's eyebrows.

"That's not entirely true, Mother. I have changed. I'm not the same person you knew back then." He paused as Margaret's expression sobered, then pressed on. "When you and Father dismissed me from the family, everything I knew about the world changed, too. I had to become a different man."

"I understand," Margaret said.

"The thing is, I *like* who I am." Emmett cast his gaze down at his hand around Jae's. "I like my life and the people in it. And I don't care about the things I can't change or fix or even forget. Everything that's happened in my life got me here today and I'm genuinely okay with that."

"I'm glad, son. Truly."

Jae caught his bottom lip between his teeth. He'd never heard Margaret refer to Emmett by anything even remotely like an endearment before. From the way Emmett's cheeks colored, Jae suspected it'd been far too long since he'd heard his mother speak that way to him either.

"I don't know if there is anything I can say to you that will make up for the way your father and I made you feel." Margaret clasped her hands together. "I'd like to try, though. You and I ... well. We may never get to a point where things are completely healed between us. You're right about that, Jae," she said, her eyes flicking for a moment to Jae. "But I hope we can make things better," Margaret said to Emmett. "If anything is left of the young man you used to be, then I believe you'd hope so, too."

Emmett nodded, the movement very slight. "Why now? It's been over ten years since things fell apart, Mother. What makes you want to change them?"

Jae's heart cracked at the question, but even more at Emmett's matter of fact tone and Margaret's quiet sigh.

"You said it yourself, Emmett. It's been over ten years. Long enough for the child I raised to become a stranger to me," she said. "Being here this summer, seeing you with the people in your life, has made me realize I missed out on watching you become the man you are, and for reasons that seem so terribly unimportant now. I can't fix anything that happened in the past—I'd never consider even asking you to try. I think we can change what's happening right now, however, and I'd like to try if you're willing."

Emmett stayed silent for a long time, seeming to study his mother. "Let's talk next week," he said at last. "There's a place over in Amelia's neighborhood that serves a great daily catch."

Margaret's face lit up. "Or I could come to you. Just tell me where you'll be cooking on the day you want to get together and I can meet you there. It seems I've been missing out on a food truck wonderland—why not start with one of yours?"

* * * *

"Not sure I can feel my feet," Emmett said as he and Jae boarded the elevator late that evening. "That's a crack on these shoes, by the way, as opposed to your dancing skills."

"Well, good." Jae hit the button for his floor, then propped himself against the side of the car. He slid his arm around Emmett's waist as Emmett leaned into him. "You're the one who insisted on sticking it out after the cake cutting business." Glancing over, he grinned when he saw that Emmett's eyes were closed.

"Because I wanted cake," Emmett replied. "And to watch your brother do the Chicken Dance. *And* Amelia toss the bouquet."

"I still say we could have given the bridesmaids a run for their money."

"God, no. Kaylee plays semi-pro soccer. She'd easily tackle either one of us to the ground *and* make it hurt."

Jae muffled a laugh against Emmett's shoulder. "Good to know. Thank you for saving me from getting my ass handed to me."

"Anytime." Shifting, Emmett turned and raised his arms, sliding them around Jae's neck as he kissed him, gently at first, then deeper when Jae opened his mouth. Emmett groaned softly as Jae slid his tongue between Emmett's lips, and he clung to Jae, his half hard cock pressed against Jae's hip.

Lust crashed through Jae with a force that stole his breath. Dropping his hand, he palmed Emmett's ass through his tuxedo trousers, a thrill running through him when Emmett moaned. The elevator slid to a stop and chimed, and that was the only thing that enabled Jae to stop. He gave Emmett a tug as the doors opened.

"C'mon."

Stepping out of the car, they navigated the hotel's long corridors, neither speaking until they stood before Jae's door.

"Do you want to grab your bag from Ty's room first?" Jae asked, unable to stop his smile when Emmett gave a vigorous shake of his head. "You're welcome to wear my stuff, of course."

"I don't give a damn about clothes right now, because my plan is to keep us both naked for as long as possible, Jae." Emmett made his eyes big. "Unless you want to play Scrabble, that is, in which case I can wear a hotel robe."

"Sadly, I forgot to bring any board games," Jae said. "But I'm sure we can find a better use for the hotel robes."

He reached for his key card but then Emmett moved into Jae's arms and he lost himself in the touch and taste he'd craved so much, gasping as Emmett moved his hands up under Jae's jacket, his touch like a brand on Jae's skin through his shirt. Jae bit back a curse.

Pushing Emmett back, he fished the card from his pocket, movements brusque as he got the door open and pulled Emmett into the room. Emmett was on him before the door had fully closed, and they fumbled with each other's clothes, jackets and the keycard quickly falling to the floor.

"Fuck." Emmett went abruptly still, his breath warm against Jae's lips. He clutched at Jae's waist, his brow knit almost as if he were in pain.

"What is it?" Jae asked, his heart plunging straight to the floor. He pressed slow, chaste kisses on each of Emmett's cheeks. "What's wrong?"

"Nothing. Just good to touch you again." Emmett's voice was gruff. "I missed you. So much. It hurt when you told me to stay away."

Jae took Emmett's face in his hands. "I'm sorry. I didn't know what else to do. I've never felt like this about anyone, Em, and I couldn't tell you."

"I know. How could you have?" Regret shimmered in Emmett's eyes. "I told you often enough that I didn't believe in love, even when it was obvious the words were making you uncomfortable. Of course, you thought I'd never want more from you than sex."

"Yes. And I do want more. I think I have from the first time you kissed me. I just didn't know what to do with that. So, I backed away and hoped it would be enough to keep us both from being hurt." Jae sighed. "I know now it was more to keep *me* from being hurt than anything else."

"Did it work?"

"No. I just hurt us both. Because I already loved you and

knowing there was no way to go back terrified the crap out of me."
Jae watched Emmett's eyes go wide but saying the words out loud
at last was just too goddamned good. "Nothing either one of us did
was ever going to change that."

"Oh, Jae."

The gravel in Emmett's voice hurt to hear and every part of Jae
longed to soothe him. "It's okay, Em. It really is. I'm not afraid of
the way I feel anymore."

Gathering Emmett close, Jae laid him out on the bed then
climbed onto the mattress beside him, kissing and nuzzling until
the tension in Emmett's body was gone and Jae himself felt loopy
with lust.

"I want whatever you want," he murmured in between kisses.
"Sex or sleep or talk, you pick. I'll even call down to the hotel shop
for a Scrabble board if you really want to play." He smirked at
Emmett's snicker. "I need to call down there for condoms and
lube anyway."

Now Emmett pressed his head back into the pillows and
laughed. "Actually, you don't. I picked up some travel-sized
supplies before we came up here along with my very own
toothbrush."

"You're so smart. It's one of the things I like best about you,
you know."

"Mmm-hmm, yes I do. To answer your question, I'd like all of
the things you mentioned and in *that* particular order. But not just
for tonight." He smoothed the hair back off Jae's forehead. "For as
many nights as you want me."

For a second, Jae couldn't speak. "Emmett," he said at last, his
voice hushed. "I'm going to want you forever. In every part of my
life. You think you're ready for that?"

"Yeah, I am. I want you in my life too, Jae." Emmett gave him
a beautiful smile. "I want to make you feel good."

"You do," Jae said. "Every time you touch me."

The emotion shining in Emmett's eyes was like a balm on Jae's
soul. His mother had been right. Emmett was in this, too—Jae
knew it deep down. Whatever page either of them happened to be
on in this love story they were writing together, Jae could trust
Emmett with his heart.

As they peeled away what remained of each other's clothes,
Jae's skin prickled under Emmett's caresses. Emmett caught Jae's

lips with his own and hauled him close, slotting their groins together and writhing against him. Both were breathless when they broke apart and the awe in Emmett's face humbled Jae.

"I love the way you look at me," Emmett whispered. "Like you're holding something rare."

"Because I am. I told you before that I've never had feelings like this for anyone, and I meant every word."

They made out for a long time, touches easy and unhurried, so Jae felt absolutely wrecked on desire when he finally climbed out of bed to find the condoms and lube in Emmett's jacket pocket. He set a hand on Emmett's shoulder and stopped him from rolling on to his belly, drawing circles into the overheated skin of Emmett's chest.

"I want you like this," Jae said, "so I can watch. I want to see your face."

Color flooded Emmett's cheeks. He lay back against the pillows once more, one hand splayed wide over Jae's thigh as Jae sheathed himself. Slicking his fingers, Jae spread Emmett's thighs wide, then took his time opening Emmett up. He held him close, nuzzling Emmett's face with his nose and lips, his desire coiling tighter and tighter as they exchanged kisses and Emmett's groans became constant.

"*Jae.*"

"I know, baby."

Jae twisted his fingers, his own cock jumping when Emmett let out a gasp. Jae's body hummed with need. Pulling his hand free, he gently soothed Emmett's whine, and kissed him some more as he lined their bodies up, pleased by the daze he glimpsed in Emmett's eyes and the clumsy quality of his kisses—he'd never seen Emmett so undone. Jae pressed his cock, hot and hard, against Emmett's thigh, and though Jae was trembling with need, he kept his focus locked on the man in his arms.

"Gorgeous," Jae murmured. "And mine."

"Yes." Emmett's voice shook. He pulled at Jae's shoulder, urging him to move. "Need you. Need … Fuck, please."

"I'm here."

Pressing forward, Jae locked his gaze on Emmett, his heart twisting as Emmett's expression shifted, going softer and more open, his eyes bright and adoring. Jae couldn't have spoken if he'd tried. God, he loved this. Loved this man, and these moments together. How had he ever thought he'd be able to give them up?

"Missed this," Emmett said again, "just like everything about you. Jesus, Jae, I didn't know."

He kissed Jae, emotion pouring off him in a wave so intense it nearly knocked Jae over. Jae surged forward, over and over, Emmett's arms locked around him like iron. Jae's need coiled tighter and hotter as he and Emmett moved, and Emmett uttered a strangled cry. The skin of his neck and chest flushed deep red as Jae reached between them and took Emmett in hand.

A few strokes were all it took to send Emmett flying, his body going rigid as his cock pulsed over Jae's fist. He went almost limp as he came down, limbs heavy against Jae's and his gaze unwavering. Jae bit his lip and slowed his thrusts, his body screaming for release.

"Oh, God."

"Yeah." Emmett stirred then, his grip tightening once more. He practically crooned as a shiver racked Jae's body. "That's it. Wanna feel you, baby. Come on."

Breath hitching, Jae found his rhythm again. He went faster and harder at Emmett's urging, fighting the instinct to close his eyes. Triumph warred with affection in Emmett's face as he threaded his fingers through Jae's hair, and when he tugged, the sting sent a jolt of pleasure straight to Jae's cock.

Jae fell apart, his nerves singing, the orgasm unfolding through him in a devastating wave. His movements slowed as he rode out the high and he sank with a grateful groan onto Emmett, who wrapped Jae up in his arms.

"Not sure I have brain power to get through a game of Scrabble," Jae said when he could form full sentences again. "I'm up for hotel robes and Netflix, though, and maybe a soak in that tub."

"I like the sound of that." Emmett gave Jae a sleepy grin. "I may need some help peeling myself off of this bed, so I hope you're not in a hurry."

"I'm not. I'm exactly where I want to be." Jae dropped a lazy kiss on Emmett's lips and settled back, sure of his place in the world for the first time in years.

Chapter Sixteen

One year later, September

"Hey, hot stuff. Have you seen the spray-on glitter?" Mark went still outside the A-frame's screen door, seeming to pull himself up short. Popcorn, Mark's big white dog, stood nearby, a rainbow striped bandana tied around his neck. "Those are words I never imagined myself saying."

"I don't believe it," Jae propped himself up on one elbow. "Of all the people I know, you're the *most* likely to ask about spray-on glitter."

"That's fair. Having someone like Owen in my life probably increases those chances on paper, given he always finds the best trinkets and toys, be they sexual or otherwise."

Emmett made a grumpy kind of noise from his place on the bed beside Jae. "Dude, we were sleeping."

"And now you are waking." Mark rolled his eyes, though a smile played about his lips. "Zac and Owen and I have been busy plastering the campsite with pink lights and rainbows since we got back from the beach, Emmett, and now we've turned our attention on decorating humans."

"The hell?" Emmett grumbled, his eyes still shut when Jae looked down on him. "The parade was over two months ago."

"Yes, but Pride is forever," Mark replied. "I'm fairly sure Owen and Aiden mixed up a bunch of wicked rainbow jello shots, incidentally, and it's only a matter of time before they come out.

I've locked the axes away just to be safe," he added, laughing when Jae put a hand over his eyes.

"Good man." Jae dropped the hand to the arm Emmett had slung over Jae's waist. "As far as the glitter goes, I don't remember seeing the can in here, but I'll take a look around. Em and I are cooking tonight, and it was time we got up anyway."

"Says you," Emmett muttered after Mark and the dog had ambled off. "There are plenty of leftovers from lunch that'll feed us all if, say, you and I were too naked to cook." He snuggled in closer, clearly unbothered by Jae's soft laughter.

"True. I'd like to spend a little more time with our friends before the weekend is over, however," Jae said. He rubbed Emmett's arm gently, moving his hand over skin gone rosy pink from sun exposure. "I owe them a nice time for helping me move."

Emmett rolled from his side onto his back, the arm he'd had around Jae's waist moving right along with him. Before Jae could miss that welcome weight, Emmett caught Jae's hand in his and brought it to rest on his bare chest, then wove their fingers together.

"You're right." Emmett sighed, the sound content. "Naked sandwich night can wait for after we get back home."

"I'd like that."

Basking in the happy light of Emmett's expressive eyes, Jae was mindful of the lines of fatigue that still lingered on his face, despite the nap they'd taken after a full day at Goose Rocks Beach. With New England's wedding season in full swing, the EP teams had been busier than usual with catering jobs for over four months straight and the long hours of balancing the day into evening shifts sometimes showed. Emmett had helped Jae pack in advance of his move as well, and the dinner they'd hosted after the Pride parade had been held among stacks of boxes.

Jae rubbed circles over Emmett's heart. "Sleep a while longer," he said. "I'll get the food prep started, then come get you in an hour."

"You don't have to, Jae. I was just giving Mark a hard time because he's a diva and he loves it."

"Hard agree. But I can tell you're still tired and we have plenty of time before anyone needs to be fed."

"Plenty of time, huh?" Emmett gave Jae a wolfish smile. "We could use it for something more active than sleeping, you know."

"This is true." Moving their linked hands as one, Jae reached down and palmed Emmett's cock through his shorts. He smirked at the hum that rumbled through Emmett's chest. "You know you'll be sleepier than ever after you come, right?"

"Maybe, maybe not." Emmett lifted his free hand to Jae's lips, desire simmering in his gaze. "I don't really care either way, long as you feel good."

"You always make me feel good."

Heat pooled in Jae's groin. He pressed a kiss to Emmett's fingertips, then held his stare as, together, they worked Emmett's fly open. Jae batted Emmett's hands away when Emmett reached for Jae.

"Let me do this for you," Jae murmured. He traced the outline of Emmett's hard on through his cotton boxers with his fingers, his own lust mounting at Emmett's low groan. "It's been too long since I took you apart and just watched, and I miss it."

"Fuck." Emmett caught his bottom lip between his teeth. "I missed it too. But what about you?"

"I'm right where I want to be." Jae stopped his teasing long enough to fish the lube out from under his pillow, and he snickered as Emmett hauled him a little closer. Sliding his right arm under Emmett's shoulders, Jae wrapped his left hand around Emmett and relished his shaky hiss. "Nothing I'd rather do right now than watch you come all over yourself."

"Jesus, Jae. You wanna shut the door?"

"No. Those bozos know better than to walk over here if they don't want to risk getting a show. I need you to be quiet, though, because you know Mark's not one to turn down free porn."

Emmett's laughter bounced off the cabin's walls, but quickly subsided into softer noises of pleasure, and Jae got lost in the sight of his lover giving himself over to desire. Emmett's eyes at half-mast, his pupils blown wide, with only a thin ring of blue remaining. The color that flooded his cheeks, slowly filtering down over his neck and chest. His parted lips, full and tempting, begging to be plundered with kisses both tender and rough.

Jae held off, so taken with watching Emmett that his own desires became secondary. Emmett's filthy whispers almost did him in, though, and he shivered hard when Emmett dropped his hand and squeezed Jae's ass. Jae rutted without thought, seeking pressure on his dick against Emmett's hip, and abruptly Emmett was

166

babbling, his spiral into orgasm passing beyond the point of no return.

Jae kissed him then, igniting a flashpoint between them. He swallowed Emmett's near sob and held him close as he shuddered, Emmett's cum arcing up onto his chest. Jae managed to get his own shorts open but only just before he was spilling too, the intensity of that rush leaving him boneless and gasping against Emmett's lips.

Despite a valiant effort to remain alert, Emmett quickly dropped off and hardly stirred when Jae sat up and wiped them both down. Quietly, Jae pulled the sheet up over his partner's half naked form, then found his shirt and sneakers before he tiptoed out of the cabin, making sure to close the door behind him.

Once outside, he spied most of his friends by the bocce pit that sat beside the tree trunk bar. The pit and kitchen building had been strung with twinkling pink lights and Owen and Mark were taking turns tossing the red and green balls while Popcorn watched and Zac offered commentary from his place behind the bar. As Jae drew close, he saw that all three humans were sparkling with glitter.

"I take it you found the missing spray can?" he asked.

"Actually, no." Owen grinned at him. "I had an extra, though, so there's plenty left for you stragglers."

"Excellent." Jae stepped up to the bar and eyed the tumblers before him, each filled with a brilliant red cocktail and dotted with berries. "Hey, handsome," he said to Zac. "What are you pouring back there?"

"Raspberry punch. Delicious but quite potent." Zac produced another tumbler and filled it with ice. "I'm switching to wine after this, so I don't end up face down before Aiden even wakes up again."

"Em's out too. I said I'd get him up in an hour. He'll probably be hungrier than a bear by then anyway and ready to eat everything in sight." Jae smiled at Zac's chuckling, then accepted a glass of punch with murmured thanks.

"I'm glad we were able to convince them both to come up here this weekend," Zac said. "Aiden really needed some time off, even if it's just a few nights. I think he feels guilty for sleeping so much, which is ridiculous considering how zombified I can get when I work nights."

"He's not around to see you zonked out during the day, so it's almost like it's not really happening. That's how Emmett explained it to me when we had a similar conversation. Intellectually, they know we're wrecked but they don't see us bumbling around as much so it's easy to look past it." Jae sipped his drink. "Oh, heck. This is rum. Don't let me drink too much of this or I'll be a big, sloppy mess."

"As long as you give us big sloppy kisses, baby, that'll be fine." Mark shook the can of glitter and made a waving gesture with his hand. "Now come on over here, and let us make you shiny, Jae-seong."

* * * *

As twilight purpled the sky over the campsite, Emmett and Aiden woke on their own, each seeming much better rested and eager to celebrate simply being together as a group. Emmett's playful side was in full force as he and Jae constructed big bowls of salad, and more than once Jae found himself pressed up against the kitchen counters, exchanging lingering kisses with a man who declared his intent to make up for the many evenings they'd had to spend apart during the last two months.

Emmett promised to behave when he and Jae moved out to the firepit to grill steaks and ears of corn, but only because he could talk about the new pleasure of sharing his apartment with Jae, who'd moved the last of his boxes from Beacon Hill to the Chinatown apartment only a few days before.

"You really had enough room at Emmett's for your stuff?" Aiden asked as they gathered at one of the picnic tables with their plates. "I didn't think that apartment had much storage space."

"You're forgetting the big section that's suspended over the front door and to its right," Emmett replied. "I moved my cold weather clothes and gear up there along with Jae's which freed up a whole bunch of space to store our warm weather stuff."

Zac wrinkled his nose. "I'm not sure I'd want to rely on a ladder to get hold of anything I needed to wear." Then he scowled even deeper. "I think I'm officially old."

"More like officially tipsy." Aiden set his hand over Zac's cup with a wide, teasing grin.

"I wasn't particularly attached to my furniture," Jae said over his friends' laughter. "It was easy to let go and donate. We switched out Emmett's mattress and TV for mine—"

"Jae's are, like, a thousand times nicer," Emmett added.

"—but other than a couple of pieces of art, the robot smart speaker, and my bike, there wasn't much else. Oh, also Sparky and my other plants."

Owen looked like he was trying his hardest not to lose it laughing. "Wait, do none of the other plants have names?"

"Oh, they totally do," Emmett said. "Jae's named every one of the plants I gave him and not a single one has died." He aimed an amused look at Jae. "What about your books?"

"Shit, you're right!" Jae opened his eyes wide and clapped his hands together. "Em cleared out a couple of shelves in those tall units by the window and now my books finally have a home."

"At least until we outgrow the space," Emmett said, "which could be never, of course."

"You'd better not say that around my ma." The laughter grew louder as Emmett mimed hiding under the table. "She's been sending Em real estate listings in Cambridge and Somerville," Jae told the others, "despite our literally having just moved in together and my repeated assurances that we're totally happy where we are."

Emmett set his cob of corn down and gestured to Jae with a buttery finger. "What he said. I blame my sister and Ty, of course. They're the ones who had the bright idea of moving to Cambridge and now Christina and Kun-bae are determined to get the rest of their chicks just as close. That's what Jae's ma calls us," he said, his smile adorably pleased.

Jae handed Emmett a napkin. "Never in my whole life has Ma called Ty or me her 'chicks' so I'm pretty sure she just means you. Which is so grossly cute, I almost can't handle it. But we're having the whole family over for dinner next weekend and they can ooh and ahh over your organizational skills then."

"I didn't know you needed that Sunday off for family stuff, Em." Aiden lifted his eyebrows at his friend. "You should have told me."

"I wasn't sure it'd even happen until just a few days ago," Emmett said. "Tropical storms make flying from Virginia pretty hit or miss, so Jae and I have been playing it by ear."

"I'd say dinner is a go. My brother messaged this morning to say he'd picked up Margaret at the airport in Providence." Jae reached over and set a hand on Emmett's. "Now we just need to work on 'I am so surprised' faces so no one figures out that we already know Ty and Amelia are pregnant."

"How exactly did that happen?" Owen asked.

"Em and his sister have identical phone cases," Jae said. "He set his down beside hers the last time the four of us had dinner and, oops, saw a message."

Owen aimed his finger at Emmett. "That same kind of thing happened to me with Mark's sister! We got together for shitty movie night and I accidentally picked up her phone instead of mine."

"Yes, but it seems Emmett resisted the urge to yell, 'HOLY HELL, GIRL, YOU'RE PREGNANT?' at the top of his goddamned lungs." Mark slung an arm over his boyfriend's shoulder as Owen burst out laughing, the merry noises at the table punctuated by Popcorn's barks.

"We could always tell them one of us is pregnant first." Emmett's eyes gleamed when Jae shot him a wide-eyed look. "That'd really throw them off course."

"I feel ninety-nine percent certain Amelia would never forgive us for stealing her thunder like that, Em. How about we stick to blowing their mind with your food?"

"That's very boring, Jae, though I do see your point." Emmett shrugged. "If keeping peace with the fam means dinner without the mpreg twist, then so be it, big sigh."

Talk turned to other topics as they finished the meal, but a part of Jae's brain stayed fixed on Emmett's words. He waited until after they'd loaded the dishwasher and their friends were toasting marshmallows for s'mores before he caught Emmett's hand in his own.

"Hey, Em?"

"Yes-s-s-s?" Emmett drew out the word with a silly grin. "I brought a big stash of vegan chocolate by the way, so you can have s'mores, too."

"You did?"

"Uh-huh. There's plain bars but also coconut filled, and those big, dreamy peanut butter cups you like."

"Guh." Jae drew Emmett in and kissed him. "Thank you. I love you, you know."

"I do. And love you back." Emmett's skin flushed warm against Jae's kiss. "You weren't really going to ask me about dessert, were you?"

"I was not."

Jae pulled back and studied Emmett, whose brash smile had gone almost shy. Emmett's charisma and confidence made it easy to overlook his underlying sweetness and big, gentle soul, a reality that made Jae treasure moments like this because he got to see this softer side of the man he loved every day.

"Are you really okay having the families over to dinner next weekend?"

Emmett stood straighter and blinked, clearly taken off guard by the question. "Yes, of course. Why?"

"No reason. You said something about 'keeping peace with the fam' earlier which made me wonder if maybe I'd missed some pieces when we talked about hosting." He rubbed his thumb over Emmett's fingers.

"Like what?" Emmett's expression began to relax again, despite the tiny frown lingering on his brow. "I wouldn't have said yes if I hadn't wanted to."

"Yeah? Well, okay then." Jae nodded once. "I just wanted to know that you said yes because you wanted to bring everyone together and not just to shut the rest of us up. Your mother in particular."

Emmett huffed out a laugh. "She has seemed eager to meet up with me again. More than I ever expected."

"And that's what I mean." Jae slipped his arms lower, so his hands rested against the small of Emmett's back. "Until now, you guys have always met up on neutral ground. This time …" He shook his head. "There's nothing neutral about welcoming Margaret into your home, Em, especially with me in it."

"It's our home," Emmett countered, "and I love that you're in it. Yes, you're right. I'm still finding my feet with Mother even now." He raised a hand to Jae's cheek, the last of the worry in his face fading away. "But if she really wants to get to know me then it has to be all of me. My life, my home, and the man I share them with."

Jae leaned into Emmett's touch and smiled. "I'm glad to hear that. Because there's nowhere else I'd rather be."

Fin

Open Hearts

About K. Evan Coles

K. Evan Coles is a mother and tech pirate by day and a writer by night. She is a dreamer who, with a little hard work and a lot of good coffee, coaxes words out of her head and onto paper.

K. lives in the northeast United States, where she complains bitterly about the winters, but truly loves the region and its diverse, tenacious and deceptively compassionate people. You'll usually find K. nerding out over books, movies and television with friends and family. She's especially proud to be raising her son as part of a new generation of unabashed geeks.

K.'s books explore LGBTQ+ romance in contemporary settings.

Contact

Newsletter: https://mailchi.mp/308e1be9c54a/colessignup

BookBub: https://www.bookbub.com/profile/k-evan-coles

Goodreads:
https://www.goodreads.com/author/show/16711208.K_Evan_Coles

Instagram: https://www.instagram.com/k.evan.coles/

Pinterest: https://www.pinterest.com/kevancoles/

Facebook Profile: https://www.facebook.com/kevancolesauthor/

Facebook Page: https://www.facebook.com/ColesKEvan

Facebook Group:
https://www.facebook.com/groups/kswhiskeywordscafe/

Twitter: https://twitter.com/K_Evan_Coles

Blog: https://kevancoles.com/

#wickedproud

Also by K. Evan Coles

Wicked Fingers Press (Self-Published)

~Stealing Hearts ~
Thief of Hearts (Novella)
Healing Hearts (Novella)
Open Hearts (Novel)

Overexposed (Novella, 2021. Also included in the Working Stiffs
COVID-19 Charity Anthology)

A Hometown Holiday (Short Story)
Moonlight (Short Story)

Pride Publishing (Totally Entwined Group)

~ Tidal Duology w/ Brigham Vaughn (Novels) ~
Wake
Calm

~ The Speakeasy w/ Brigham Vaughn (Novels) ~
With a Twist
Extra Dirty
Behind the Stick
Straight Up

~ Boston Seasons (Novels) ~
Third Time's the Charm
Easy For You To Say (TBD)

Off Topic Press (Self-Published)

Inked in Blood w/ Brigham Vaughn (Short Story)

http://www.kevancoles.com

Author's Note

Thank you for reading! I hope you enjoyed Jae-seong and Emmett's story. Please consider adding a short review on Amazon and let me know what you thought—I would love to hear from you.

If you enjoyed this book, check out Mark and Owen's story, *Thief of Hearts*, the first book in the Stealing Hearts series, available in paperback and ebook on Amazon and Kindle Unlimited.

https://www.amazon.com/gp/product/B07NGQP7N1/

Some hearts are made to be stolen.

Mark Mannix doesn't believe in love or romance, which is ironic given his birthday falls on Valentine's Day. As he approaches forty, Mark is perfectly content with his life and nursing career in Boston, and—outside of his long-time friend-with-benefits, Alistair— prefers his hookups to be one-night stands.

When Mark's plans for New Year's Eve fall through, he attends his sister's party and meets Owen Todd, a graphic designer of Caribbean descent. Owen is more than a decade younger than Mark and, at first glance the two men appear to have little in common. The chemistry between them is potent, however, and Mark breaks his no-strings pattern, seeing Owen week after week.

A connection forms between the two men, leaving Mark in uncharted territory and drawn to Owen in ways he's never known before. Even so, Mark continues his hookups with Alistair but is startled when Owen withdraws out of a desire to protect himself. His foundations shaken, Mark must decide if he can watch Owen walk away or … if the time has come to follow his heart in a new direction.

Thief of Hearts
K. Evan Coles

Excerpt

Chapter One

"Did you bring the wine?"

Mark Mannix shifted one of the cloth grocery bags he'd been lugging and heard a *clank*. "I hope that's what's in these, because they're fucking heavy. And hello to you too, by the way." He raised an eyebrow at his sister. "Mind letting me in? I don't want to stand out here in the hallway while your neighbors gawk."

Lauren snickered, but she held her front door open wider so Mark could cross the threshold into her apartment.

"Thank you." He leaned in for a hug. He hadn't planned on spending New Year's Eve with his twin sister and her fiancé in their Boston waterfront condo. He'd *considered* it until an opportunity more debauched had come along, just as it had for the last several years running. Mark's plans for debauchery had fallen through this year, however, and now here he was with Lauren and Keith, helping them prep.

"You're welcome." Lauren kissed Mark's cheek, then stepped back and held out her hands. She was still clad in a bathrobe and her hazel eyes sparkled with good spirits. "I'll take your coat if you'd bring that bag to the kitchen. Keith is making some kind of cocktail with merlot, Campari, and limoncello and he wants to try the recipe out on you."

"Sounds interesting, I think." Mark set the bags down so Lauren could help him peel off his black wool coat. "He couldn't just make sangria?"

"Apparently not. Keith marches to the beat of a slightly dented drum and if he wants to research drink recipes on YouTube, who am I to stop him?" Lauren gathered the coat over her arm and Mark headed for the kitchen with a laugh.

"You made it!" Keith gave Mark a big sunny smile the moment

178

he stepped through the kitchen door. "Thanks for bringing more booze. You're a lifesaver."

"You're welcome." Mark handed a couple of the bags off to Keith. "I used to pick this stuff up for Mom and Dad, too, so I knew where to shop. I was going to make some cranberry cream cheese dip, by the way, but Lo told me your need for bubbly was infinitely more dire."

"My girl knows me well." Keith's dimples showed. Like Mark, he wore a dress shirt and jeans, and his big frame practically vibrated with good-mood vibes. At six foot four, he seemed to fill the whole kitchen. "I'd have been more than happy to eat your dip, because yum. You should make it the next time we get together for Shitty Movie Night!"

Mark shook his head. "I'm thinking we'll do spaghetti and meatballs that night, so better not. I can make the dip right now, however. I'd already bought the ingredients, and I brought everything along."

"This is just one of the reasons I love you, Mark. And as a thank-you, I'm going to be your personal drinks butler for the next hour. I'm glad you decided to come." Keith patted Mark's shoulder. "You'll know half the people we invited from work anyway."

"So I gathered from what folks were saying." Mark said. He and Keith worked together as nurses at Mass. Eye and Ear and Mark felt sure his friend had extended invitations to everyone on the staff.

Keith smirked. "Lauren invited some of her co-workers, too, and they're mostly dudes. Maybe you'll find someone fun to start the New Year with, hmm?"

"Don't let my sister hear you say that," Mark warned, but Keith just scoffed.

"She knows you have sex. We're both aware that's why you were going to blow us off in the first place, as usual. Alistair waved a naked party in your face and you folded like a cheap suitcase."

Mark snorted out a laugh. "It's not a naked party. It's a drag ball. And, really, can you blame me?"

"Nah. Kind of shitty that he pulled out at the last minute, though." Keith sniffed. "I know you guys are just casual and all, but Alistair strikes me as kind of a douche."

"You've never met him."

"I know this. Despite you and he screwing around for years."
Keith made little effort to hide his disdain. "I'm not sure what you
think that says about the guy, Mark, but to me it says 'I'm a
douche.'"

"He's a good guy," Mark insisted. "Yeah, we're friends with
benefits, but he's always been really decent about the friend part."

"Eh, fine. I still think you can do better, man."

Just then, Mark wondered if Keith didn't have a point. It had
been shitty of Alistair to leave Mark high and dry like this. Not that
Mark wasn't capable of entertaining himself, but the disappearing
act didn't meet the criteria of "good buddy" in any way. Mark
needed a drink before he started thinking such thoughts, though,
and he set about helping Keith make that happen.

Lauren popped back in, clad in a shiny dress that put stars in
her eyes, and the three chatted while they finished the party prep.
They laughed and joked so Mark hardly noticed the passing time
and in what seemed an eye blink, the apartment had filled with
people. True to Keith's word, many were friends and coworkers of
Mark, and greeted him with unbridled delight.

"You're very popular."

Mark glanced up from the cocktail shaker he'd been using to
concoct another drink and met a pair of dark, smiling eyes.

Happy New Year to me. Hello there, Tall and Handsome.

"I'm not supposed to be here," Mark said to the young man at
his side. "I work with a lot of these people and they're nice enough
to not hold it against me for nearly blowing them off. Can I interest
you in an Italian Sangria?" Mark gestured to the shaker.

A grin lit the elegant angles of the young man's face. "Is that a
thing?"

"It is tonight." Mark topped the red wine and orange juice he'd
already poured with Amaretto, limoncello, and Campari, then
replaced the shaker's cap. "I'm not sure where Keith found the
recipe but it's quite tasty."

He also pulled himself straighter, very aware his new
acquaintance stood at least an inch over his own six feet. The
young man's all-black ensemble lent him a striking edge too, as did
the tight platinum-tipped curls on his head.

"Should I be nervous?" The young man's expression turned
teasing, and mmm, his voice was like honey and smoke. "I know
you're Lauren's brother, but for all I know you could be mixing up

furniture polish."

I wonder if he asked Lauren about me.

Mark pushed the thought away. "These drinks are far tastier than polish," he said. "And, Keith mixed one for me earlier which, as you can see, has not killed me." He rattled the shaker, then strained its contents into an old-fashioned glass and added two fat cubes of ice from the bucket.

The young man set his beer bottle down and accepted the glass, his gaze on the foamy red concoction. "Is it really called Italian Sangria?" he asked.

"No, but I haven't bothered trying to come up with something more clever. Keith swears it's named after Benito Mussolini, but I think he's full of shit."

The young man smiled and sipped the drink, and the obvious pleasure on his face sent a pulse of warmth through Mark. "Not bad at all."

"I thought so, too. So, you know I'm Lauren's brother, which probably means you know my name is Mark."

"So she said. I'm Owen."

Mark shook the hand Owen extended. "That's much easier than what I've been calling you in my head."

Owen raised an eyebrow. "Which is what?"

"Tall and Handsome. Both true, but a bit of a mouthful." Owen's raspy laugh made Mark's nerves zing.

"I can't promise to answer to Tall and Handsome, but I won't hold it against you, either."

They spent the next hour or so chatting while they moved around the party with their drinks and sometimes plates of snacks, neither straying very far, like magnets drawn together. And though Mark was being less than sociable toward the rest of his friends, he doubted anyone would blame him, because Owen was stunning. His tawny brown skin and lush lips were flawless, and the spray of tiny freckles across his nose almost too appealing.

Owen worked as a designer in the Creative Department for Lauren's firm, Bloom & Glass. He'd come to the party with another pair of co-workers, one of whom was also Owen's roommate, and he was smart and funny, a combination of positives that pinged Mark's attraction in very nice ways. Owen was also eleven years younger than Mark's thirty-nine. Mark didn't consider the age difference to be a non-starter, but it had been a very long time since he'd chatted up a man who didn't live on his own.

Regardless, Mark found Owen as easy to talk to as he was on the eyes, and they settled into a cozy corner of the living room with a view of the harbor and chatted about whatever came to mind.

"Do you and Lo work together a lot?" Mark asked, then shook his head at himself. "Sorry, force of habit. I meant Lauren."

"No, we don't," Owen replied. "We're grouped on the same project teams but we tend to be on opposite ends of the process. Lauren does the writing and I work on marketing collateral for the final product—physical things like pamphlets and brochures if they're needed, but also web content and applications."

"Sounds interesting and very much something I'd be terrible at." Mark shared a smile with Owen. "I couldn't draw a straight line if you paid me, so it's probably better I went to nursing school."

"Lauren said you're a specialist, too."

"I'm a Nurse Practitioner. So Extreme Nursing, if you can imagine such a thing." He smirked at Owen's soft laughter. "Keith and I work together at Mass. Eye and Ear. We're both in Emergency ENT, so it's all ears, noses, and throats."

Owen nodded. "Cool. You've had some famous singers as patients, right?"

"Yes. But most of the people who pass through the department are tense because they're in pain or worried or both. The vibe isn't exactly fanboy central."

"There you are." Lauren slid into the seat on Mark's other side. "I wondered where the two of you had gotten to." She grinned at Owen, her cheeks pink. "Please tell me Mark's being nice to you."

"He's good at mixing drinks, so he'll do," Owen said. His wink made Mark's stomach do a giddy flip.

"I'm a fucking delight," he declared, but Lauren rolled her eyes.

"You're an epic pain in the ass," she said. "I've hardly seen you since people starting arriving and I thought maybe you'd gotten bored and left."

"I wouldn't do that without telling you," Mark chided. "I'm not that rude. Besides, I've been mixing drinks for Owen and he is the opposite of boring."

Lauren hummed. "That's nice to hear, given your twenty-second attention span." Her gaze shifted to Owen. "Mark gets flighty when he hangs out with straight people for too long."

"Oh, sweetie, you are so cut off." Mark made a playful grab for her glass but while Lauren blocked him and laughed, the fondness in her gaze tugged at his heart in a nice way.

"I'm glad you're here," she said. "Especially since this is the first New Year's we've spent together in a while! And even more so because this is nowhere near as fabulous as your original plans."

"Eh, it's not so bad. And I'm glad too." Mark was surprised to find he meant it, not only because he loved his sister and Keith, but because his evening was turning out very pleasantly, thanks to Owen. On impulse, Mark dropped a quick kiss on Lauren's cheek. "Thanks for hosting. And for inviting me. And for your fiancé, who taught me to mix these weird-ass drinks."

Lauren smirked. "You're welcome, doofus." She got to her feet, eyeing Mark and then Owen. "If you two decide to ditch us for something cooler, I won't blame you. I know this is sort of tame for handsome boys like yourselves. But say goodbye before you go so I can hug and embarrass you properly."

"Where were you supposed to be tonight?" Owen asked after Lauren had slipped off again.

"In Providence with a friend of mine. We had tickets to a drag ball with a Moulin Rouge theme." Mark nodded at Owen's knowing look.

"Nice. Not sure I would have pegged you as a fan of musicals."

Mark laughed. "I'm not, but I am fond of a sparkly corset."

"So what happened?"

"My friend decided Rhode Island wasn't grand enough and booked a trip to Reykjavik for the week." With Mark's other friend, Ellis, no less. Mark had known Alistair and Ellis were screwing around, of course, but that didn't make him any less annoyed that he'd been left behind. "I'd have loved to see Iceland with Alistair, but I'm working tomorrow and that means no overseas trip for me."

"Hmm." Owen furrowed his eyebrows. "How come decided not to go to Providence anyway?"

"There didn't seem much point. Alistair changed his mind about the ball at nearly the last minute and most of my other friends had already made plans. Going solo to a drag ball isn't my idea of a good time. What about you?" He eyed Owen's stylish clothes. "Do you and your friends have plans beyond Lauren and Keith's?"

"There's talk of after parties and a trip to Chinatown for some late-night eats," Owen replied, "but I'm down for whatever. I'm…flexible."

The moment caught and hung between them, buzzing with energy, and Mark returned Owen's slow smile. "My favorite."

He liked this young man. The way Owen smiled, his raspy voice and laugh, and the way he moved his dark, liquid eyes over Mark with obvious appreciation.

"The fireworks go off soon," Mark said. "You want to step onto the balcony and grab a spot before it gets too crowded? The view is fantastic." Pleasure unfurled inside him at the way Owen's eyebrows rose.

"That sounds good."

"Okay." Mark pushed to his feet. "Grab your coat and meet me in the kitchen."

Working to be stealthy, Mark and Owen lifted a bottle of wine from the refrigerator and glasses from the counter, and while Mark suspected Keith spotted them, he and Owen ducked out on to the balcony without being stopped. The shock of quiet, chilly air made a bracing change from the heat and noise of the party, and made Mark feel hyperalert.

Owen set the glasses on the patio table and stepped up to the railing, unabashed in his admiration of the view of the wharfs across the street and Boston Harbor beyond. "You were right. This is gorgeous."

"My sister wants to keep this apartment forever, just for the view." Mark worked at the foil on the bottle.

"I don't blame her. I'm surprised she and Keith don't live out here."

"Pretty sure fear of hypothermia is the only thing that stops them. It's not bad tonight, though."

"Agreed." Owen met Mark's glance with a sweet half-smile. "What about you? Is there a view at your place that can beat this?" he asked.

"I'm biased, but I'd say mine's better. I live in the West End and my side of the building looks out over the Charles River." Mark popped the cork. "The balcony's small, like the rest of the place, but it works for me. The critical thing is that it's quiet and has a big bed where I can sleep until the cows come home on my days off."

Owen made a soft, thoughtful noise. "Sounds nice." He patted his pocket then, and shot Mark a sheepish smile. "Sorry—force of habit. I've been smoke-free for two weeks, but the habit dies hard. I've got it down to herbal cigarettes now and while I don't like them much, it feels like progress."

"I get it." Mark said. "I quit a few years ago myself. I don't need to tell you you're better off."

A pause fell while he filled their glasses, but it wasn't uncomfortable. Inside, the crowd was gearing up for the countdown, their excited voices muffled but still audible through the glass door.

Owen lifted his drink and narrowed his eyes at its contents, which looked very dark in the dim light. "Is this a red wine?"

"Yes. It's sparkling Shiraz." Mark held his own glass aloft and watched the streetlights below make the deep ruby-colored wine glow. "My mother was very fond of the bubbly on holidays, but she liked to switch up from whites now and again. Sparkling Shiraz at New Year's was her favorite."

Inside, the crowd started counting backward from ten.

"I've never had it," Owen said. "Then again, my family doesn't drink wine, so you could say I'm still broadening my horizons."

"Does that make me a bad influence?" Mark shared a smile with Owen and the countdown hit five.

"I guess we'll have to see."

They tapped their glasses together while the party behind them erupted in cheers and calls of "Happy New Year," and, a moment later, the sky over the harbor before them exploded with light and color.

Made in the USA
Monee, IL
17 December 2020

53935322R00115